BREAKING THE STORM

SEDONA VENEZ

WANT FREE SEDONA VENEZ
BOOKS?

Sign up for Sedona Venez's Newsletter and receive FREE BOOKS. In addition to the free stories, you will also get special pricing, exclusive previews and news of new releases.

GET A FREE SEDONA VENEZ BOOK!

Join Sedona's mailing list to be the first to know of new releases, free books, special prices and other author giveaways.

https://sedonavenez.com/free-book

"Tis better to have loved and lost than never to have loved at all."
—**Alfred Lord Tennyson**

CHAPTER 1

I TUCKED my legs under me as the crisp fall air whipped around the terrace. "Now this is living," I murmured under my breath, enjoying the lush gardens that offered a feeling of complete privacy amid the hectic vibe of the Upper East Side of Manhattan.

This was my quiet time.

My fifteen minutes of solitude.

The lull before the storm.

There was no Mom, Aunt Lia, or my cousin Light barging onto our shared terrace in hysterics about some Credence O. business conundrum. And there were no phone calls from escorts whining about a fucked-up assignment or demanding a pay raise.

All was right in my world, at least for a few more precious minutes. Then all hell would break loose again, and my life would resume its breakneck reality of dealing with the drama and chaos of business and family.

"Stormy? Where the hell are you?"

Shit. Light's on the move, and she sounds like she's in a fucked-up mood—again.

"Your time is up," Light barked as she swayed in, looking like she'd just stepped off a runway, with not one shiny, jet-black strand of hair out of place. It never ceased to amaze me how she could look like the picture of calm and coolness, while inside, she was a churning slew of tumultuous emotions.

Sighing heavily, I sank lower into a lounging position. "Fifteen minutes—that's all I asked for, and you couldn't even do that."

Light clutched the two champagne minis to her chest like bars of gold. "No, I couldn't. I'm not equipped to deal with the hurricane brewing downstairs in the office." She handed me a bottle as she plopped down beside me. "Three more escorts didn't show up for their assignments. The phone is ringing off the hook with pissed-off clients. And I just ran out of alcohol. This shit is going down the toilet, and the night's still young."

"What did I tell you about raiding my refrigerator? These were gifts from Noah." Noah was my friend and the enforcer for alpha Ryker Alfero, the leader of the toughest New York wolf-shifter pack.

I tried to snatch the other bottle from her hand, but she dodged my attempt. That was the downside of living with family—no privacy, the constant invasion of my space, and the pilfering of all my expensive stuff. It didn't matter that, apart from work, I shouldn't have to put up with this annoyance in our expansive five-story townhouse with an elevator centrally located, providing access to all levels.

"Didn't you hear the part about me running out of alcohol?" Light mumbled.

"Go to your mother's wing. Her place has all the good stuff."

Mid-sip, Light shot me an evil glare. "She changed the code to her floor. Damn witch."

I smirked at her. "Now why the hell didn't I think of that?"

She looked at me cheekily. "Because I'm your favorite cousin. You love me and adore my charming company."

I eased off the chair. "Nope, that's not it. It's because, if I did, you would whine like a little puppy, annoying the hell out of me," I responded before picking up my cell and striding off the terrace and into the elevator.

Light followed me. "That's a real bitchy thing to say, but true."

My mind went into business mode, lining up all the calls I had to make to settle the tornado of chaos. One of them I didn't relish making at all. The elevator door slid open into the large, stately, polished, pine-paneled office.

Reading my mind, as usual, Light blurted, "And we're calling that she-wolf first."

I refused to let Light drag me under in her sea of rage. Ignoring her, I let her anger over the dangerous Lacie predicament roll off me like rivulets of rain. I didn't need Light hassling me over the fact that, if I didn't handle this situation correctly, it would bleed into every facet of our lives. It was an outcome that, knowing Lacie Gilden's devious mind, was exactly the goal she was hoping for—total anarchy.

"Will you just let me handle this, Light? I don't need you riling me up. I just need to clarify the legal ramifications of her actions. That's it."

It was a conversation I dreaded, and it didn't help that Lacie and I had a terrible history. Our past had exploded into a cataclysmic, bloody brawl in high school. Everyone in our witch coven knew the Gildens were as ruthless as they came, and it didn't help matters that they were our direct business competitors. Their business had gone to great lengths to steal our clients and employees by using tactics that would make even the most hardened criminal grimace with shame.

Light curled up on the large sofa, sucking down the last drops of champagne, desperation written all over her face. Instantly, I knew she was hurting from the daily strain of keeping the barrage of human emotions from driving her crazy, and no amount of alcohol could mask that.

I was really worried about her because she had been born with the worst luck of all the members in our family. Light was an empath with the ability to sense all human emotions. The constant influx of feelings was overwhelming to her, with no remedy to prevent them from making her completely insane. We all tried different methods to help. The only thing that worked was dulling her senses with alcohol—and me soothing her through our bond connection.

So, I did what I always did.

I lowered my mental walls, allowing her to take a few sips of my emotions to put her mind in a calm, neutral state. It would cause me horrible, migraine-inducing side effects later, but I would take one for the Credence team.

Light latched on to our connection with a sigh. She needed it to take the edge off her instability. My stomach heaved as my emotional state fluctuated from angry to delirious with each pull. It was too dangerous for me to let our connection linger, so I quickly severed it, immediately settling my emotions.

Light's fingers trembled as she took a large gulp of champagne. "Thanks, Stormy."

Brushing back the strands of hair sticking to the sweat on her forehead, I asked, "Why did you let it get so bad?"

She leveled me with an irritated stare. "Because I'm tired of being a burden. I'm tired of everyone in this family treating me like I'm some incompetent hag who's one step away from going psycho. I'm just damn tired of not being treated as an equal around here."

Shit, not this again. I could almost hear the woe-is-me violins playing in the background. "Okay, first, you are an equal. Our mothers made it legal by giving us equal shares in the business. Second, without your marketing genius, we wouldn't have as many new clients as we do. So, stop fishing for compliments already." I picked up my cell. "Now, I need to get myself mentally prepared and in control to make this fucking call."

"See? That's your problem. You always have to be in control. For once, will you just let go? Unleash those well-manicured claws and let her know you mean business. Otherwise, I will." She flexed her fingers around her bottle. "Gladly."

I scoffed. "Uh-huh, that's exactly what we need. Both of us getting crazy on her ass." *Nope, that wouldn't be good.* Light and I could get downright mob-like when we put our minds to it. It was a state we hadn't been in since college. Well, at least I hadn't. I was no longer the wild, impetuous girl who allowed emotions to dictate my life. I'd put that shit aside when I graduated from college.

No, this situation demanded meticulous calm and stealth. And if that didn't work, I wasn't above deadly intent mode.

The gloves were off for messing with our bread and butter. And I would not let some spiteful backstabbing witch taint our reputation just because she held a grudge against my family and me. We'd worked too hard to maintain our reputation as Credence Other Corporation, New York's most sought-after secret Other escort service. We provided over-the-top discretion and exclusivity to our clients—Other males who preferred Other females, but without all the drama of unnecessary attachments when they were in town on business and needed Other arm candy.

My heels clicked along the inlaid wood design flooring as I walked toward the French doors with beautiful views of the trees, lush foliage, and picturesque 64th Street. Taking a deep, cleansing breath, I clenched and unclenched my fingers before tapping the numbers on my cell.

"Hello, Stormy Credence." Lacie's answering purr was like fingernails on a chalkboard. "To what do I owe the pleasure of a call from the elite Credence O. Corporation?"

I gritted my teeth, pushing down the rising anger. "Lacie, it's unprofessional and against the Other Council rules to call our escorts, pressuring them to leave our employment."

Lacie laughed mockingly. "I can't help it if they're interested in making actual money without all the ridiculous Credence O. restrictions."

I wanted to reach through my cell and choke the hell out of her.

"Restrictions, as in ensuring our clients are clear that we are not a prostitution service?" I asked.

Lacie clucked her tongue. "*Prostitution* is such an ugly word. My business provides a service of pleasure that demands high compensation," she responded with an air of arrogance.

"Put whatever pretty spin you want on it. It's straight-up prostitution," Light interjected.

I quickly cut her off before she launched into a full-on verbal attack. "Look, Lacie, if they want to join your family's prostitution ring, I don't care."

Light snickered as she poured more champagne into flutes.

I winked at Light before continuing. "But as you are fully aware, all our escorts are under contract, and severing it incurs a hefty fine." I paused dramatically. "So, when I garnish their wages, fingers will start pointing to their new employer—you—to pay the fines for them. Now, I really don't want this to get nasty, like bringing-your-ass-before-the-Other-

Council ugly. But I won't hesitate if you don't back the hell off."

I was bluffing. Going before the pompous members of the Other—wolf-shifters, vampires, and assorted supernatural beings who blended in, coexisting with humans—Council would be as enjoyable as going to the OB-GYN.

Lacie's voice was crisp. "You can't threaten me, hybrid."

"This hybrid just did. Next time, think about the ramifications before you go fucking with our business."

"You bitch!" Lacie sputtered.

Without another word, I ended our call.

"Thank goodness we're done with that trash," Light muttered as she turned on the flat-screen television.

"For now," I countered. We would never get rid of Lacie or her family. Walking over to my desk, I picked up the two newly signed contracts with freshly inked names—Ryker Alfero and Brad Camero.

Damn, this is a freaking nightmare.

What were the odds of having two alpha shifters demanding escorts on the same night?

Pressing my finger to the biometric lock on the safe, I pulled open the door, placing the contracts inside before slamming it shut.

A commercial blasted my ex-boyfriend's rock song from his new hit album.

"God, if I hear that song again, I'm going to scream," I complained.

"I thought you'd be happy for him." Light looked at me pointedly.

"I am. He's worked hard for his success." Knox Gunner was a singer, entertainer, and television personality who was most known for fronting a world-famous rock band. His unequivocal ascension to A-list rock superstardom was fast, and America couldn't get enough of him. "But damn, his songs have scored so much airplay this year that they're stuck in my head."

"Making it all the harder for you to move on," Light added.

"I've moved on. But I will not lie—every time I hear his songs, it's a bitter reminder of what I did to him." And the memory of the hurt that shone in his eyes the night I broke up with him.

"Did to him? Or for him?" Light asked. "Because as I see it, his ass should be grateful that he's alive instead of taking a dirt nap."

"Do you know you have the logic of a psychotic woman?"

She shrugged. "What can I tell you? I keep it real simple. I spill fewer tears that way. Now, get over here." She patted the space next to her. "My favorite show is on." I walked over and sat down beside her.

Light was right. I'd done him a favor by letting him go, or at least that's what I'd tried to convince myself.

CHAPTER 2

"Move it!" I screamed over the thumping beat of the music, pulling along the bane of my existence, Light. "The Battle of the Bands is about to start, and I want to wish Knox luck before he goes on."

Light skidded to a stop. "If I move any faster, I'll twist my ankle."

"I told you not to wear those shoes tonight," I rebutted, glaring down at her cute but ridiculously high stilettos.

"But they're my hundred percent chance that I'm going to get fucked tonight shoes." She waggled her brows while gyrating suggestively in sync with the thumping music.

"I'm not in the mood for jokes, Light." I stepped closer. "Not when I have to break up with Knox tonight."

"About time. Seven months together is too long. Plus, I don't like that we can't read him, Portia, or Wyatt. It's fucking weird that our gifts don't work on them."

She was right. There was no way that both our magical abilities were malfunctioning in the same group of people. Light could sense human emotions, but she couldn't sense anything from Knox and his friends. I had the gift for reading auras—Others had blue auras and humans green—but with Knox and his friends, it was as if a veil shrouded their colors from me.

"They're either hybrids," Light announced, "or Others with alpha blood."

Our abilities didn't work on hybrids, Others with alpha blood, and a small percentage of humans.

"Or he could just be human. Frankly, it doesn't matter now, Light. It's over tonight."

"It better be because you and I know that if you continue down this path, you'll fall in love with him and he'll end up like they all do—dead."

"This is so fucked up." I hated what we were, a bloodline of hybrid witch fae born shadowed by a century-old curse that killed any human we fell in love with.

She grabbed my hand while looking pointedly at me. "No, what's fucked up is if we don't cut them off before we get attached and start spouting stupid words of love. Let him go." She released my hand. "Look sharp. Wyatt's headed our way."

Turning to face in the direction Light was staring, I saw Wyatt, guitarist and Knox's closest friend, parting the crowd like a ship slicing through the sea.

"Well, if it isn't Stormy and her sidekick, Lightning," he said, coming to stand in front of us.

I rolled my eyes. His amusement over our names was wearing real thin. *Shit,* it wasn't our fault our mothers thought it was cosmic and damn near amusing to name us after inclement weather. It was bad enough that I'd caught shit from classmates over my name, Stormcloud Credence. But Light, whose full name was Lightning, was the butt of every joke imaginable.

Light pointed at him. "Hey, asshat. What did I tell you about that?"

"I can't help it, Lightning." His eyes got all smoldering. "Your name makes me fucking hot."

He tried to grab Light's waist, but she was quick, skirting away like he was a leper.

"No touching." Light held her cup in front of her like a shield. "I'm here for the drinks, not to be pawed by the likes of you."

"That's what you say," he replied, then eyed me. "Knox's been waiting for you. He's been fucking crazed. I don't know what fucking spell you put on him, but fix it."

Spell?

Did he know what I was?

No, he couldn't. But he was eerily perceptive, which made me uncomfortable. And it didn't help that he was always looking at me with that snide glare I hated.

"Spells don't have shit to do with it," I said. "I'm his genie lamp. He rubs me in all the right places, and I grant him everything he desires."

"I know." He smirked. "I heard you two last night. Keep the porno moaning down to a dull roar next time."

My eyes narrowed. "Jealous?"

"Can't be jealous of something that will be over by next week." He looked me up and down. "You're an unnecessary distraction, Stormy, and I don't like it."

"Who gives a fuck what you like or don't like?" I stepped closer.

Light looked from me to him with interest. She knew I was close to throttling his ass. And she was always ready for the thrill of a good bloodbath.

He sneered. "I don't get why he's with you. You're not even his type."

His evil smirk said it all. He'd hit my weak spot. I knew I had more breasts and ass than most of the thin, half-naked, cosmetically enhanced groupies who hung around Knox and his band.

"Wow, Wyatt. I guess it should flatter me that an ass like you actually thinks I have that much power over a guy like Knox. Let me clue you in. The more you and your she-bitch, Portia, try to push me away from him, the tighter we get. It's the fucking law of attraction, which makes me wonder if you're concerned about him, or if you're only worried about me taking away your one-way meal ticket out of poverty?"

"Just because he fucked—" His nostrils flared. "No, scratch that. Just because he went down on you doesn't mean you're an authority on all things Knox."

My mouth flopped open as my temper spiked, going from a slow simmer to an all-out boil.

How the hell does he know that?

Was Knox talking about me to his friends like I was some fucking notch on his guitar?

"Oh, hell no, guitar boy," Light chimed in. "Don't talk to my cousin like that."

"I just call it like I fucking see it, Light," he responded with a decidedly cruel tinge to his voice.

I cocked my hip. "Has it ever occurred to you that Knox might not like the pressure from you and Portia riding his coat-tails like he's some sort of messiah, leading you and his groupies to the promised land?"

Wyatt flinched like I had physically bitch-slapped him.

Aha! I'd found his soft spot.

And being the bloodthirsty witch I was, I went all in for the kill shot. "You know, sometimes pressure can make you do some necessary things, like getting rid of cumbersome baggage."

Knox was talented. Everyone knew that. And grudgingly, I had to admit his band was just as talented. The band was comprised of Wyatt, the guitarist, Josiah, the bassist, and Aiden, the drummer—friends who were so different in personalities that the fact that they were so tight made little sense. It was a mystery I'd given up probing after Knox had been so vague about the origins of their friendship.

Wyatt's eyes narrowed. "Did he tell you that?"

Not in so many words, but I could see the strain of Knox fighting hard to keep the band together. In my eyes, mission impossible. And trying to win tonight's last round of the Battle of the Bands was another heavy weight on his already overburdened shoulders. Winning tonight would mean scoring a record contract, and that would be one step closer to his dream of finally getting his voice and music heard by a larger mainstream audience.

Arms pulled me back roughly. I looked down at the muscular forearms. The right had a black-and-gray guitar tattoo etched across it, and the left had a black wolf howling at the moon. I loved the feeling of comfort and warmth as his taut body molded around mine like a glove. I actually sighed, sinking into him like a warm bath.

I just loved his touch.

Simply, it made me crumble.

"Hi, Knox." Light rolled her eyes with a smile, nudging Wyatt away. "Bye, Knox. Come on, Wyatt. I need another drink."

"I'll catch you later, Stormy. Our conversation is far from over," Wyatt stated firmly.

I eyed him. "I look forward to it."

Light wiggled her fingers before dancing off into the crowd with Wyatt's eyes fixed on her ass.

Knox pulled me into a secluded corner before saying, "You look beautiful," with his eyes locked on me with his usual scorching intensity. "Is all this for me?" His sexy deep voice was electrifying, like thunder, making my stomach clench and toes curl like a well-sated cat.

Tilting my head back, I wrapped my arms around his waist. "Of course, and you haven't seen nothing yet. Wait until I get you alone tonight. I'm going full-throttle sexy on your ass." That really meant I was finally going to have more than oral sex with him, giving me something I could remember when I walked away, forever.

He whispered into my ear, "Hmm, I can't wait," before nibbling on it.

I was almost purring when he reached up, gently pulling my hair loose from my standard tight ponytail. He loved it loose, had said it made me look like an exotic temptress. *And for our last night together, what Knox wants, he will get.*

He wrapped the soft length around his hand, tipping my head back to meet his sensuous gaze. "So, how did your contemporary dance competition go?"

I was happy that he cared enough to ask because my dancing was as important to me as his music was to him. He understood how much my dancing, a fusion of styles dubbed "contemporary/pop," meant to me. Dancing had been a part of my life since I was born. It was my way of escaping the pressure of my family and bloodline. Over the years, my dance skills had gotten so refined that several renowned dance companies had asked me to join their ranks, which I wanted more than my next breath. But a professional career as a dancer was not in the cards for me. After graduating from college in a couple months,

I was duty bound to help run Credence O., my family's escort business.

I reached up, running my fingers across his hair. "You'd know if you took the time to answer your cell."

He nipped my full bottom lip before running the tip of his tongue along it torturously slowly. "Portia had us rehearsing all day," he whispered against my mouth. "No avoiding the question. How did you do?"

"Well, why don't you ask the slave-driving bitch who answered your cell?" I pushed him. "She was more than happy to tell me you were too busy to talk to me."

I despised Portia, the band's personal manager and all-around spiteful hag. It didn't help that Portia enjoyed pointing out—every time Knox was out of listening range—that she and Knox had once been pretty steady sex buddies, which annoyed me even though their affair had been over months before he'd met me.

Knox didn't see her as an issue. To him, she was the past. Men were naïve that way, thinking just because they'd closed the book on a sexual relationship, it was a done deal and history. What they didn't get was, for most women, it was only over when she closed the emotional and physical doors on any possibility of salvaging the relationship. And those doors were wide open in Portia's mind. That much I knew from the way her lustful eyes followed him whenever they were in the same room. Portia definitely wanted more than a business arrangement with Knox, and I was in the way of her having that and more.

"Portia knows I hate it when she answers my cell." His jaw clenched.

I snorted. "Once again, Portia the dictator is up to no good. And to answer your question, I placed second."

"You're number one in my eyes." He kissed and nuzzled

my neck before giving me his "I will fuck you where you stand" stare.

Trailing my fingers across his chest, I said, "That's what you say, rocker, but once you win tonight and move on to the rocker hall of fame, I'll be nothing but a distant memory." I waggled my eyebrows. "But, hopefully, a hot one."

"You don't honestly believe that, right?" He traced a finger across my cheek.

I debated whether I should be brutally honest.

I settled for just honest.

"Knox, men disappoint." *All the time*, I deliberately left unsaid.

"That was the past." His eyes narrowed. "You and I are the future. And regardless of what happens tonight, I'll still want you, Stormy." His hand grazed my back. "Fame won't ever change that. You know we can have something good here, right?"

I resisted the urge to lower the walls around my heart, hoping for something unattainable—love. There would be no happily ever after for us because, tonight, I'd have to walk away from him, never looking back.

I swallowed the painful lump of emotions clogging my throat. "Nothing lasts forever, Knox. I graduate in a couple months, then I'll join my family business. And you have to move on and pursue your music career." Stretching up, I tried to smooth away his scowl. "Knox, all I want for you is success, for people to hear your amazing voice and songwriting talent."

"And why can't you fit into that equation?" He combed his fingers through my wild mass of thick auburn hair. "Do you know you're the first person in my life who believes in me without reservations? Who accepts me, wanting nothing in return?"

"You deserve that and so much more," I croaked.

"I never believed that until you came into my life."

And soon, I'd be walking away from him.

He ran his hands over my curves. "You deserve better than me. You're smart, sexy, caring, honest..."

My heart thumped wildly because I wasn't honest. If I were, I would have told him about the Credence Curse, but I couldn't.

He continued, "And me? I'm just a street thug who jumps from job to job, waiting for this music thing to kick off."

"But you're so much more, Knox." And he was. I'd never forget the first time I saw him singing his heart out onstage. It wasn't just his looks that had drawn me to him like a magnet; it had been his voice. And I'd been happy to dance to it. Out of the blue, our eyes had locked and stayed that way throughout his performance. That was how I'd met him.

I still got a tingle down my spine when I remembered how mysterious he'd seemed when he walked right up to me and actually started a genuine conversation that didn't involve dirty sexual innuendos or empty promises. It was then that I'd realized he was a real-life badass without the idiot factor. He was brooding, intelligent, and oozed rugged sexuality—a wickedly enticing combination.

Who could have known he'd actually want me, a college girl who loved the anonymity of not being that "Credence fae witch hybrid." He didn't know that Others used to hunt and kill witches like my family for sport and that Others hated us because, in their eyes, fae witch hybrids were an abomination. I blossomed during the temporary reprieve from having to explain the often-embarrassing behavior of my mother. This was my time, and I'd been reckless and free, immersing myself in my passion for dancing and music without having to suffer her oppressive disappointment.

It didn't matter that Knox initially thought I was a bored

rich girl trying to live out some fantasy with a starving musician. A month later, he'd realized I just liked him. It was uncomplicated, and that was what we'd both wanted. At least, that was what I'd convinced myself.

I wasn't ready to admit to Light or myself that my feelings for Knox were getting dangerously deep, waiting to lay siege to my heart.

I was falling for him, and that was foolhardy.

The rules were clear. Falling in love would obligate me to expose what I truly was, setting in motion his slow march to death.

"I see all good things happening for you." My voice was thick with emotion. "Regardless of what happens tonight."

He kissed each of my fingers, one by one. *Damn, he is really adorable beneath his tough veneer.*

"I don't know a fucking thing about love." His jaw tightened. "Living on the streets when my mother died was tough, not that she'd ever given a shit about me. And I've done some pretty fucked-up shit to survive. I'm not proud of it, but it's the truth."

I whispered, "Don't do this, baby. I don't need an explanation. We all have ghosts from our past." *Some more than others...*

He continued, as if each word were painful to utter aloud. "I'm fucking tainted. And to be honest, I don't think I could ever truly trust anyone. I'm too rough around the edges to give you the love you need." His fingers slid through my hair. "But if you give me a chance, I'll work hard to be the man you deserve. And if that's not almost love, then I don't know what is."

I rubbed his arm, loving the way his eyes went all warm at my touch. It was times like these when I wished there were a future for us. But I knew better.

Fate is a bitch.

"No response?" He arched a brow. "I'm trying here, Stormy."

"I know." I sighed. "Can we talk about this later?" Because I didn't want to lose sight of what I had to do later tonight. "The Battle of the Bands finale is real important to you." I kissed him with a loud smack. "Just think, you could win a record contract tonight. You worked too hard for this opportunity just to let it slip through your fingers."

"Maybe, Stormy." He ran a hand over his hair with agitation. "Maybe we'll win the Battle." He looked around at the packed crowd of excited bands through the plume of smoke. "There's just some heavy competition performing tonight."

"And none of them is as talented as you." This was the truth.

His unique voice meant there was no singer like him. It was like pure, hard thunder with a sensuous kick at the end. When combined with his raw sex appeal, I swore it was like an ice cream cone on a summer day, delicious with every lick and even better going down.

I rubbed my thighs together, getting hot from the memory of exactly how super talented his tongue game was. His eyes narrowed, his nostrils flaring, like he could actually smell my sensual scent of need.

I ran my tongue over his lips before saying, "Playtime is over. Go play some music."

He scowled jokingly. "You're a pushy little thing." He nipped my bottom lip. "It's kind of hot." His lips curled up into a slow, sexy smile. "Thanks for being here, Stormy. It means a lot."

"I think I might faint. You actually said something sweet." I softly punched him in the chest. "And what's the deal with leaving me tickets at the door? You didn't have to do that."

Knox was struggling, even though he worked several jobs. He couldn't afford to pay for tickets.

"And that's why I did." He looked at me pensively. "You don't ask for a fucking thing, Stormy. You put up with me not being able to take you out on a decent date like that punk Luke did."

"Luke and I are no longer friends, so let it go."

His lips curled up snidely. "Are you sure about that? Because Portia..."

I pulled away from him completely. "You need to stop listening to her."

I knew Portia was the culprit, starting rumors that Luke and I were together. All lies, but it didn't help that Luke was stalking me. Luke couldn't—no, wouldn't—accept the fact that I wasn't interested in him romantically.

Knox scowled. "Something about him feels off. That dude is fucking psycho."

That was true. Luke was turning out to be more mentally unstable than I'd originally suspected. But I knew that Knox's hatred of him came more from the fact that everywhere Knox and I went, Luke would show up.

"Why are we talking about this?" I asked. "The past is the past."

"You're right." His face softened slightly as he pulled me against him. "I apologize for being a major ass." He cupped my face, landing a soft kiss on my lips. "Do you forgive me?"

"This time. But I'm done talking about Luke. You either trust me or you don't."

He sighed heavily. "Stormy, you know I don't do that trusting shit."

That was another red flag that our relationship would never work. We both had major trust issues.

"Yeah, well, if I were going out with Luke, I would tell you.

I don't play games, Knox." I had bigger issues to deal with, like ensuring I wouldn't end up insane from the strain of constantly being on guard around him. "Like, if you were still sleeping with Portia, I would want to know."

"Portia and I were over way before you and I met. It's all business for me." He ran his fingers through his hair. "But for her, it's all personal. And she's bitter right now."

"Bitter about me," I responded flatly.

"Exactly. Her mood swings and manipulation are tearing the band apart." He rubbed the back of his neck. "I would fire her, but that would break up the band."

I blinked. "Let me get this right. She's using the band as leverage to get back with you?"

His expression was grim. "I suppose that's one way of describing this shit. She's dangerous and desperate, a combination that might drive her to do something I know she would regret. But I'll fix this. I promise."

I didn't push the issue because, after tonight, he and I would be over.

"I know you're used to more, and someday, I'm going to give it to you." He paused. "Your family must hate that you're with a guy like me."

"It's not about them."

"Why is it that every time I mention your family, you avoid the topic?"

I shrugged, my heart thundering in my chest.

Not this again.

"Believe me, there's nothing special about my family."

Other than we're cursed descendants from a long line of powerful fae witch hybrids, doomed to kill every man we fall in love with. No biggie.

His eyes narrowed. It was as if he could sense my unease.

"What? Your mother won't approve of you bringing home a tattooed rocker guy for dinner?"

Nope, quite the opposite. Mom would love him. Just not for me. More like for her.

Knox was everything she loved in a man—young, wild, and rough around the edges. She would suck him dry.

He stared at me, waiting for me to say something, not that I would or could.

How could I even begin to explain the basics of the secretive world I live in?

He would think I was insane if I told him this world not only comprised humans but also beings called Others—supernatural beings coexisting with humans—like us. *And my family. How could I even explain Mom's eccentric, extravagant lifestyle?* Or that she was an unabashed Domme—a female sexual dominant who rotated through young sexual submissives faster than the speed of light?

I cringed at what he'd think of Mom and Light's mom, Aunt Lia, who ran Credence Other Corporation. But despite my family's wealth, we were outsiders among Others because of our fae ancestry. And the last nail in the coffin of craziness was that, in a few months, after I graduated from college, I'd have to learn the family business with full expectations to take it over, like an insane rite of passage.

Nope, I like the persona I created better—Stormy Credence, the fun college party girl. It was just simpler that way.

"Look, it's not you." My voice cracked. I cleared my throat and started again. "My mother is different." *Very different.* "I'm just not ready to unleash her on you." *Or any human.*

She was just too much of everything. Which was the exact reason I'd intentionally told him very little about my family. He knew my parents were no longer together, that I hated my father and had absolutely no contact with him, that my mother and aunt ran a successful company in Manhattan. And that I was an only child with two cousins, including Light, and two aunts, including Light's mother. Of course, I didn't mention we were the last of the Credence bloodline, a topic that was way more morbid, complicated, and darker than I cared to delve into—ever.

I liked him not digging into my family dynamics. He just accepted. I also didn't dig into his family life. He had none. His mother died years ago and left him nothing, so he lived with Wyatt in a run-down apartment.

I broke out of my trance when I heard Portia purr, "Knox, it's time."

My eyes narrowed as she strode toward us like a toxic dark cloud of dust, wearing jeans so tight I wondered how she could even walk without tearing the seams like an angry green monster. My lips pursed with disgust at her body-hugging, ripped-from-the-neck-almost-to-her-belly-button black T-shirt with a faded eagle. It was just tacky. I didn't like her. Shit, no female who encountered Portia liked her. She was too phony—from her overinflated breasts to her ass implants. Even her ombre-blond hair mixed with god-awful jet-black highlights was made up of hair extensions. She deliberately ignored me as usual, letting her obscenely long fake nails trail along the bunched muscles of Knox's shoulder.

He shrugged away from her touch. "No hello for Stormy? She's standing here."

With an air of forced nonchalance, Portia mumbled, "Unfortunately."

"What did you say?" His voice rumbled like a freight train.

"You know how I feel about her, Knox." She jammed her hands on her narrow waist. "And I would take great pleasure in making her—" she stepped forward "—disappear."

"Don't even dare." His voice boomed as he pushed me behind his wide, muscled back.

I tugged on his shirt, trying to step around him as he clutched me against his back with arms of steel. I was more than capable of defending myself against her.

"You won't always be there to protect her, Knox. She's nothing but a weak..."

Oh, hell to the no.

"Please let me go, Knox. I'll show her weak!" I bellowed.

Knox pinned me to his side. "If you even breathe on Stormy, I won't be responsible for what I do to you."

Portia's mouth formed a big O of shock as she held up her hands and stepped back. "Don't you see what she's doing? Destroying everything. She's not worth it." She pointed at me with her ugly finger. "Plus, she's playing you off that boyfriend of hers. I've seen them together."

"What?" I huffed. "That's a damn lie."

I could tell he was furious by the way his body convulsed as he tried to get his temper under control, and it didn't help that we were drawing an interested crowd.

"Stop, Knox. She's not worth it." I wrapped my arms around his waist, relieved when I felt his anger ebbing away.

"You are fucking close to being dropped, Portia," he warned.

She let her cool mask slip, showing the real Portia—the spiteful Portia. "You won't. You can't. Not after what I've done for you." She stamped her foot like a spoiled child throwing a tantrum. "You fucking owe me, Knox."

What the hell?

He owes her what?

"I don't owe you shit." His fists clenched and unclenched. "So, don't even think, not for one second, that I won't walk away from you." He widened his stance. "There are managers who would be more than happy to take your place. Never forget that."

"Look, I'm sorry." Portia swallowed nervously. "We've come too far, Knox. For years, it was just us." She gave me a look filled with raw hatred. "Then she comes along, and you lose sight of what we've worked so hard for."

"You mean what *I've* worked so hard for." His voice was as hard as ice.

"Come on." Portia's eyes looked desperate. "Let's close the deal. Knock this shit out tonight."

"You answered my cell." It was a flat statement.

"You were busy." Her voice squeaked.

"I determine when I'm busy. And I'm never too busy for Stormy. Got it?"

Her jaw tightened. "Yes, got it. Now, can you get ready?"

He shook his head with disgust. "Bye, Portia. Go do your job and get out of my face." He spun around and pushed me against the wall, his broad back blocking her view.

I peered around him. She was still standing there, staring.

I looked at her pointedly. "Can you go away now? We were in the middle of something here."

If looks could kill, I would be dead. She huffed, stomping away in a cloud of skank.

Opening my purse, I reached in, pulling out my good-luck gift. Something I'd seen him eyeing at the pawnshop for a while. "Open your hand." I shoved the wide silver skull ring into it.

He pulled me against him, hugging me tightly. "This is the best gift I have ever received."

My breath caught in my throat at the raw emotion in his voice.

"It's nothing. Just something for good luck," I replied.

"It's everything. Thank you," he answered before his warm lips kissed my neck, sending a tingle of pleasure through me.

"Knox!" Wyatt yelled. "We're on soon."

Knox pulled away from me slowly. "I've got to go."

"Go." I trailed my fingers across his cheek. "I'll be the girl in the front, screaming at the top of her lungs."

"And I'll be the man singing his heart out for his woman."

That was the first time he'd called me "his woman." His words made me feel overwhelmed and terrified.

His lips devoured mine before breaking our kiss.

I walked away before I did something stupid, like tell him how I felt. My mind wouldn't let me reveal that, not tonight or ever.

I pushed through the crowd and skirted around the corner.

Portia stalked toward me. "Are you done filling his head with bullshit of happily ever after?"

I tracked her movements with my eyes, not trusting her one bit. "Okay, are we really doing this?" I took off my earrings, sliding them into my jeans pocket, getting ready for anything.

Her eyes widened with shock. "So, the rich girl is tough, huh?"

I wanted to laugh.

She didn't know just how tough. The one thing Mom had prepared me for was the ability to protect myself under attack. She wasn't taking any chances with her only daughter. Others were dangerous and took weakness as an invitation to maim—or worse, kill. And killing witches, especially rare fae witch hybrids, was a trophy kill. So, the prerequisite for granting me permission to move away from home and getting access to my trust fund was my promise to continue my biweekly defensive training sessions with Noah, my childhood friend.

Despite my initial resentment at being forced into training, I never missed our sessions. In fact, I enjoyed the no-holds-barred ruthlessness of them. It was all brute force with a little blood thrown in for good measure, and I enjoyed it. And just thinking about handing out a well-deserved ass-kicking to Portia made my pulse race with anticipation.

"Don't let the pretty clothes and the smile fool you." I strolled around her. "It's really not my style, fighting like a couple classless backstage groupies." I stopped, strategizing how far I could lodge my foot up her skinny butt. "But I'm not opposed to finally having a reason to kick your ass. If you want to take it there, then let's go. If not, step out of my way. I have to get ready to cheer on my man."

She spat on the floor.

My eyes widened with disgust. You could take the girl out of the streets but not the street out of the girl, and Portia was a straight-up street urchin.

"Not as soft as I thought you were." Portia wrinkled her nose. "I wonder if Knox knows his pretty little trophy girlfriend is a street fighter?"

I shook my head with disbelief. She was truly a piece of work. I saw the way she'd bully Knox's groupies. It bordered on abuse. Portia was dangerous, a woman who had grown up on the streets like Knox. She was used to doing anything and everything to get what she wanted. Unfortunately, I had grown up around a lot of women like her. Most of them Others who were rotten to the core and had no qualms about using their bodies, beauty, and powers to manipulate people around them like pawns on a chessboard. And that was what Portia was—a master manipulator.

Portia flicked the strands of my hair with a taunting glare.

I swatted her hand away. "Stop stomping those man-sized feet encased in cheap-ass shoes and get to the fucking point, Portia."

She smiled at me with eyes saturated with pure hatred. "It won't last."

I didn't act coy about what *it* was. "It? Believe me, my relationship with Knox will last as long as I want it to. And neither you nor Wyatt have the balls to chase me away. Trust me on this." I stepped up in her face, trying not to gag when I smelled a sickly sweet scent wafting around her. The aroma was eerily haunting and clingy. "When will you finally get it through your head that I won't go away just because you still want him? He. Doesn't. Want. You."

Portia's face flushed with anger. The air was so thick with rage and tension, I could almost taste it like a bitter pill.

"You are not one of us, Stormy. And we only stick to our kind."

My eyebrows rose. "Kind? Are you serious? What does that even mean?"

She sneered. "You do not know what and who you're messing with, rich girl."

My stare was unwavering. "Exactly what type of prescription drugs are you on? Because you sound totally deranged."

She glowered at me. Frankly, it was unnerving.

I'd had enough of the cat-and-mouse game. "Okay, so are we done here?"

"For now," she responded before stomping away.

"Truly insane," I mumbled under my breath, marching out from backstage and immersing myself in the throng of gyrating drunk bodies. One of them was Light. She was at the bar, as usual, holding court with an entourage of men circling her like sharks, as the boom of the music filled the club.

I walked behind her, flicking her hair. "I'm here. Now the party can begin," I said, giving her a wink.

The sharks stopped mid-swim, focusing on me with interest.

"Not going to happen." I waved at them. "Bye now." Leaning over, I smiled at the bartender, screaming over the noise, "Two beers."

"Yay! Beer." Light grabbed her cup of beer as soon as he'd put it down. "Stormy, check out the pretty auras on those two." She sloshed her drink, pointing over at two menacing-looking guys—one with blond hair and the other black—with blue auras, which meant they were shifters. They eyed the crowd with disdain as they bulldozed their way through the people who were heading backstage.

Oddly, I'd seen them before. They had been hanging outside Knox's apartment, just watching. When I'd told him about them, he'd shrugged it off but gotten oddly silent.

"I saw the skank known as Portia stomping away in a plume of anger," Light stated flatly. "You two got into it again, huh?"

"Yep." I grabbed my cup of beer and pulled Light through the crowd toward the front of the stage.

"Oh, I almost forgot to tell you," Light started. "The cackling hens called from Vegas last night."

I almost choked on my beer. "What did our mothers from hell want?"

"Your mother had a premonition, something about a bird—no, an eagle. Then she babbled about how you need to watch your back and that the Credence Curse is about to rear its ugly head again."

"What?"

Light's eyes were a little dazed. "Huh?"

"Light, did it even occur to you to mention this earlier?"

She blew a strand of hair from her forehead. "Why? You're not in love with Knox."

I wasn't yet. I took a sip of beer, staring into space. But if I didn't break up with him tonight, it would only be a matter of time before my heart dragged me to a place with Knox that would lead to love and regret. Right after the show, I had to break up with him.

I swallowed anxiously before the lights flickered. The music lowered.

Happy for the distraction, I pointed to the stage. "It's about to start."

Light pointed to the other side of the club. "Isn't that Stalker Luke talking to Portia?"

My gaze focused on Luke—aka Stalker Luke—who was standing against the wall with his friends, the Ivy League squad, and Portia, who was practically climbing him like a tree.

Luke was what I called a chameleon. He was anything he thought you wanted him to be in order to snare you, a fact I'd found out the hard way. When we'd first met in psychology class, I found him intriguing because he was handsome and attentive. We'd become fast friends until he'd made a point of letting me know he wanted more than friendship. Then I had to have the awkward talk with him, making it clear that I didn't see him as anything more than a friend. And when I'd met Knox and made it clear—again—that Luke had to leave me alone, he still pursued me with a creepy, stalker-like focus.

"What is he doing here?" I hissed, trying not to make further eye contact. He was like a dog who would construe my acknowledgment as an open invitation to come over and play.

Light shot him the bird.

I slapped her arm. "No! He'll come over."

"It's too late. Stalker Luke is sauntering this way."

I sipped my beer, staring at the flickering stage lights.

"What's up, Stormy?" Luke greeted me cheerfully.

"It's Stormcloud." I glared at him. I was in no mood to be polite. He was here to start trouble. I saw it in his deranged, beady little eyes. "Only my friends and family call me Stormy."

"I thought we were friends." He leaned against the stage, trying to prevent my escape with his body.

I shoved away his arm that had been preparing to wrap itself around my waist in the most inappropriate way.

"Why are you here, Luke?" I asked. This wasn't amusing. This was the second time he'd followed me to one of Knox's gigs. The first time hadn't been pretty and had ended with Knox backing him into the wall, almost choking him to death.

"Portia invited me." He looked over at Portia, who waved at me mockingly. "She thought I would enjoy the show."

"Didn't get enough of an ass-kicking last time? Go away, Luke." I shoved him.

"Knox is playing you, Stormcloud." He cut a sidelong look at Portia. "They're still sleeping together. And I'm going to be here for you to lean on when you find out," he finished before stomping off.

"This is chaos," I muttered.

"Yup," Light replied. "All because of one person—Knox. Cut him loose."

The rightness of her words sent a shiver through me. Something in my soul knew that shit was about to get worse if I didn't break things off with Knox.

We both looked up when a man strode onto the stage, smiling like a game show host. The crowd roared and cheered.

"Ladies and gentlemen, welcome to the New York Battle of the Bands finale. A big thank-you to the three major record labels for providing judges for tonight's matchup." He pointed grandly over to the side of the stage. "And please don't forget the judges will take into consideration the crowd's response for each band. After the last band has played, the judging will begin. This year, we have a lot of talented bands waiting to rock for you tonight. Each band is hoping to win top honors and the grand prize of a recording contract with one of the major labels. So, let's rock!" He walked off the stage, and the lights dimmed.

I tried to get excited as I listened to the thumping sounds and vocals of the first band, an all-female group. They were fantastic, but still not good enough to win. By the time the third band played, I'd had several more drinks and was on my way to being totally buzzed on alcohol, so I stopped drinking and just danced like I was starring in a music video.

Half an hour later, they announced Knox and his band. I screamed at the top of my lungs, happy to see him perform for the last time. When he stepped onto the stage, my heart stopped like it was my first time seeing him. He grabbed the microphone and looked directly at me. "Tonight, we're performing something new. It's a song I wrote for the storm that blew into my life, changing everything about me for the better." Then he sang in that seething, sexy way that made me melt.

"There was no me before you.

You brought me something I didn't think I ever wanted.

The roar of the Storm.

The thunder.

The lightning.

And when the clouds rolled in, all I could think about was the break in the Storm.

My Storm.

Breaking the Storm."

The song revealed everything he couldn't relay to me except through his music. By the time he finished hitting the last note, I was an emotional mess. I hadn't even realized tears were streaming down my face until I tasted their saltiness on my lips. I dashed my tears away, clapping and screaming so loud my throat and hands hurt.

The emcee returned to the stage. "All right, time to judge."

The crowd was a rowdy mess when he called out each

band's name. Everyone had his or her favorite, stomping and yelling like crazy. The judges deliberated for a long period before passing an envelope with the winner to the man onstage. He opened the envelope and smiled. My heart dropped when he didn't announce Knox's band as the winner.

The crowd booed the winning band, shouting Knox's name over and over. The mayhem was deafening. Cups of beer flew onto the stage, and security stepped up to stop a near riot.

"I'm going backstage," I announced to Light.

Light grabbed my hand. "To comfort him? Or to break up with him?"

I swallowed hard. "I can't break up with him tonight. Not after this setback."

"If not now, when, Stormy? You're just prolonging the inevitable. Break it off now."

Tears pricked the corners of my eyes because she was right. I had to do what I set out to do tonight, break up with him. Pushing through the crowd, I made my way backstage, my mind raging against kicking him while he was down. But I knew it didn't matter whether I left him tonight or tomorrow or the day after; it would still hurt the same.

Turning the corner, I skidded to a stop when I saw Wyatt stumbling around, drunk, clutching a bottle of liquor.

"Hey, Wyatt. Where's Knox?"

He pointed down the hall. "The manager's office."

Wasting no time, I walked that way. When I finally reached the cracked-open door marked *Manager* and heard Knox say, "What the hell are you doing? Put your clothes on and get out, Portia. I didn't ask for this. I'm not interested."

"I know you didn't ask..." Portia answered. "I wanted to give myself to you. And I thought—"

"That's what you get for thinking. Like I've said several times, I'm not interested in you, Portia."

"But what about us?" Portia begged.

"There hasn't been an 'us' for over a year. We're just business. Now, get the hell out. I want to be alone."

"How about I go out there right now and tell Stormy that you've been lying about who and what you are? About what we all are?"

I swallowed hard. It was like the cosmic universe was giving me the perfect opportunity to finish what I came here tonight to do. Break it off with Knox.

My fingers shook as I steeled myself for the best acting performance of my life.

I pushed the door fully open and tried not to flinch when I saw Portia standing in front of Knox. She was naked from the waist up.

Contorting my face into a fake mask of blind rage, I said, "So sorry for interrupting your consolation prize for losing the Battle of the Bands."

Portia smirked at me while reaching up to stroke his chest. He shoved her hand off.

"This is not what it looks like," Knox said.

I didn't let on that I'd heard their entire conversation before busting in.

"Really? Because it looks like I've interrupted your secret hookup with your skanky whore. We're done, Knox." Turning, I stormed away, searching through the crowd for Light. I did what I'd come here to do, and now it was time to get the fuck out of here. My eyes locked on Luke, who was leaning against the wall, waiting. He strode in my direction, his eyes filled with an "I told you so" gleam.

I held up my hand in his face. "Not now, Luke," I snapped while looking around frantically for Light. My breath hitched when I caught sight of Knox marching toward me with a thunderous expression on his face.

Luke wrapped his lean arms around me, then kissed me on the lips.

Luke's body sailed into the crowd like a bowling ball knocking down pins. The crowd cleared as Luke's body skated across the floor.

Frozen with shock, I stared at Knox. He was angry, bordering on feral. It took a lot to rattle me, but his expression made my knees almost wobble.

"You, don't move," Knox demanded before storming over to Luke, yanking him up and twisting his arm behind his back at a painful-looking angle.

"Don't touch her, ever. Stormy belongs to me," Knox hissed.

I watched in horror as Wyatt and Aiden struggled to pull Knox off a laughing Luke. Finally, when they did, Luke wiped the blood from his mouth with the back of his hand. "You did it to yourself, asshole. Thank you for making my job of getting her back so much easier."

Knox lunged at him, but Aiden and Wyatt grabbed him tight.

Light ran over to me with wide eyes. "What the hell is going on?"

"I did what we Credence women always do, fuck everything up." I turned on my heel, practically sprinting toward the club's entrance.

I made it all the way to the sidewalk, breathing in a lungful of air, before Knox grabbed my arm.

"Get the hell off me," I demanded.

He backed me against the side of the building, caging me in. "Explain."

"I caught you with Portia, and you want me to explain?"

"Did it ever occur to you, you saw exactly what she wanted you to see?" he asked.

I desperately wanted to tell him the truth about the Credence Curse, but my family forbade it. Now, with me out of his life, he was safe and could be happy with another woman.

"I saw the truth. You and I don't belong together." I pushed against his chest. "We're done."

"You don't mean that."

"But I do. Leave me the fuck alone."

"Stormy, I really don't need this shit right now."

I was emotionally and mentally exhausted by this conversation and just needed to go home to bawl my eyes out.

"Move, Knox. Now!"

He stepped back, allowing me to sidestep him. I straightened my clothes, spinning on my heel to find Light and get the fuck out of here. He clasped me gently, tucking me against his chest, wrapping his arms around me. I almost sighed contentedly as my back pressed against him familiarly.

"Don't leave like this," he whispered into my ear in a husky voice filled with raw emotion.

My body and mind wavered for a second before I shoved down the pain of loss. "I really don't know what type of women you're used to dealing with, but I can't—no, scratch that. I won't get past this. You and Portia have fun." I pulled away with pointed finality.

My heart was racing when I spotted Light standing next to the waiting car service.

"Let's go," Light ordered while opening the back door and sliding inside.

"Stormy, don't walk away," Knox pleaded.

Please don't cry, I chanted over and over in my head. A sob escaped.

Before I could get inside the vehicle, Knox stepped behind

me, the heat of his body pressing against mine. Swiveling around, I said, "Don't," then shoved him back.

"Stay," he asked, running a finger across my cheek. "Talk to me."

"What do you want from me, Knox?"

"Everything."

"I have nothing left to give." He didn't understand that I was doing this for him. I was saving his life.

He reached for my hand. I evaded his touch.

"We can work this out," he insisted.

"Wait." I looked him up and down with a fake expression of contempt. "Did you honestly think you and I would actually skip into the sunset like some ridiculous reality-show couple?" Each word was like a knife in my chest, painful and biting, like a slow crawl bringing my soul closer to death. "You're a starving artist. I need someone rich, like Luke. And from what I've seen tonight, you're not worth my time or effort. Goodbye, Knox Gunner."

I hopped into the car, pulling on the door to shut it, but he stubbornly held on.

"This is not the end, Stormy." His eyes were hard. "It's only the beginning. I'll be back to claim what's mine—you." He slammed the door before hurrying away.

"Go," Light ordered the driver, who wasted no time and peeled away.

My head fell against Light's shoulder as tears streamed down my cheeks.

"The pain will pass," Light whispered while stroking my hair.

"I know," I whispered, but deep in my heart, I knew that I'd never be the same woman again.

Knox had ruined me for any other man.

CHAPTER 3

PRESENT DAY…

My thoughts snapped back to this moment in time.

It made no sense, ruminating on the past. My relationship with Knox would have ended no matter what I did differently, so it was best just to accept it and move forward.

Sighing heavily, I focused on the bubbly host on the screen who was smiling like she'd won the lottery before saying, "Hello, my lovelies. Gigi Bordeaux here to rock your world with the hottest celebrity news. Women are fainting at this latest tidbit. Sexy Knox Gunner is coming to the city so nice you have to say it twice—New York, New York."

Gigi leaned forward, displaying breasts spilling out of her too-tight blouse. "And last night, fans got a scrumptious taste of the wickedly sexy superstar performing his scorching popular hit single at the music awards. And let me be the first to say, congrats, Knox, on winning an award for Song of the Year and Best Rock Album. His performance was the kickoff for his long-awaited world tour, set to start next week in New York before making its way around North America, with stops in Chicago, Los Angeles, and Las Vegas. And tickets are hot, hot, hot—" she made an exaggerated sad face "—and, unfortunately, sold out."

She licked her pouty lips, staring dead at the camera before flicking her hair like she was in a shampoo commercial. "But hold on to your designer panties. I've scored the hottest interview yet. They have granted me a coveted sit-down with Mr. Hotness himself. Knox. Knox, baby." She leaned toward the camera, batting her fake eyelashes. "It will be backstage and real personal." Her voice got husky. "Stay tuned, ladies." She fanned herself dramatically. "This is going to be a hot one."

I scoffed before getting to my feet and heading toward my desk to grab my cell.

"You hear that, Stormy? Knox is in New York." Light gave me her best beauty-contestant smile. "And guess what? You're in luck. I have a connection that can get us front-row tickets and VIP backstage passes."

"Not that I'm remotely interested in *your* connection, but whom did you have to blow to get access to the God of Rock?"

"Not that I'm opposed to giving a well-deserved blow job, but it wasn't required." She rolled her eyes. "Wyatt called me this morning to say he was in town and would love to take me out to dinner."

"Wyatt?" I arched a brow. "I didn't know you still talked to him."

"Oh, don't give me that hurt look like someone just stole your fucking bike. I haven't talked to him since you broke up with Knox. But, out of the blue, I got the call."

My brows furrowed. "I thought you hated him."

She shrugged. "I do. He's a conceited bastard that I'm playing like a Ken doll." She winked at me. "Besides, with

Knox back in town, my week just got a little more interesting. Can you imagine the reunion this will be? You. Me. And Knox? Just one big dysfunctional reality show."

I looked at her over the rim of my reading eyeglasses. "The possibility of running into Knox in person would be as enjoyable as a root canal. So, the answer is hell no."

"Oh, come on. There's no way in hell we'll see him. Besides, I heard his opening act is smoking hot, so we can act like wild groupies for one scandalous night." She winked. "With no freaking repercussions and all the hot rocker sex we can handle."

"No." Pursing my lips with displeasure, I thumbed through my cell contacts. "One, I'm not interested in doing the groupie thing. Two, you and I have way too much work to do." My heels clicked as I paced back and forth with my cell on speaker. "Celina? Where in the hell are you? You missed check-in."

Light propped her feet on the couch with her eyes fixed on the television. "Oh hell, Stormy, you sound too whiny. Put more Domme in your voice, like our mothers. Trust me on this —our ladies love it." She suggestively waggled her eyebrows.

I gave her an irritated glare before continuing, "Celina, call me ASAP. We have a legacy client looking for a wolf-shifter escort for his friend. It's a birthday gift. So, get your cosmetically enhanced ass ready to meet him, pronto." I slid my finger across the screen, ending the call.

Light clapped her hands. "That's it, girl. Tough. Hot. Kick-ass Domme."

"Are you trying to make me kick your ass?"

"What?" Light responded with her usual mischievous smile.

"Dragon witch," I barked into my cell, calling my mother—the witch from hell. And just like the last five times, it went to voice mail. "Why in the hell is she not answering her cell?"

"Coven retreat," Light chimed in.

"Coven retreat? It can't be that time of year already."

"Yes, Stormy. They go to the same retreat every year. Witches gather. Discuss Other business. Get drunk. Get laid. And come back home, well fucked and smiling like the Cheshire cat." She sighed loudly. "I'm so damn envious, and I can't wait until our moms retire so we can finally get our invitations."

I snorted. "As much as I adore a good lay, you couldn't pay me to spend three weeks locked at some retreat with those backstabbing women." Only the top Other escort service businesses got invited to a three-week retreat at a luxury resort. It was a mixture of business and a lot of pleasure, with mostly cougar Others on the prowl.

Pulling my bra strap-length thick auburn hair away from my neck, I sighed out in frustration because it was irritatingly hot on my neck, which was the prime reason I always wore it pulled back into a sleek ponytail. It was less of a hassle.

"Okay, so let me get this straight. Mom leaves a frantic voice mail about needing to leave town to take care of an emergency and leaves this dress—" I gestured to the garment I was wearing "—with instructions to get my ass to Ryker Alfero's party, all because of some witch retreat?" It wasn't my job to meet and greet clients; that was Mom's and my aunt's responsibility.

"Pretty much." Light looked me over with a wicked smile. "But you've got to admit, she has impeccable taste. Look at you. You look like a sex kitten. Meow." She swiped her hand like a cat. "Damn, your body is just sinful. And I'm envious as hell." She eyed my eyeglasses disapprovingly. "Will you take off those cock-blocking glasses?"

"I'll have you know, I've been told these glasses make me look like a naughty teacher who's about to hand out a punishment to a bad boy." I pretended to slap a ruler in my palm with a stern glare.

Light squinted. "Okay, keep them on. You need all the help you can get to counteract the judgmental air you get every time you're around Others."

"It's hard not to judge people who are hypocritical elitist assholes who look down their noses at hybrids like us, yet are more than happy to use our services to find them escorts."

Light shrugged. "Not all of them are like that, just the prejudiced asswipes on the Other Council. And they don't fucking count."

I glared at her. "They do count because they control everything that happens behind the scenes. If we weren't damn good at what we do, they wouldn't have shit to do with us. They need us because we fill the female Other shortage gap. So you bet your sweet ass, every time I get the opportunity, I'm going to stick that shit in their face. Without us, our family of female fae witch hybrids, they wouldn't have a chance in hell at finding those pretty little females they parade around like show ponies."

"Okay, that's true. But wolf-shifters are sexy as hell."

My body stiffened as I tried to calm my breath. *Oh shit. Not again.* The last time Light had had an affair with a wolf-shifter, it was disastrous.

"Light, please tell me you haven't been having sex with wolf-shifters again."

"Oh, don't get all uptight and righteous with me. I didn't say I've fucked one lately. But god..." She grinned. "You don't know what you're missing. The sex is hotter than hell."

My mouth tightened. "I don't care how hot the sex is. It's not worth the involuntary side effect of binding with his crazy ass forever. Besides, there are rules, Light, to protect us and them."

Light ticked them off on her fingers. "No sex with the same guy more than once. No relationships with humans. Ensure limited sexual contact with Others." She dismissed me with her hand. "Too many damn rules if you ask me."

"Our lives aren't that bad." I cringed inside because, in reality, they were, but I tried not to dwell on something I couldn't change. None of us could. "The Credence women are powerful, confident, successful, rich, and beautiful."

"And don't forget bitter," Light added before taking a sip of champagne.

"We're bitter because we're ashamed that we have fae blood."

"You got me there," Light agreed.

"Shifters hate us because we remind them of a time when the fae kept them in cages and made them fight for food. The vampires despise us because we remind them they were once slaves to the fae. And witches envy us because the fae chose our ancestors to breed with. But none of the Others gives a shit that the fae wronged our family. Think about it. Centuries ago, the fae forced our ancestors to have sex with them because they wanted to leave a trace of their bloodline in the human realm before they went back to their realm."

Centuries later, the tension between our family and the Other community was ever-present, no matter who much we tried to be amicable.

Light chimed in, "And to make matters worse, they are using our Credence Curse to keep us in line."

"Exactly." The Credence family made an oath to the Council that we would ensure we killed no human men because of the Curse. That oath was the only thing keeping the truce between us intact.

Light scoffed. "But the only reason the Credence family made the oath of ensuring the Curse never reared its ugly head again was because our ancestors were emotionally broken from losing every man they loved. Shit, they threw their hands up in the air in defeat and came up with some fucked-up rules that don't make a bit of sense. Now we're stuck living a loveless life. This shit is not healthy."

"Has it ever occurred to you you're being selfish? Do you know how many women would kill just to have the life we live? We have more money than we could ever spend. We age significantly slower than humans do. It's a win-win situation."

"This—" Light gestured wildly at the hand-painted walls, expensive furnishings, and Louis XIV-style Rouge Royale fireplace "—doesn't mean shit if we'll have no one to share it with. Face it. We're going to die alone, and no amount of money is worth living a life that is emotionally empty."

"Do you really think I like the fact that I'll never have a man to share my life with?" After Knox, I learned not to dwell on a situation we were born into and couldn't fix.

Light glared at me with more clarity than I'd seen in months. "Yes, I think you do."

I placed my hands on my hips. "If you think I enjoy living my life like some emotional leper with no chance in hell of having companionship, then you don't know me. And I thought you did."

"Oh, I know you well, Stormy. And what I know for sure is that you live your life in this shell, not willing to show anyone you care. Dammit. Make some fucking mistakes. Let yourself feel again. Do something, because it's breaking my heart to watch you wither away, pretending all you need is your career and money."

My heart had frozen over after Knox, and nothing was going to change that fact. "And what would be the point of that? Unlike you, I care if I hurt a human."

Light pursed her lips. "There's nothing in the rules that says we can't have fun."

"Okay, so you find a guy. You get attached. Then what?" I arched a brow. "You can't build a life with him because you eventually have to walk away."

"Exactly. You just said it. We walk away. But at least we experienced it. We understand we will not skip off into the sunset in some fucking fairy-tale, happily ever after ending. But we can have fun while it lasts and then move on to the next man."

Light was out of her fucking mind. I didn't have the emotional bandwidth for that shit.

"That's bullshit. I will not open myself up for the experience. All I need from a man is straight-up S-E-X."

Light's face flushed. "No, what's bullshit is you walking around living this half existence because you're scared that one day, S-E-X will turn into love."

"That's never going to happen. I'm happy with what I have —my career and my family. And if I need a warm body, I'll have it for one night. Then I'll be the one walking away, well fucked."

Light smirked. "God. I can't stay angry with you when you say funny shit like that."

"Good." I flicked her hair playfully. "Now let's drop this horrid topic," I grinned at her before walking away to check my makeup in the full-length mirror. Frankly, I didn't even recognize myself tonight. My pouty lips glistened with lip gloss, making them look sensuous, and my almond-shaped hazel eyes were sultry. I loved looking sexy, but my hectic work life didn't exactly incite the need for sex-on-a-platter makeup.

"Why does my mother act like I'm a kindergartner who needs her to pick out my outfit?" I asked. Unlike most mothers, who encouraged their daughters to cover up, Mom's motto was less was more, tight was right, and classy was the fine line between stripper-wear and couture.

"She knew you would've worn a stuffy business suit if she didn't."

I glared at her over my shoulder. "And what's wrong with that?" That I had to go braless to wear the body-hugging black silk gown with a wide-set neckline that reached my belly button annoyed me. Thank goodness it had a sheer mesh overlay to prevent an embarrassing boob falling-out incident.

"If you haven't figured it out yet," Light replied, "we sell sensual indulgence." Her smile disappeared when she noticed my frown. "Hello? Where's the sexy, fun Stormy who would hang out with me all night in the club?"

"She grew up and started taking life seriously." I tapped my bottom lip. "Brought about by years of working overtime to keep up with all the tasks my mother, aunt, and cousin—" I looked at her pointedly. "—refuse to touch."

"Blah, blah, blah." Light's lips pursed with disapproval. "Embrace your hotness, Stormy. Live a little. You're so uptight, you make a nun look like a stripper."

My eye twitched with annoyance. "Well, one of us has to take shit seriously around here."

"Another dig at me?" Light wrinkled her nose. "It doesn't matter because I'm comfortable with who I am."

I smiled mockingly. "A wild party girl who loves to prank call me at three in the morning, singing horribly off-key?"

Light held up her hand. "That was once. Okay, twice. Anyway, that's off topic." She sighed. "I just wish you would loosen up. Work those curves. Sway that hot ass. And for good-ness' sake, have some rough sex, like real soon, because you're getting fucking cranky from cock withdrawal."

I dropped down on the sofa with a weary sigh. "I have sex

every night—lots of it." And it was very good, not great, but I'd learned to pick my battles.

Light snickered. "Sex toys don't count."

"It's the best kind of safe sex." I winked at her. "Besides, cock withdrawal is not a medical condition. It's a state of knowing when to stop trying to attain something that doesn't exist—a real man who gets me." I plopped my feet onto her lap. "And I'm a hard woman to get. I'm like an onion—way too many layers."

Light pushed my legs off her lap. "It might help if you ever got out of the office. You know, actually go out and get back into the dating game. This time, aim for someone not so boring. Tom screamed vanilla."

I arched a brow. "Really?"

Light smirked. "What?"

"What?" I mocked her. "Tom wasn't a relationship." I snorted loudly. "He was my fuck buddy—you know, the type of buddy you call in a pinch."

Light rolled her eyes. "You only called him when your toys were on the disabled list."

I pointed at her. "Exactly. And I've yet to meet a man good enough to put them into retirement." I paused. "Shit, find me a man who could do that, and I'd have a toy-burning party, wearing nothing but stilettos. I'll give you one better. Find me that man, and I'd strut around Mom's BDSM club, butt-ass naked in those stilettos. Either way, I'd be smiling like I'd won a beauty pageant." I did an exaggerated beauty-contestant wave.

Light laughed huskily. "As much as I love you, if that man actually existed, I'd kick your ass to get at him first."

I shook my head. "Proving the fact that a good lay is hard to find."

Light scrunched her nose. "Shit, there's no disputing that fact. I just want you to acknowledge Tom's fucking boring."

I shrugged my shoulders. "That's what I liked about him. There was no chance in hell of me falling for him. Something you should take heed to."

"Oh, hell no. The Credence rule says no relationships or bonding. It says nothing about picking absolute snoozers in bed. Shit. If I can't have a decent fucking relationship, then at least I can have hot sex."

I fluffed my hair. "He's not that bad in bed."

Light's brows hit her hairline.

"Okay, yes, his tongue game was horrible." I shuddered with distaste because it was so bad, I'd told him to cease any further attempts.

Light gestured for me to continue.

I held my hands out in defeat. "Okay, he's bad in bed."

"Exactly. It's time to rotate back on to the dating market." She looked at me matter-of-factly.

"So says the woman whose longest relationship was with that champagne glass in her hand," I responded coolly.

Relationship conversations weren't one of my favorite topics. It rated as high as ex-boyfriends. Once the relationship was over, I'd erase them from my memory bank like yesterday's trash. It was easier that way.

"Let's move on."

Light pursed her lips. "It's the Credence Curse. You fear it striking again, like it almost did with Knox."

"Oh, fuck the Credence Curse. We have blamed everything from the inception of time on the Curse," I snarled. "Mom trips on the curb? It's the Credence Curse. A boyfriend's cock accidentally slips into another woman's mouth? It's the Credence Curse. Enough already. Off with their heads—literally." I made a chopping motion.

Light quickly sat up, spilling her drink. "Off with their

heads? Oh, sweetie, you'd better get some sex, like real soon, because you're getting bitter and crazy."

My eyes narrowed. "I'm not bitter or crazy. I'm just keeping it one-hundred-percent real." Sauntering over to the desk, I picked up a bottle of champagne and filled my glass. After draining my glass, I looked at her with satisfaction as I filled it up again before giving an air toast.

I hated living under the doom and gloom of the Credence Curse.

A curse Great-great-great-great-grandma Elizabeth Credence caused when she fell in love with a human and refused to marry the warlock her family had promised her to since birth. Elizabeth's marriage to the warlock would have united two powerful covens, but she chose love instead. That love was the root of the Credence Curse.

Incensed that Elizabeth rebuffed her son, the warlock's mother cursed Elizabeth and the entire Credence bloodline.

A curse that doomed any human we fell in love with to a sudden, horrible death. And there was plenty of evidence throughout history that the Curse was real.

Elizabeth's human husband got struck by lightning while riding a horse. Years later, her daughters Mary and Claire fell in love with and married humans. Mary's husband slipped down a hill and broke his neck. Claire's husband drowned in a lake. Claire had two daughters, Solista and Mercy. After getting her heart broken by a shifter, Solista fell in love with a human who died after being trampled by his horse.

After all those deaths, the Credence women finally took the Curse seriously and forbade anyone in the bloodline to fall in love with a human. Well, that and the Other Council didn't like the unwanted attention our family was getting because of the bizarre deaths, which was why our family made an oath to the Council that we would ensure that we killed no human men because of the Curse.

"Stormy, you're not the only one who's almost gotten caught by the Curse. Just let it go," she stated flatly.

I gritted my teeth. "I have."

"You haven't. Zero worthwhile boyfriends are a testament to that fact." Light sighed. "You dated Tom because all he cared about was his career. You need someone who will let you put your guard down and encourage you to make some dirty minor mistakes."

"Oh, hell to the no. That's a deal-breaker." I took a huge swallow of champagne, letting the bubbles roll over my tongue.

"Okay, but can we agree with my original assessment that you're a sexual submissive? Then all will be right in my fantasy world."

"I can't be sexually submissive to any man. I love control too much." In fact, I craved and demanded it.

"You just haven't met the right man to earn your submission." Light scowled. "I can't believe Tom left you for that submissive whore."

"We were over way before he left." That was the truth. So, it hadn't hurt that he'd left me for a woman who was everything I wasn't—blond, thin, and submissive.

"That goes to my original statement about you needing a good lay," Light responded.

"I'm not the only one who needs that."

She shrugged. "I'm on a cock hiatus. Pacing myself."

"Can you tell me how we moved from our mothers ditching us for a witch retreat to my lack of a good lay?"

Her eyes widened. "It's all related. And please don't act like they haven't done crazier things. We'll fill our entire life with years of therapy sessions, all because of those two insane hags," she grumbled. "Can you believe they're sending me, of all people, to some stuffy charity ball to meet some heavy-hitter tiger-shifter who's in town?" She crossed her arms. "I don't do stuffy."

I choked on my drink. "Wait, you get a tiger-shifter, and I get stuck with a wolf-shifter? How is that fair? We have three tiger-shifters on our roster and only one wolf-shifter—a missing one, at that."

"Don't ask me. They passed out the assignment, and now I have to spend a perfectly good Friday night completing it. Thank goodness Rhia and Bethany were available to come with me tonight."

"Am I the only one who realizes shit is falling apart?" I responded with annoyance. "This is critical meltdown time. I feel it, and it's making me fucking nervous."

Light brushed her hair from her brow. "Do tell, wise one."

My eyes opened wider with shock. "Celina is missing. And Jack is calling me like a jilted lover. I can't hold everything together on my own."

"Alone?" She raised her hand. "I'm your partner. Stop panicking. Celina isn't missing. You know how flighty she is. She's probably on some fabulous vacation with one of her wealthy lovers. And your father..."

I gave her an evil stare.

Light held up her hands defensively. "I mean Jack—he's probably looking to get some money from you."

Yes, that was definitely what it was. Jack always popped back into my life at the most inopportune times, just like a pimple on prom day. Either he'd spent all his gambling winnings, or one of his many women had thrown him out after discovering what a big asshat he was.

For the life of me, I just didn't understand why he'd called me after the last time we'd spoken. I'd clarified that he needed to lose my number. It was pretty pathetic when a man made a point of telling everyone who listened that he wanted nothing to do with his child, but then made no bones about the fact that he would try to use me as his own private bank when his funds got low. No, I knew the real Jack—the despicable, evil man who hid in a handsome shell. Jack wished I'd never been born, and I wished Jack would wither away and die like the piece of trash I knew him to be.

He was the first man in my life to hurt and disappoint me.

I was the child he hadn't wanted, and it was a hurt I locked away. But every time he resurfaced, it was like a Band-Aid being ripped from unhealed flesh. His emotional neglect left lasting scars on my soul. It had seared lasting childhood memories into my brain from the last time I saw him.

I was ten, scared and hiding behind a weeping willow tree, watching one of many heated arguments between my parents.

Mom was yelling. Her porcelain skin was flushed as she shook her hands in his face. Her fingers were twitching, as if she were one step away from doing something terrible—like casting a wicked spell to render him speechless, which would have been practically community service because everything that came out of his mouth was vile.

Jack was the name I'd known my father by since birth. As usual, he was drunk, angry, and harassing Mom for money. He was worthless.

Mom's fiery-red mane flew around her like a cloud of embers as she paced back and forth, waving the piece of paper in her hand like a fan. "Look what I got in the mail this week. They sent it special delivery to my office." She crumpled the letter and tossed it in his face. "You're sleeping with Selma Gilden?"

He took a big swallow of scotch, eyeing her with barely veiled hate. "Ava, why does it matter? I was just your sperm donor. You made it very clear you wanted nothing more from me."

She laughed. "It's so convenient that you remember that fact when one of your little tarts flaunts that you're sleeping with them. And when it's time to beg for money, you're more than happy to remind me of my stupid mistake in choosing you."

He smiled cruelly, narrowly standing, mumbling incoherently under his breath. I never understood how such an outwardly beautiful man could be so ugly on the inside.

She looked at him with disgust. "Selma is my biggest nemesis. She's crowing over the fact that she's banging the father of my child, and you have the nerve to ask why it matters." Her face was enraged. She poked him in the chest before responding, "Her family is our biggest business competitor. They have been for centuries. They've done everything in their power to destroy us."

He poured more scotch into his glass and drank it down like it was a glassful of water. "Ava, I don't give a shit about Other business. Never did. Never will."

"Why are you here?" She quirked a brow. "I locked up the valuables, so there's nothing to steal."

His fists clinched. "I need money. I've worked hard for it."

Mom laughed tauntingly. "You haven't worked a day in your life." She jabbed his chest furiously. "You gamble and whore around Manhattan. If that's what you call a job, then sign me up."

He grabbed her hand roughly. "You knew what you were getting when you got involved with me."

Her green eyes narrowed on his painful grip on her hand. "It would be in your best interest to release me before I do something I won't regret."

"Threats from the fae witch? Well, that's hilarious. I'm not scared, Ava. If you want to fight, let's fight. But don't bring magic into it, because being torn apart by a wolf-shifter trumps witchcraft any day."

She scoffed. "What do you know about shifting? You're an alcoholic half-breed whose major talent used to be he was a good lay." She looked at him like he was shit beneath her designer stilettos. "Even that skill was limp and lacking a month later."

He smiled contemptuously, "It wasn't lacking, honey. I just didn't have proper motivation."

"You're wolf trash, Jack, a major mistake, but I got something out of it I will cherish forever—Stormy."

His smile disappeared. "It's always about Stormy, one of the last surviving heirs of the Credence bloodline." He laughed cruelly.

She smirked. "Really? You're jealous of your own flesh and blood? Fascinating."

He smashed his glass on the ground. "It's always some game with you. You're the ultimate manipulator. Always have been and always will be." He paced back and forth while Mom looked at him like a specimen under the microscope. "Breaking news. No man will ever love a Credence woman. You're just too damn hard to love."

Mom tapped her foot impatiently. "Please, Jack, you knew it was never about love for me. I needed what was between your legs. Stormy was more than worth the hassle of having to deal with you."

"Yes, how could I forget? You wanted a child who could carry on the Credence name." His gaze flipped from her to me. His eyes were icy and glassy. "I never wanted Stormy. You did."

She arched a brow. "Are you done?"

I ran over to my mother, grabbing her around the waist. Mom rubbed my head softly, looking at him with cool eyes.

"Good. Now leave, Jack, and never come back or contact Stormy. Ever."

"I haven't wanted shit to do with either of you for years, Ava," he responded before striding away on wobbly legs.

Even that young, I refused to cry. "How come he doesn't love me, Mommy?"

She stroked my hair. "He doesn't even love himself, baby. How can you expect him to know how to love you?"

If you didn't learn from the past, you were doomed to repeat it. And I, for one, had no intention of letting that happen. I had a lifetime of hard-knock lessons I held close to my heart.

I scowled, hating the fact that I'd let my mind wander... again. I didn't linger in the past; it'd already happened. I couldn't change it, but I learned from it, determined to move forward to a bright future. A lonely but prosperous one. I would stay focused on keeping our business successful, building on to the empire that had made my family wealthy. And to do that, we needed to gain the respect of our employees —the escorts. They were the rare commodities that didn't respect Light's or my authority—yet.

I moved back to a safer topic, our missing employee. "Celina knows the rules. Notify us if she's going out of town. And as flighty and scatterbrained as she is, she always does that." A shiver ran down my spine. "No. Something's wrong. And it's not the time for something to be wrong. She's the only she-wolf escort we have."

"Stormy, will you shut it? You're killing my buzz." Light took another big swallow of champagne. "Why are we still talking about this shit?"

I blew out loudly. "Ryker wants an escort for his best friend. Some freaky birthday present."

She gave me a look of confusion.

I continued, "Ryker Alfero, alpha of one of the largest and

most powerful wolf-shifter packs in New York? He's the fucking leader of the Other Council." Everyone knew about Ryker's fight for alpha position of his pack. When a bloody wolf pack battle killed his father, Ryker had challenged his uncle for alpha position and won.

Light rolled her eyes. "I know who he is. I just can't figure out why you didn't tell me the problem half an hour ago instead of babbling."

My mouth dropped open in shock. "What? Did you think I was searching for Celina because I was looking for sex advice? We need her."

Light drained her glass. "Give me the rundown again."

"I have limited information from Mom. All I know is he's requested a she-wolf for a best friend who's in town for a couple weeks. It's some surprise birthday present for him."

Light's eyebrows furrowed. "His contract covers non-pack members?"

I shrugged. "Unfortunately, it does. And since they have handed you the easier assignment, I'm stuck going to the party to meet them to ensure they're clear on the parameters of our services." I rubbed my head, feeling the start of a major migraine approaching. "Ryker's too powerful for us to mess this up." Not to mention, our families had a terrible history.

Light got up and grabbed her tablet from the desk and started flicking through the file of escorts. "Okay, we've got a couple shifters available at the end of this week—a tigress and a jaguar. So, you bat those gorgeous hazel eyes, smile, and run your tongue over your full pouty lips, all sexy-like. Then casually have Ryker's friend look through our roster of shifters and hope like hell he goes for the bait and switch."

"What planet are you on? Ryker's contract specifically states we must provide a female wolf. That means we're royally screwed, because I'm not trying to piss him off by telling him we don't have something we're contractually obligated to provide."

Light inhaled sharply. "I heard he has a wicked temper."

"Okay, thanks for adding, Light." I paused. "If I don't find a female wolf, we are both screwed, partner." I sighed heavily, already tired of a game our ancestors had played for centuries. Only this time, it was our turn to play. And if we lost, we would be the first Credence generation to change history and not in a good way.

"Shit. We're fucked."

I clapped my hands. "Finally, I get some concern from you. It's not just me, baby. It's you and me in this clusterfuck. So, hold on for the wolf-shifter ride because it's going to get real bumpy."

CHAPTER 4

"HELL, why do they do this shit?" Light exclaimed. "They're getting more devious every day."

"Just another test to see if we can handle this business. I just hope I survive the bloodbath of being mauled to death by an alpha wolf-shifter."

"You're not getting ripped to shreds by some crazy wolf-shifter." Light grabbed her cell, shouting, "Crazy witch," voice-dialing Lia, her mother and my aunt.

"What, Light?" Lia responded in an annoyed voice.

Light screamed, "What the hell, Mom?" She was actually hyperventilating, while I was thinking about how to avoid a pissed-off shifter who could rip me to pieces.

Light continued her hysterics. "You and Aunt Ava promised a big, badass wolf-shifter a female wolf we don't have."

I pulled her cell closer. "Aunt Lia, where's my mother?"

Mom interrupted in a husky voice like some sultry kitten, "Calm down, sweetheart. Why are you screaming? I'm right here. You've always been such a high-strung little witch-in-training."

I would not fall for her distraction techniques. No, this time, I focused on not wanting to die. "Mom, why is your cell turned off?"

"Jack is phone-stalking me again. Something about wanting to meet me to discuss important business. Well, that will not happen." She sighed. "What do you want, honey? We're very busy."

My patience was running thin. "Didn't you hear what Light just said? We don't have a female wolf. Credence O. rule—always deliver what's promised to the client. We can't deliver!" I shouted.

Aunt Lia responded nonchalantly, "Improvise, darling."

My gaze slid to Light before replying, "Improvise? That's your answer? I can't conjure up a female wolf. Believe me, right about now, I wish I could."

Aunt Lia chimed in with an annoying singsong voice, "Improvise."

Mom laughed before she said, "You're a big girl. Both of you are. Credence women have been dealing with Others for centuries, doing what is necessary to keep our business successful. Don't be the one Credence to fuck this up." Her voice was calm and collected. Nothing ruffled that woman's feathers.

Aunt Lia piped up, "Well, darlings, we've got to go now. The party is starting, and we need to get first dibs on the desirable men."

Light whispered, "We're fucked."

I refused to give up. "Are you testing us?"

"We don't have time for games, Stormy," Mom responded. "You should know that, especially with the family business, but we question your ability to run this company without us. I mean, just listen to you two. You're panicking over a missing she-wolf. Tradition is tradition. You must prove you can run Credence O. without our intervention. No exceptions."

"Hmph, especially for someone who's turned her nose up at who we are and what we do while reaping the rewards," Aunt Lia said.

I squirmed. "I've never turned my nose up." Well, not exactly. "I've managed the funds. I've made excellent investments, doing everything you two refused to do by actually focusing on something other than entertaining clients."

"*I'm never using magic, ever. Boo-hoo.*" Aunt Lia mocked me—and my decision never to use the craft.

"That's my choice, and it has nothing to do with my right —" I looked over at Light "—*our* right to claim our legacy, taking over the business. By Credence law, you two must transition the business over to us and then fade into retirement."

Light chimed in, "Poof! Bye-bye, Mother."

Mom laughed. "I believe these two are the worst of the Credence bloodline. And let's not talk about the sad fact that there's no mate potential. The Credence bloodline will die with them." She sighed loudly. "It's damn depressing."

I rolled my eyes. I hated the fact that it was an accurate statement. We were literally the last of the Credence family. If we didn't produce children, the bloodline would die with us, not that we succumbed to pressure. I wasn't even sure I wanted children—a fact that I would never tell Mom for fear she'd have a heart attack.

Aunt Lia responded, "I know. No grandbabies. God, I'm going to be sick."

"Damn drama queens," I snapped. "I don't hear Aunt Trulista whining about the last of the bloodline."

"Tru is too busy with coven business," Mom responded evenly. "Besides, she did her part by providing a Credence heir. It's not her fault Sky is as hopeless as you two. For goodness' sake, this isn't rocket science. Find a man and have a child."

Light snapped, "We've got plenty of time."

"Please," Aunt Lia replied. "You think *committed* is something they do to crazy people. And poor Stormy hasn't gotten laid in so long that if she cracks open her gorgeous legs, you'd see cobwebs and dust."

Mom's laughter was smooth as molasses. "Good one, sister."

Listening to them was annoying as hell.

"Not everyone believes an excellent date means a night at a BDSM club with a seedy wolf-shifter licking her stilettos." I smiled wickedly. "Or that foreplay begins at the sound of the come-and-get-it dinner bell."

Light and I high-fived. It was like a tag team—us against our mothers.

Light chimed in, "Dinner served. Ring. Ring. Ring."

Aunt Lia laughed. "Insolent little witches. Admit it, you both just gave up on trying to find a man. It's sad, really."

Light's eyes went wide. "For the last time, I'm on a man break. Stormy's the one who's avoiding finding a man."

I gave her the evil eye. "Remind me later that you have an ass-kicking coming to you."

Light shrugged. "I'm just saying. You're ready. I'm not."

"You both are ready. The time for casual fucks is over. Take the leap of faith and find the one."

Regardless of all the trash talking, I loved them, but they expected us to give as hard as we got. In my family, toughness and resilience were rewarded. The weak did not inherit the earth.

"I really don't care what you say as long as you get your skinny butts back to Manhattan. We've got a major crisis here," I countered.

"There's no *we* about it." Mom's voice got deep, showing

playtime was over. "You two have a major crisis, and you will do what I instructed. And each of you handles your assignment."

"Don't you use your Domme voice on me," My voice was just as hard. "It doesn't work."

"Oh, don't you fear, smartass. One day, a Dom will have you scurrying for cover." Mom sighed heavily. "I'm bored, sister. Shall we go over the rules of engagement?"

They actually cackled in a creepy way. *Shit. This was trouble.*

I looked worriedly at Light. "We know the rules, Mom."

They had drilled us about the rules since we were young.

"Quiet," Mom barked. The command was icy and impatient.

I blinked, gritting my teeth, readying for a major battle.

Mom continued, "Rule one: there is no fraternizing with clients. This includes sex, dating, and the fuzzy area in between. We don't shit where we eat. Rule two: don't mess with the family business. That means do whatever you need to do to keep the client happy. Our reputation is everything."

"Our girls are the cream of the crop," Aunt Lia said. "We attract and keep the very best. That's how we've maintained our legacy contracts with the damn awful blue-blood Others for centuries. Remember that."

Mom interrupted, "Rule three: what we promise, we deliver. If it means selling your soul to the underworld, so be it. If it means promising your firstborn, kiss your baby goodbye. Rule four: we don't break up marriages or relationships. Single and available is all we match. We don't care how much money they have or promise. That's off the table, period. Rule five: break or destroy the business, and we will break and destroy you. This is our legacy, and blood won't mean shit if you two fuck this up. You get me, ladies?"

"Yes," we said in unison.

"Lovely," Mom said.

Aunt Lia interjected, "These rules are the same ones handed down from generation to generation. When my mother lectured me on the rules, I was just as insolent and resentful as you two are. But I learned the hard way this keeps order and structure within the Credence family and among our employees."

This was the major take-no-prisoners Credence test. I felt it in my bones.

"I mean, how hard could this possibly be?" Light asked.

"Exactly," I agreed. "The escorts have the simple part. All they do is look pretty as arm candy. We do all the hard work."

Aunt Lia laughed. "Is that so? There's so much you two smartasses don't know about what it takes to be an escort. Humility. Intelligence. Negotiation skills. And submission." She sighed. "Oh, Ava, how could they not know this?"

"This is exactly the reason our escorts don't respect them," Mom replied.

I rolled my eyes. "They don't respect us because they know they can run to you with the slightest complaint about us, and you'll take their side. And please don't act like they're rocket scientists or out to create world peace. All they care about is the money."

Inwardly, I cringed when I remembered the last test Mom and Aunt Lia had given us. It had been an epic fail when Light and I had hosted the monthly escort dinner for the first time. Typically, it was an extravagant bonding event Mom and Aunt Lia hosted, where the escorts would give the status of assignments and gossip about which Other millionaire and potential client was in town and who had gotten mate-claimed. But when they'd found out Light and I were hosting, half of them hadn't shown up, and those who had had treated us with outright hostility.

Aunt Lia responded, "And you don't?"

"I'm honest about what I want," I countered. "I don't wrap it up in pretty bows and hope a man gets it. This is who and what I am. And I know for sure I'm not looking for some shifter or vampire that's a start-up man."

Aunt Lia bellowed, "What the heck is a start-up man?"

"I can't wait for this explanation." Light drained her glass.

I shot her an annoyed glare. "A man who's finding himself sexually, financially, and emotionally."

The instigator, Light, prodded, "Please break it down for me, Stormy."

"I'm not trying to be a teacher in bed. I want someone to teach me. I'm not trying to be a man's financial provider. He needs to come to me ready to be an equal partner. And I don't do broken men. Fix your issues before you approach me."

Light looked on with awe. "Damn brilliant and hard-core."

"Stormy, that's the smartest thing you've said during this entire conversation," Aunt Lia responded.

"Don't encourage, Lia," Mom ordered. "Now, on to the tiny matter of our retirement. We decide when we retire. Do you think it was easy to get our mother to turn over the business to us? No, we worked our gorgeous asses off to show we understood it was a privilege and not a right. We proved we understood everything the Credence bloodline stood for. And when we showed the Credence business and legacy would not die with us, then and only then was the business ours."

"Now it's time for you to prove the same," Aunt Lia finished.

Light's eyes looked like a kicked puppy's. "Hey, we work our asses off every day to do just that."

"Prancing around the office in designer suits, playing

director of marketing, doesn't count, Light," Aunt Lia chastised. "Rolling up your fucking sleeves and dealing with the clients and escorts does."

I laughed. Light gave me a middle-finger salute.

"What the hell are you laughing at, Stormy?" Aunt Lia asked. "You hide behind your laptop all day and night, playing director of operations. Turning out damn metrics reports that have nothing to do with the reality of our world. Spend five seconds dealing with our escorts, and you'll be tearing out your hair. In fact, how about you deal with our overprivileged clients who think they walk on water? Then you'll truly understand the difference between what's written in their contract and the reality of implementing it. Believe me, there's a big, fuzzy gray area that reality doesn't account for."

Mom interrupted, "Three weeks. That's what you two have to prove you deserve the keys to the castle. Running Credence O. is difficult, but you'll discover that all on your own. Just one mistake can turn a business that's existed since the horse and carriage was hot into dust."

"We've got to go, darlings," Aunt Lia exclaimed. "This year's theme is sexy human sacrifices, and we want first pick."

My eyes widened with outrage. "What? You're going to kill humans?"

Mom laughed hysterically. "See, Lia? This is a prime example of what denying your bloodline will do to you. Turn you into an educated idiot. Stormy, if you had shown the least bit of interest in the craft, you would know we don't use harmful spells unless absolutely necessary. And it will be absolutely necessary to turn you two into donkeys if you destroy our business."

"Educated idiot?" I frowned. "I'm not the only one who went to college. You have an MBA, not that it's required to wield a flogger."

"She's joking, Stormy. Don't get your panties in a bunch," Aunt Lia said. "And sexy human sacrifices is a BDSM theme."

"Great, more sex," Light muttered. "That's all you over-sexed hags need. Do you know how many nightmares I've had since I saw you at that club with your sexual submissive?" She shivered with disgust.

"Oh, quiet. Don't be jealous of your mother, baby. I'm finally getting some," Aunt Lia cooed.

Light leaned against the desk. "Mom, please. You have more sex than I do."

Mom said, "That's so true."

I threw my arms up with frustration. "I give up. They're certifiably crazy."

"Bye, sweetheart," Mom said. "And don't destroy the business while we're gone."

Our call ended.

Light walked over to the couch and threw herself onto it. "We're so screwed."

"We can handle this," I replied, ignoring the foreboding vibe of disaster floating around me.

Our mothers had totally plotted out their divide-and-conquer strategy by having Light at one event and me at another so we couldn't combine our best skill sets—my negotiation skills and Light's people skills—in order to succeed tonight. Together, we balanced each other. Separately, we were a total disaster. But tonight, we had to win, which meant I had to step out of my comfort zone because failure was not an option.

CHAPTER 5

NOTHING WAS GOING RIGHT TONIGHT, and it was freaking me out.

I called Noah—my childhood friend and member of the Alfero pack—to pick his brain for tips on handling Ryker, only to find out from his personal assistant that he was unavailable because he was out of the country on urgent business. Then my visit to Celina's penthouse had resulted in the doorman telling me he hadn't seen her in days. *Why did Celina disappear without a word?*

So lost in thought, I was startled by the sound of ringing that echoed throughout my car's speaker system. I groaned when Light's name displayed on the console, dreading what I knew would be more bad news.

Pressing the button on my steering wheel, I answered, "What's up?"

"Are you there yet?" Light whispered.

"No. And why the hell are you whispering?"

"I'm on the terrace, hiding behind a huge potted plant."

"What's going on, Light?"

"I have a hostile tiger-shifter on my hands. And do you know why? Because his mother thought it would be a fabulous gift to match him with a nice tigress while he's in town." Her voice started rising in an unusually panicked manner. "But guess what she failed to mention? That he's already mated to a human, a human she hates."

I banged on the steering wheel in frustration. "That's exactly why I despise these 'I-want-to-set-you-up-without-your-knowledge' matches. Someone always gets fucked, and not literally either."

Light shuffled her cell. "Hold on, it gets worse. I called his mother and politely explained we're not in the business of breaking up relationships and we only match single clients, but she's not having it. She threw a hissy fit, threatening to petition to the Other Council for breach of contract."

Great, this night keeps getting better and better.

The Other Council rarely took on minor disputes like this, but I was sure they would reconsider their position once they'd heard this was a complaint against Credence O. I could just hear the circus music.

I drummed my fingers on the steering wheel. "Our contract specifically states we only match single clients. Just apologize to him and leave the party. I'll have Reason deal with his mother in the morning and explain the finer things in life, like the heavy penalty fee she owes us for misrepresenting her son's availability status and wasting our time."

"Um, Stormy, there's more, but please don't freak out."

"Just tell me, Light."

"Some guy named Jeff Hunter just called my cell."

"And?"

"He claims to be a reporter, and he's asking a lot of questions about Celina, like what exactly her position is at our company."

I jerked the car, barely missing plowing into another one. "Why is this shit happening?" I pounded the steering wheel with each word.

"What do you think he'd say if I told him Celina is a wolf-shifter and one of our top escorts?" Light laughed hysterically while I battled the urge to hurl. "Stormy?"

This is bad. We listed escorts on our books as personal assistants. And in the real world, personal assistants didn't make as much money as ours did.

"I'm here, but I can't process the mess that's unraveling before my eyes. I just need to focus on what I need to do to save this deal with Ryker. Then we can focus on everything else later."

"I'm not trying to add to the drama, but I have a bad feeling about this Ryker deal. So, you'd better fluff up your hair, reapply your lip gloss, and show some cleavage to make it happen."

It wasn't my style to use sexual ploys to get over on a client. But tonight, I was going to make an exception. There was just too much at stake not to.

"Already on it." This entire night was really pushing me way past my comfort zone. My idea of Friday night excitement was crunching numbers and going over contracts with a glass of wine, a bowl of fettuccine, and my favorite reality show blasting. I didn't do parties or social gatherings. "Let's just get through tonight without either of us having a nervous break-down. We'll deal with everything else tomorrow morning." I pulled up to a palatial estate. "I'm here."

"Stormy, you're going to be fine. Now go into that party and show them what you're working with. And don't forget I love you."

"Love you too," I responded before ending our call.

I unlocked the door and stepped out, allowing the valet to

take my convertible, then wasted no time following the eclectic guests to the entrance of the party. My mind was so engrossed in preventing myself from running in the opposite direction that I bumped into a tall, dark-haired, olive-skinned man blocking the entrance and checking the guest list. I recognized him from somewhere; I just couldn't figure out where. Beside him stood two burly but well-dressed men in black. I read their aura, and all three were blue, which meant they were Other.

The dark-haired man's eyes roamed up my body before stopping at my face.

"Hello, I'm Stormy Credence."

"Uh-huh." He gave me an amiable smile. "I know who you are. In fact, most Others know who your family is. My name is Bones, and I'm a member of Ryker's pack. He's waiting for you."

I controlled my nervous twitch at the mention of his name because I'd heard Ryker was a major ass. I just hoped Ryker's friend was a relatively young shifter who was working his way up the ranks in the pack. It would make it a lot easier to convince him to choose another escort.

"Thank you," I responded coolly.

He smirked before nodding over to security. One man grandly opened the heavy mahogany doors.

I'd just stepped over the threshold when Bones said, "Ms. Credence?"

I looked back at him with an arched brow. "Yes?"

"It's going to be a real long night, in more ways than one. If I were you, I'd grab a glass of champagne before meeting Ryker."

My eyebrows rose. "I'm sorry. What—" My jaw dropped when the two guards gently nudged me across the threshold before stepping back outside and firmly shutting the door in my face. Guests' heads snapped around to look at me as I stood there with my hands on my hips, fuming, listening to their distinct laughter outside.

What the hell is so funny?

I was so tempted to go back out there and ask them, but I didn't want to make a bigger scene, something I knew the dynamic trio of stupid would relish.

I glued my feet to the ground when the door popped open, and Bones walked in, barely suppressing a smirk.

"And what was all that about?" I commanded.

"Now, if I told you that, this whole thing wouldn't be as fun, would it?" He winked at me before striding away.

I confirmed it. He was a smug asshole.

Smoothing down my dress, I started strategizing and sorting through all the information I'd memorized. Before becoming leader of the Other Council and alpha of the Alfero pack, Ryker had been one of the top cardiologists in America.

He'd given it all up to run his wolf pack and take over his father's successful property development business. Ryker had no kids, was unmated and unmarried, but he had plenty of bedmates—humans and wolf-shifters. He was also used to getting what he wanted, so I knew navigating the waters of renegotiating his escort request would require using skills I deplored—flirting, fawning, and batting my eyelashes as if his manly prowess enamored me. Those were skills Mom and Aunt Lia had perfected and used cunningly, all with the goal of getting what they wanted. I could use my looks and femininity to get what I wanted, but it wasn't my style. Using my brain to outthink and outwit a person was my go-to strategy, but that wouldn't be sufficient tonight. Shifters were very sexual beings. And if I wanted to get anywhere with Ryker, I'd have to work my womanly wiles like a pro.

My gaze wandered over the ballroom, taking in the well-dressed guests milling around, sizing one another up like cattle.

Most auras were green for humans, with a smattering of blue for Others.

Not wanting to look as anxious as I felt, I grabbed a glass of champagne to keep my hands from twitching nervously as I weaved my way through the eclectic crowd. My eyes narrowed when I saw Bones talking to a tall, heavily muscled, impeccably dressed man. When his eyes locked on to me, I knew instantly he was Ryker from the way he strode over to me like some sort of marauding Viking.

I tried not to blink in shock. He was the opposite of what I'd envisioned a doctor to look like. He was massive, like an MMA fighter. But he was exactly what I'd envisioned him to be as an alpha, from his well-groomed dark beard and short jet-black hair to the scar across his left eyebrow and the snake tattoo on the right side of his neck.

"Stormy Credence." His deep voice rumbled as his sea-green eyes scanned me from head to toe. "I'm Ryker Alfero."

"It's wonderful to meet you." I quickly extended my hand while scanning his aura. And just as with all alphas, something veiled the color of his aura from me.

He grabbed my hand, bringing it to his lips. "Simply love-ly." He smiled in a slow, sexy way that, under different circum-stances, would have even made me give the wolf-shifter a try.

Pulling my hand back, I leaned in, allowing my body to graze his broad chest. "And just so we're clear, I'm definitely not on the menu."

"Well, that's a fucking shame." He sniffed the air. "The Credence women pique my interest."

Eyes on the prize, Stormy, I chanted in my head.

"Thank you, I think." I put on my best game face. "So, Ryker." I smiled. "Can I call you Ryker?"

"Darling, you can call me anything you want."

I laughed. He was suave; that much was true. But I needed

to focus on getting this deal closed. Then I could walk away and let Celina handle him and his friend.

I arched a brow. "I would love to meet my new client to discuss expectations."

"Of course. Follow me." He started walking, and I kept up by his side.

"Your family has had a contract with Credence O. for centuries. So, I'm surprised it's being used to provide an escort for your friend," I stated as we flowed through the party.

"My friend serves an important purpose, so I want to keep him happy."

I frowned at his cryptic response. "Do you care to elaborate?"

Ryker shrugged his wide shoulders. "We have eclectic taste in women." He pressed his palm to the center of my back, guiding me over to a deserted section of the room. "But the companionship of a female wolf has totally eluded him. Hence, my gift to him."

My body stiffened when I felt the oppressive weight of a hard stare that seemed to follow my steps. Casually, I glanced around, trying to act indifferent, when my breath caught in my throat. I stumbled forward. Ryker caught me before I splattered onto the floor.

My eyes locked on to the one man I never wanted to see again, the man who was now walking through the party with a beautiful, waif-thin woman clinging to his arm.

Knox Gunner.

What in the hell were the odds of seeing him again?

CHAPTER 6

I FOUGHT the rising panic and emotions that came flooding back like it was yesterday.

Relax.

Without thinking, I blurted out, "Knox."

I steeled myself for a gaze of hatred, but when Knox's sea-green eyes met mine, they were neutral. "Stormy," Knox acknowledged, then he looked over at the woman still clinging to his arm like a life preserver. "Later."

She looked at him with a wistful expression before sauntering off.

Inside, I was a churning pool of mess as I pulled on my neutral mask, a mask I'd used so many times to hide the hurt and loneliness that were like a sharp ache that never seemed to go away. That pain only grew stronger with our reunion.

Ryker tilted his head and studied us. "Great. You know each other. We can begin with the business at hand, his selection of an escort."

"I don't understand." I blinked in shock, trying to process what he said. "Knox is your friend?" This couldn't be right. Knox wasn't a wolf-shifter or a member of Ryker's pack. If he was, it was Other protocol for Ryker to introduce Knox as either a shifter or a member of his pack.

Tired of the guessing, I scanned Knox's aura and saw nothing. No blue or green aura.

"Stormy?" Ryker called out, interrupting my musing. "Is there a problem?"

My eyes locked with Ryker's. "I'm not sure he's the type of client we do business with."

As far as I was concerned, Knox was human, and our business did not take on those clients. Credence O. was not in the business of sex for pay, but we knew that clients and escorts had sex by mutual consent. Shifters were notoriously wild and rough in bed, and if Celina and Knox had sex, she might reveal that she was Other.

Ryker leveled me with a cool stare, crossing his muscular arms. "Our contract states we will provide an escort at my request. This is my gift to my friend. And you will fulfill my request." He smiled, but it sure as hell didn't reach his eyes.

Ryker had to be out of his damn mind to think I would provide a female wolf to a human. We serviced Others only.

I pressed my lips into a thin line, and then I said, "I'm sorry, but I have to decline your request for *obvious* reasons." I raised my chin, placing my hands on my hips, not caring that I was openly defying him.

"Why? Is it because I'm not rich enough?" Knox asked in a low tone. "I guarantee you I'm wealthy enough, even by your standards, Stormy."

Some nearby partiers stopped to look at us. *Shit, now we're making a scene.*

I gave Ryker my best polite smile. "Can we talk somewhere private?"

"Sure, let's go to my office," Ryker responded before they both walked away, leaving me to trail contritely.

"Yep, this keeps getting better and better," I mumbled under my breath, walking through the crowd like it was a slow march to my execution.

Minutes later, I stepped into the luxurious office to find two belligerent men glaring at me. I shut the door and stared at them.

"What the hell is going on, Stormy?" Ryker asked. "Are you trying to piss me the fuck off by insulting me?"

"I'm not trying to insult you or our long-standing business arrangement." I smiled coldly. "But the type of woman Knox needs is not in my employment. My business provides refined escorts for companionship at social events, nothing more. Now, if Mr. Gunner is looking for a no-strings-attached sexual liaison, then I'm sure he won't have any issues getting that elsewhere."

"Let's cut the shit, Stormy," Knox said, never taking his eyes off me for a second. "This isn't about sex. It's about unfinished business between us, and I'm back to claim what's mine."

Mine? He was talking about me. My fingers started trembling until I clamped them together as I tried to remember how to breathe.

Ryker gave us an impatient glare. "I don't know what's going on between you two, but I know my contract specifically states you will provide an escort for Knox, starting tonight. Now, if Knox says he isn't interested, then I'll dissolve the agreement right now." He then stared at me. "If not, then you'd better provide an escort by the end of this party, Ms. Credence. Do we understand each other?"

Shit, shit, shit.

My lips wobbled into a half smile. "Unfortunately, the type of escort you requested is currently unavailable."

Ryker crossed his arms. "Don't make me destroy your company, Stormy. One call and I'll ruin all the legacy contracts that make your family filthy rich. So, I advise you to come up with a reasonable solution to this problem." He nodded at Knox before walking out of the office, slamming the door.

My blood curdled with rage. This could not be happening. That one call would destroy our business. It was a damned-if-I-do-and-damned-if-I-don't situation.

Fuck it.

"What type of woman are you looking for, Mr. Gunner?"

He tilted his head and studied me. "I want a woman who will be completely at my mercy."

I didn't respond right away. Then he leaned into me, invading my space until the warmth of his body was a burn against my skin.

He carried on. "Someone to play with." I jumped when a hand circled my nape. His touch set my skin aflame. "Do you want to play with me, Stormy?"

I locked eyes with him, seeing the searing demand in his sea-green eyes. "Are you serious?"

He leaned forward and growled, "Very," against my ear before nipping the lobe with his teeth.

I forced myself to step slightly away from him. "Does that line really work with women?" I asked, crossing my arms over my chest.

He inhaled sharply, as if he could actually smell the desire flowing through me like rich, dark honey. "I think you know." He raised a brow. "Do you want me to help you relieve that burning need?"

Ignoring his comment, I sat on the sofa with more calmness than I felt as I pulled my tablet from my bag. I bit back a smart retort when Knox sat next to me, crowding my space with his long legs splayed.

He was trying to ruffle my feathers.

No, he *was* ruffling my feathers.

Slowly crossing my legs with a self-assured smile, I swiped my finger through the photos of the bevy of gorgeous shifters on our roster. "Before we start our negotiations, I'd like to reiterate that we at Credence O. do not advocate sexual interactions with clients."

He arched a brow.

I wanted to smack the sarcastic smirk off his face. "But we are realistic about the sexual appetites of our clients. So, what our escorts do with clients must be discussed at the first meeting with your assigned escort."

"Tsk-tsk," he started with a wicked gleam in his eyes. "Come on, Stormy. Why play games? It's obvious the attraction between us is still there."

I extended my tablet to him. "Show me what type of woman you want."

He grabbed the tablet, making sure his long, thick fingers stroked mine. I released the tablet before jumping up to walk over to the side bar filled with an assortment of expensive-looking bottles of spirits.

I poured myself a much-needed glass of Bowmore scotch, wasting no time taking a gulp. I sighed when the smoky, spicy, and vanilla flavor notes rolled over my tongue.

"The woman I require must be everything I want and need for the entire time I'm here."

I straightened my back.

"You'll be that woman. My perfect little submissive."

Ripples of arousal went through my body before panic set in. I knew when we were younger Knox was in the exploration stage of the D/s lifestyle, so his words didn't surprise me, but I refused to let him manipulate me into some simpering submissive.

I turned and pinned him with a glare that made most men curl up and wither away. Knox was not most men.

"Oh, fuck you, Knox. It will not happen."

His lips twitched. "You'd be surprised at the kinds of things I can make you do."

I barely held back from throwing my glass at his head. "Not going to happen."

"What happened to, *What the client wants, the client gets?* Well, this client wants you." He rolled up the sleeves of his crisp, tailored white shirt, displaying the tattoos on his muscled forearms.

"I'm not for sale, Knox."

"All your escorts have a price, including you," he said evenly.

I stared at him with my lips pursed in disbelief. "You don't have enough money to make me do the depraved things I don't doubt you want."

"Haven't you heard? I'm a rich man now, something you told me you needed in your life."

I squared my shoulders and took a deep breath. "Okay, Knox, you win. I get it. You're angry over what happened between us. I broke up with you, but that was over five years ago. Get over it."

"That's it?" He bit out the words, tight-lipped. "No mention of you being mad at me for allegedly cheating on you with Portia? After all, that was the reason you cited for breaking up with me at the time." His eyes were calculating, as if he knew something I didn't.

I stiffened, and my eyes narrowed. *Did he know that I'd falsely accused him of cheating just as an excuse to break up with him?*

No. That's impossible.

There was no way he could have known I'd been eavesdropping outside the door for a while before bursting in on both of them.

I blew out a breath. "You want an apology for breaking up with you the way I did? Okay, I apologize. But I wasn't the only one who fucked up. You did, too—a fact you have conveniently forgotten." Not true, but I didn't really give a shit about the truth right now.

Tone just as flat as ever, Knox said, "Don't play games. I never fucked Portia while I was with you or after you."

"I don't care, Knox. This is strictly business."

"I forgot you do that," he grumbled, not hiding his discontent.

"Do what?"

"When you get emotionally vulnerable, you erect a wall between us."

"This is bullshit!" I muttered under my breath.

"Is it? Because you hid the truth about who you and your family really were."

"I never lied to you, Knox. I told you what you needed to know."

"Needed or wanted me to know?"

"I..." I started, and Knox held up his hand.

"Here's how I see it, Stormy. Before you broke up with me, I was totally upfront with you about wanting a future with you, and you used that as an excuse to push me away. When all you had to do was tell me the truth. The truth about how you felt. The truth about who you were. And you did none of that."

"I didn't mean to hurt you, Knox." That was the truth. I came so close to falling in love with him it terrified me.

"Well, you did."

My heart plummeted at the raw emotion I heard in his voice. "I'm sorry."

He kept his answer short. "Yes, me too."

"What do you want from me, Knox?"

"I already told you. I want you as my submissive. You will do anything and everything I say. This is not negotiable. What's your answer?" His words sent a shiver through me.

"No."

When his cell buzzed, he dug it out of his pocket and looked at it. "It's Ryker, and he's pissed with you. He wants to know if we've resolved our differences." He paused. "What should I tell him?"

My irritation swelled. This was my worst nightmare come to life. In our business, reputation was everything. I couldn't be the one who single-handedly destroyed it over pride.

I sighed in resignation. "I agree to your demands."

"Wonderful." A smile twitched across his lips before he texted Ryker back. "I told him we resolved our disagreement." His cell pinged. "And he just replied that he's pleased." Leisurely, he got to his feet, shoving his cell into his pocket. "Now, back to our business. Come here, Stormy." He beckoned me with his index finger.

I crossed my arms over my chest defensively. "Hell no. Don't talk to me like that."

With an aggrieved sigh, he said, "Enough." He pointed to the spot in front of him. "Here. Now, Stormy."

Straightening my shoulders slowly, I plodded toward him, a frown on my face. I had to fight the angry tremble threatening to overtake my body. Even after all these years, the pull between us was still there.

"Let's set expectations, shall we?" He lifted an eyebrow and waited.

He traced a finger across my lips.

My resolve almost faltered beneath his steady, authoritative regard. "Let's," I responded with an attitude. "Under no circumstances am I having sex with you, and there will be absolutely no kissing. Regardless of what you and Ryker think, we don't sell sex. We sell companionship without the drama. That means, under the terms of the contract, I will make myself available for any social or business event you need me to attend with you. Anything else is off the table."

"Denial is pointless, Stormy."

With no warning, he caressed my lips with his own. I kept my mouth firmly closed. Undeterred, he nibbled and sucked my lips. My breath became ragged. My nipples tightened. And warmth pooled between my thighs. Knox was kicking through my defenses, demanding my submission.

My mind and body fought for control.

My body won.

My mouth opened, giving his tongue entry. His tongue slid over mine, seeking to claim every inch of me. With his fingers tangling in my hair, he angled my head back, granting himself deeper access. His growl vibrated through me, strumming over my pussy like his fingers on a guitar.

He gave me one last swipe of his tongue before he retreated. "You'll belong only to me in every sense of the word."

I clenched my thighs, hoping to stop the rise of desire.

Catching my chin, he bored his gaze into mine. "Do you understand what I want?"

My pulse sped up at his question. I knew exactly what he wanted.

My family was a walking commercial for dominant and submissive relationships.

Mom and Aunt Lia had years of experience as Dominants with submissive men. Men who would let Mom and Aunt Lia dominate them in any way they chose. And Light was a submissive all the way. She was just waiting for a worthy Dom. And me...I couldn't see myself trusting any man enough to submit, to kneel at his feet and relinquish my power.

"Everything you say is law. And my body belongs completely to you."

"See?" He brushed a hand against my breast, and my nipples stiffened immediately. "I know you better than you know yourself. I know what's important to you. Power. Order. Authority. But I'll let you in on a secret. Your submission to me is more important." Steel laced his tone.

"What are we doing here, Knox? Trust is the basis of a real D/s relationship. That's something we don't have."

"So, we'll build it." He smiled, and my heart skipped a beat. "We'll push the boundaries." He reached out and pulled me flush against him.

Fear raced through my body.

He was going to pick at my heart and soul like a vulture.

My body would be his tool, his weapon.

"Choose this, Stormy." His gravelly voice sent vibrations of lust throughout my body. "Don't let your brain talk you out of something you need." He rubbed a strand of my hair between his thumb and forefinger. "If it's closure you want, then grab this with both hands."

My heart thumped hard in my chest. "This is not closure. It's unearthing shit I buried years ago."

"Denial, again." He tilted his head and studied me. "Let's put all the shit on the table, shall we? You falsely accused me of cheating on you, and then you broke up with me." I tried to interrupt, but he stopped me. "Don't, Stormy. You pushed me away because you did not intend to take our relationship to the next level. At least admit that much."

I wanted to scream that I had to end it to keep him alive because I was so close to falling in love with him. He didn't understand that my love would have been a death sentence for him. But no man could understand the burden I carried like a cross on my back—the Credence Curse, the family secret.

This reconnection between Knox and me was going to happen. Only this time, I was too emotionally broken to fall in love with him.

But he was right. We could both get closure, with a lot of passionate sex thrown in. In the end, we could both walk away and put a period at the end of this mess with no regrets and no hatred.

I nodded slowly. "Okay, let's do this. But get one thing straight. Me breaking up with you had nothing to do with money. You might not believe it, but it's a fact."

His slightly mocking smile returned. "You will be at my beck and call at all times. I have a five-night concert tour and several events I'm committed to attend. After that, we'll play it by ear."

"At all times? I have a business to run."

His nostrils flared, and every muscle in his body seemed to tense, straining against his dress shirt. "A business you won't have if you fuck me over on this deal. Are we clear?"

I stepped back from him. "Crystal."

My body was stiff, like a tightly strung violin, because I knew he planned on shattering me like fine china.

And I refused to let my heart and soul get broken when his game was over.

CHAPTER 7

I WAS TOTALLY SCREWED, and with no sleep last night, I was cranky.

No matter how many scenarios I'd concocted in my mind, there was no way I was getting out of this Knox debacle unscathed.

I'd been staring at the contract for hours, scanning for anything that would give me a way out of being Knox's sex toy, and I'd found absolutely nothing.

Desperation had set in, and it tempted me to beg Reason to find some loophole, something I knew didn't exist in any of her ironclad contracts, which was why we paid her outrageous legal fees. She was that good of a lawyer. I tried to calm myself before calling her.

On the second ring, she answered, "Stormy?" She yawned loudly.

"What's the deal with not responding to my text about last night's tiger-shifter fiasco?"

I heard shuffling before she responded, "Stormy, it's

fucking six o'clock on a Saturday morning. Sleep for me is a necessity."

I chortled. "Oh, don't pull that vampire shit on me. You're a hybrid vampire—a latent one, at that. You don't need to sleep through the daylight."

"Now you're just being mean by pointing out all my genetic flaws," Reason joked. "You're lucky I'm not a sensitive girl."

I smiled, enjoying the banter. That was why she was my best friend, and I loved her like a sister. Practically growing up together had formed a tight bond between us. Her family was made up of a long line of lawyers who had handled all our legal affairs for centuries.

"Please," I teased. "If you could, you would have a T-shirt printed, boasting your hybrid status."

Reason was the black sheep in her family. Her mother was a human, and her father was a vampire. Reason's birth was a shame to her blue-blood family, which had done everything they could to ostracize her. Her saving grace was that her father was an influential and ruthless man who loved her more than life and did everything in his power to make her fit into the vampire world. But Reason wanted no part of it, totally ignoring his attempts, much to his frustration and embarrassment. She was like me. We lived more comfortably in the human world.

"So, what happened last night?" I prompted.

Reason shuffled her cell. "A client ignored civility and got into a scuffle in a club with another music artist over who had the right to take over a damn VIP section." She scoffed. "What morons. Anyway, both camps started brawling like MMA fighters. They tore the fucking club up. They injured patrons and employees. And of course, my client called me, all panicked about getting arrested." She sighed. "I told him to leave the club before the media got wind of it. So, in a nutshell, I had to disturb a perfectly good Friday night to go sweep things under the rug again. The life of a celebrity lawyer sucks, my friend."

I swung around to look at the morning sunshine. "What are you complaining about? You're a well-paid celebrity lawyer. Suck it up, buttercup."

Reason responded with a laugh. "It's more like being a well-paid babysitting service that keeps me rolling in the bucks. It would surprise people the magnitude of shit that doesn't get into the papers, all because of my creative sweeping abilities."

I rolled my eyes. "Blah, blah, blah. Stop bragging. Back to my contract issue."

"It's airtight. I'll call Tiger Lady this morning and explain the finer things in life, like the huge penalty fee associated with lying and wasting company time. Then I'll hit her with the fact that there's also a fee for any hint of her defaming Credence O. And if that's not enough, I'll also point out that if we have to bring this shit before the Other Council, my legal fees alone will drag that bitch under."

I cringed at the mention of the Other Council. "Well, let's hope it doesn't come to that. Credence O. can't afford a scandal."

I absolutely hated the Other Council. They were the governing body of the Others that helped enforce the most important rule—Others did not reveal their existence to humans. Too many members of the Council hated my family. The only redeeming factor was that Aunt Trulista had a seat on the Council, and she would ensure we had a fair Council hearing if it came down to that.

I continued, "Call Tiger Lady and let me know if I have to get involved."

"Okay. Talk to you later, baby cakes."

Our call ended, and I whirled around when I heard a rustle. Light sauntered in wearing low-slung sweatpants, a tight white T-shirt that read *Bite Me,* and shadows under her eyes. It looked like I wasn't the only one who'd had a rough night. Light carried two extra-large cups of what I knew were lattes and an expensive black shopping bag from an exclusive boutique in SoHo that catered to celebrities.

I grabbed a cup from her hand. "Thank you."

She plopped down into the chair in front of my desk and sighed. "It's six in the morning. What are you doing up so early?" She took a huge swallow of coffee.

I looked at her with an arched brow. "Working."

She took in my scrubbed-clean face and hair pulled back into a tight ponytail. "You look like shit. What time did you get in last night?"

I didn't need her pointing out the obvious. I looked like crap and felt like it too. "Are you the damn warden now?" I complained while sipping my hot coffee.

"What flew up your ass this morning?" she demanded, throwing the bag at me. "This is for you."

"What is it?"

"Open it and find out. Some hot-looking guy just dropped it off a couple minutes ago."

I eyed it like something was going to jump out and bite me.

"Didn't you hear the doorbell?" she grumbled. "Freaking ringing disturbed my beauty sleep." She took a sip of coffee. "All I know is whoever sent what's in that bag has damn good taste. A pair of panties in that shop costs a pretty penny."

I pulled out the card and read it aloud. "*Stormy, my driver will be at your house at 9:00 p.m. sharp. Wear everything. No panties. KG.*"

I pulled out the backless nude dress that was so short, if I bent over, you would see my ass, which was probably the point.

Light took a large sip of coffee, eyeing the dress enviously. "Ooh-la-la, that dress is smoking hot. Me likey. But who's KG?"

"Knox Gunner."

Light choked on her coffee. "I'm sorry. What are you talking about?"

"The client is Knox Gunner. Apparently, he's Ryker's friend."

"Holy smokes. And...?"

"He's still pissed at me because I broke up with him." I bit my bottom lip. "Well, that and all the ugly things I said to him about him not being rich enough for me, like Luke."

She waved her hand impatiently. "That was years ago. Both of you need to let that shit go."

"I have no issues doing that. But because of Ryker's refusal to budge on the escort issue, that was not an option."

"Wait. Ryker pushed for this?"

"Yes. You interested in taking on the alpha?"

Light sat back tiredly. "Oh, hell no. He's too much of a project, and I'm not willing to put in the work. Instant gratification—that's me all the way." She plopped her feet on my desk. "Now, how do we solve the female wolf issue?"

"I sort of resolved it," I answered over a mouthful of coffee.

She leaned forward with wide eyes. "Sort of? This should be good."

"I made an agreement to be Knox's escort instead of a female wolf." I took a big sip, looking at my nails like I had the best manicure ever.

"Holy shit. When I said break some rules, I didn't mean all of them."

Swinging the leather chair around, I walked over to the

safe, pressing my thumb to the sensor to open it and placing the Alfero contract back in before slamming it shut. "I had no choice. I'll honor the contract. He'll get bored within a couple days. He'll chalk it up to getting his revenge and move on with his life. I can deal."

"You can't have sex with him. Shit, you can't even go out with him. It's the Credence rule."

"I made that very clear. No sex. No kissing. Straight business—and I guess lots of humiliation."

"He's a Dom?"

I nodded.

She clapped her hands with delight. "Oh damn, this keeps getting better and better. I told you it would happen."

"I'm not a submissive, Light. I love power and refuse to relinquish that to anyone."

Light looked at me with disapproval. "Stormy, get over this prejudice you have against submissives. They hold all the power. It's just not supposed to feel like it."

I knew what he truly wanted. "He wants me to feel powerless, but I'm not sure how far my dominant personality will take this shit before calling it quits." I wasn't a quitter. I was just realistic about the power he held over me. It made me fucking uncomfortable.

She arched a brow. "I'm sure he thought of a way to ensure that wouldn't happen," she stated flatly.

I looked at her with shock. "How do you know?"

She shrugged. "He wouldn't be much of a Dom if he hadn't."

"If I quit, he'll ruin the business by essentially tarnishing our name."

She raised a brow. "Oh, that's hard-core. But it also means he wants you bad." Light's eyes searched my face. "Would it be so hard to see where this takes you?"

She was right. I wasn't a prude. And if I were truthful with myself, I wouldn't mind closure with Knox. In fact, I needed it. But D/s wasn't something remotely on my wish list.

"But how do you just go from everyday dominant to submissive in the bedroom?" I really didn't understand the mental switch.

"What I do in the bedroom does not reflect who I am in everyday life. I am a feminist, and Dom/sub play does not impact that." Light took another sip of coffee. "I don't feel diminished or lesser because I'm a sub. In fact, it's quite empowering. It makes me feel very sexy and turned on. It's exhausting to be in control all the time—at work, in bed. Let Knox drive for a while. Admit it, this is the sweetest deal ever."

"But it will not be easy, Light. You know me. I'm an Aries. We don't give control. We take it."

"Well, welcome to a whole new frontier, baby, because the power dynamic has just shifted in Knox's favor."

"Yeah, that's what makes this so fucking scary."

Her lips twisted into a smirk. "So, you're going to be a rock star's groupie for a while. Wow, lucky you. And you know blow jobs count as sex? Just so we're clear."

I ignored her, looking at the dress again. "How the hell did he know my size? And I'm not wearing this shit. If I bend over, you'll see my ass cheeks."

"But your ass is so cute," Light cooed.

I threw a paper clip at her. "I'm thrilled this is so amusing to you. I don't like this shit at all—telling me what to wear, where to be. It's infuriating."

Light smiled cheekily. "This is exactly how our escorts feel with every client. But the difference is they enjoy it."

"I'm not an escort."

"Look, Stormy, stop complaining. The worst that can

happen is, at the end of this assignment, you learn something about yourself."

"And that is?"

"That's the journey you have to take. It's not ideal. I recognize that. But you need to loosen up a bit here," Light emphasized. "Besides, I think we both agree you and Knox have some unresolved issues. Just fix them. And move on."

"It's easy for you to say that when you don't have to put up with the depraved things I'm sure he's planning for me. I can deal with straight-up sex, but the other stuff is more challenging for me."

"He might go easy on you since you're a newbie. But either way, several rounds of rough-and-tumble sex might make you a new woman."

I rolled my eyes heavenward. "So, your answer to this mess is to fuck it out? And whoever's left standing wins?"

"Yeah, there's nothing a good lay can't resolve. Just don't get all emotionally involved." She looked at me pointedly. "The sweetest revenge is turning the tables on his ass by getting something out of this deal—no-strings-attached sex from the hottest man alive."

I couldn't help but wonder how Mom would've handled this, but I wasn't Mom. I knew this. And she wouldn't be around to clean up our messes forever, which was something she'd been trying to tell us for years. No, this Knox issue was one I had to fix myself. I'd never understood the lifestyle of our escorts—didn't want to. But it was hypocritical of me to want to bask in the money that had come from their efforts while I looked down my nose at them for it. Light was right. I had to do this.

"The goddess of fate has truly screwed me over." I wrinkled my nose. "There's nothing left to do but go through with this."

"Exactly. He wants to make you squirm. But think of this as

a fantasy rock camp, except with a one-hundred-percent chance of getting laid."

"You know our mothers would kill us if they ever found out about this, right?"

"What happens when the hags are away stays between Team Us."

CHAPTER 8

I CLENCHED my teeth as I sat in the SUV, refusing to get out.

This is ridiculous.

I stared at the entrance, trying to calm the disturbing anticipation that was building in preparation for finally seeing Knox again.

"Ms. Credence?" The driver looked at me in the rearview mirror.

"I'm ready."

The driver swiftly stepped out, opening my door. Placing my hand in his, I allowed him to escort me out.

He smiled. "Have a nice evening, Ms. Credence."

"I don't know about that," I mumbled under my breath as I walked away.

Stepping into the restaurant, I scanned the auras in the space. Most of the auras were blue, which meant lots of Others frequented this place.

Proudly, I lifted my chin as the men's eyes narrowed with interest.

I looked good tonight, that much I was sure of, but I was

such a nervous wreck about seeing Knox again that Light had had to help me get ready.

My thick auburn hair flowed around my bare shoulders. The backless nude dress was a pleasant contrast against my skin, something Knox had somehow known, which told me he'd picked out the skintight dress that hugged all my curves in all the right places. I'd finished the look with my favorite designer stilettos.

The lighting was dim, like some upscale club, setting the mood for an anything-goes vibe. I looked around the well-known private restaurant owned by a former model named Vivica, who was also a vampire. It was more of a VIP restaurant patronized by the rich and famous Others and humans, and the waiting list was long. But the difference between this restaurant and other celebrity-frequented restaurants was that everyone who came here wanted their privacy because of the acts that took place on-site.

Sexual acts performed onstage for all to see while patrons ate and watched. Given proper motivation, guests might also have their own private show in their own secluded booths.

A tall, pale redhead dwarfed by two burly men walked straight toward me with an enormous smile on her face. "Stormy Credence. I'm Vivica, owner of this sinful establishment." She gestured dramatically. "Welcome to Redemption, darling." She patted each man's arm before they fanned out, watching the crowd like some sort of personal security.

Vampires weren't friendly, but I sensed no falseness in her tone, so I smiled back. "Thank you."

She circled me. "Oh my goodness. You look so much like your mother," she gushed with a sultry voice.

I arched a brow. "Minus the attitude, right?"

"No, darling, I can tell you have the same spitfire attitude."

I looked around at the celebs sauntering around inconspicuously. "Look, nothing against your beautiful restaurant, but this place has more celebrities than a rehab facility. And it's really not my scene."

She puckered her pouty lips. "Then why are you here, darling?"

I nervously adjusted my hem. "I'm meeting someone. Not sure if he's here yet."

"Oh, Knox is here, darling. Waiting for you. Impatiently, I might add." She looped her arm through mine. "Come with me."

We walked through the extravagantly designed restaurant, draped with rich fabric across the ceiling. The whole middle section of the floor was wide open, making way for the strange circular configuration of several booths with high backs and wide sides facing a large platform, which obstructed the view and any chance of voyeurs.

Vivica practically glided across the floor. "I bet you didn't know I used to work for Credence O.," she stated matter-of-factly.

I glanced at her with shock. "Really?"

"Uh-huh. I was one of Ava and Lia's best girls. But this was way before you were born."

I knew vampires were eternally youthful, but Vivica looked about my age.

Vivica laughed. "The stories I could tell you about your wild mother and aunt. We used to raise hell on assignments. And your mother had clients lining up to book her."

I almost tripped at her revelation.

Mom worked as an escort?

What about all the rules she'd droned on about not breaking?

Oh, what a hypocrite. Wait until I tell Light.

"I guess she didn't tell you about that, huh?" She winked at me.

There was no sense in pretending. "No, she didn't."

"I was really rough around the edges when they took me in and gave me a home and a life direction," she recounted. "I went from a distrustful, resentful vamp who thought the world was out to get her, to a woman who was ready to embrace life. When I found my mates, it was time to quit. So, trust me when I say life is about taking chances and leaving the past behind."

When we reached the table, Knox, Wyatt, and a pretty platinum blonde with chestnut highlights occupied it. My eyes drifted back to Knox, who was looking at me pensively. He looked good enough to eat in his crisp white dress shirt that was open at the collarbone, displaying his tanned skin with an intricate wolf tattoo on the left side of his neck.

"Here she is, Knox." Vivica pushed me forward gently. "And can you stop glaring at her like you're about to eat her alive?"

"Why?" His eyes sparkled with laughter. "When eating her is all I can think about, but these damn booths don't give me the room to show her the power of my mighty tongue."

Turned on by his words, I crossed my legs.

Oh, this isn't good.

How the hell am I going to get through dinner?

"Improvise, darling." Vivica gave him an amused stare. "I permit eating on the table." She winked at me. "Have fun, Stormy. This one's a keeper."

Knox stood impatiently, ushering me into the booth, and I sat down. "You're late. Don't let it happen again."

I ignored him, smiling stiffly at Wyatt. "I didn't know you were joining us."

"I'm not. We're leaving." He nodded over at the annoyed blonde.

"We can stay for a bit." The blonde offered her hand to shake. "I'm Knox's personal manager, Harper Ducaine." She looked me up and down. "And you are?"

Instantly, I could tell she was prepared not to like me. "Stormy Credence." I nodded toward Knox. "His groupie for the evening."

Harper's face lightened as she chuckled. "No offense, but you don't look like his typical fan."

Utterly mystified, I stared at her. "Really? What did you expect?"

She tapped her lip with fake seriousness. "I don't know, less brain and wit. Frankly, he's aiming too high with you—too beautiful and intelligent for the likes of him." She jabbed a finger in Knox's direction.

I smiled. "Don't let the dress fool you. This is my groupie disguise."

Wyatt snorted. "It's nice to see you again, Stormy, but I have a date with Light."

I was against it, but Light was a big girl and could handle herself.

"It's not a date," I cautioned. "It's her granting pity to a loser on a real slow date night."

He arched a brow. "Still don't like me, huh?"

I looked at him silently before responding, "There's not much to like." I wasn't sure if it was his sly smile or the way his cold eyes always seemed to examine me like a piece of meat, but there was something about him I didn't trust or like.

Harper chuckled, looking at Knox with a gleam in her eyes. "Oh, Knox, I think I'm in love. Can we keep her?" She batted her eyelashes. "Pretty, pretty please?"

"I don't share," Knox responded with his eyes locked on me.

Harper winked at me before saying, "Damn, he's so possessive."

He scrutinized me. "She's all mine for as long as I want her to warm my bed."

I knew what he was making clear—that this was a temporary thing. *A fling.* And I shouldn't get any permanent fixture ideas.

"She actually gets to warm your bed, huh?" Harper asked. "Well, this one must be very special." She suddenly looked at me. "He never brings women to his bed. It's some caveman territorial thing."

"That has nothing to do with it," Knox maintained.

"Okay then, can I join you two? I promise I won't touch her." She winked at me. "Much."

He gave an exasperated sigh. "Harper, she's not into women." He brought the glass to his lips, sipping slowly. And that was when I noticed the wide silver skull ring I'd given him years ago on his finger. He'd kept it. I swallowed hard over the lump of emotion.

Harper pouted playfully. "Are you sure? You know how good I am at converting."

"Hello?" I waved my hand. "I'm right here. Why are you two talking around me?" I glared at her. "And to answer your question, I'm only into men." I nodded toward Knox. "Present company not included."

Harper fanned herself. "Oh, honey, when Knox breaks you, it's going to be hot."

I snorted. "Not going to happen."

She arched a brow. "Do you know how many women would love the chance to warm his bed?"

"I bet he has them lining up. When one leaves, another jumps right in. He's Knox Gunner, rock star extraordinaire." I crossed my legs. "I'm not interested in being in the lineup."

She pursed her lips with disapproval. "Is that what you

think? He's a Dominant, not a whore. Wow, Knox. You've got some work to do with this one."

"I'm up to the challenge." Knox leaned back, draping his arm behind me. "I call it Project Breaking the Storm." I tried to move away, but he softly fisted my hair with one hand, bringing my face mere inches from his. "Where are you going, beautiful?"

I didn't even bother to move. I relaxed into his grip. His fingers combed through my hair. His green eyes turned emerald with desire.

I didn't even realize I was slowly moving toward his lips until Harper's voice startled me by saying, "Would you move your ass, Wyatt? I'm late."

Wyatt was trying to move while she shoved him. When they finally stood, Harper adjusted her short black dress.

She looked at Knox with her lips curled up into a wide smile. "This one's feisty. She's exactly what you need—someone to tell you where to stick it."

Wyatt smirked. "Oh, I think he knows exactly where to stick it."

Harper rolled her eyes. "What are you, in high school? Come on. Let's leave them alone."

I watched them walk away before looking back at Knox. "You got rid of Portia? That was a smart career move." I shook out my napkin, placing it on my lap.

"I had to change my life, so I fired her that night," he responded coldly. "Something you would have known had you not run away with your tail between your legs." He took a long sip of water, looking at me over the rim of his glass. "Back then, I needed a woman who would fight—for me and for us. I thought you were that woman. I was wrong."

I inhaled a deep breath and held it for a beat before speaking. "I'm not even going to respond to that."

I swallowed hard, sticking my hands under the table to hide the trembling.

He was right. Back then, I had been a coward and too scared to live with the ramifications of falling in love.

He examined me. "And just so we're clear, you know damn well what you saw between Portia and me was set up by her and Wyatt to get rid of you."

It was like a stab to the heart, hearing aloud what I already knew.

"Why are we talking about this?" I asked in a husky voice.

"Because I don't want to gloss over it like it never happened. We're both sitting here because we have unfinished business."

"Not that I'm not happy to know you fired her, but she wasn't the only one who had a hand in that shit. What about Wyatt?"

Knox slammed his glass onto the table. "Wyatt's paid for fucking around in my life. He's learned his lesson, believe me."

I doubted that very much, but that wasn't any of my business anymore. "Well, at least you have Harper."

"She gets me. That's what makes our relationship work."

I couldn't stop the creep of jealousy that snuck up on me at the way *relationship* rolled off his tongue.

He stared at me. "I don't mix business with pleasure, so don't start weaving some crazy story about Harper and me having sex, because we're not. Unlike you, I don't shroud myself in mystery, and I don't fucking lie. If there's something I don't want to talk about, I'll tell you."

"Why do you mean, unlike me?" I stared at him with my lips pursed.

"If you have to ask, then you're still not ready to come clean about everything."

My fingernails bit into my thigh. *Did he know about the Curse?*

"There's nothing to tell, Knox."

"Lies," he said with clear sarcasm.

"You're a fucking hypocrite, because if anyone who needs to come clean, it's you."

He shrugged. "My life is an open book. If you want to know something about me, just ask, and I'll be more than happy to tell you the truth. But can you say the same?"

I swallowed hard because I couldn't.

"That's what I thought," he answered.

"Okay, tell me why you shared nothing personal with me besides a bit of information about your mother that I practically had to beg you for."

Raw pain flickered in his eyes before disappearing. "Did you really need to know the woman I called mother emotionally abused me until the day she died? That she hated me so much, she actually lied and said my father didn't want me, when he was frantically searching for me?" His tone held no emotion at all. "I lived a very hard life. But that was before the music saved my life."

I knew, buried deep down inside him, it had to hurt, knowing his mother hated him so much. I knew exactly how much something like that stung. My father's hateful taunts were a reminder of the pain that ran deep.

He continued, "Things were getting complicated in my life when we met. I went from no father in my life to having one I was so proud of. But the fact remains, I never lied to you—ever." He arched a brow. "Can you say the same?"

My breath was ragged as I tried to calm the turbulence of the emotions churning deep in my gut. "If you're talking about Credence O., then that wasn't a lie. I told you my mother ran a company in Manhattan. I just didn't elaborate on what kind. It wasn't your business. And, frankly, it didn't matter."

His eyes hardened. "The truth matters, Stormy, and always will."

Yes, but the truth isn't something I could tell, a fact that I learned to live with.

I almost breathed a sigh of relief when two servers approached the table.

"Bone marrow with veal cheek marmalade, foie gras fried rice with shredded duck and coriander, crispy duck wings with yuzu kosho, grilled clams flecked with Calabrian chilies, pasta spiked with pink peppercorns, and squash-stuffed ravioli with hazelnuts," the first server announced as the second server grandly set the small sharing plates down in the center of the table. "Enjoy," the server finished with a bow of his head.

"Are you feeding an army?" I asked.

Knox smiled, a slow lifting of perfect lips to reveal straight white teeth. "I didn't know what you'd like, so I ordered some of their popular dishes for you to try."

"I see," I croaked before clearing my throat. I kind of liked that he had made sure I had a well-selected sampling of a foodie's wet dream.

The server poured more water into our glasses while the server beamed at me. "What would you like to drink?"

"I'll have a Moscow mule," I answered.

"And I'll have Jack on the rocks," Knox replied.

The two servers wandered away.

"Why are we here?" I commanded.

"To eat. I thought that was clear. It's a restaurant after all." He narrowed his eyes as he continued to assess me with a combination of curiosity and intense interest.

I knew he was toying with me, but I was in no mood for games.

Knox put a small plate in front of me, scooping up a portion of foie gras fried rice and putting several crispy duck wings with yuzu kosho onto it.

With butterflies fluttering in my stomach, I was not in the mood to eat right now, despite the delicious offering. "You know what I mean. Why this restaurant?" I brought the glass of water to my lips, sipping slowly. "I'm not a voyeur, and I don't get off on watching people perform sexual acts on one another."

I wasn't a prude, far from it. *But come the hell on. This is just not my thing.*

"How do you know if you've never tried it?"

The server arrived with our drinks on a silver tray. Swiftly, he placed them in front of us before scurrying away.

Picking up my Moscow mule, which was in a cool copper mug, I drank thirstily, feeling the smooth burn of alcohol before placing the cup down.

The aroma of the delicious rice made my stomach grumble as Knox pulled the plate toward himself, digging in. He held out a forkful of rice. "Here. Open up."

"You know I'm not a two-year-old, right?"

His voice was seductive when he ordered, "Open your mouth, Stormy."

Appallingly, something about him feeding me aroused my senses. Reluctantly, I parted my lips, allowing him to slide the fork inside. *Damn, this is good.*

"See? You can be a good girl."

He dug in and ate a forkful while watching me.

Picking up my glass of water, I gulped. There would be no more alcohol for a bit. I needed to keep my mind focused.

The stage brightened. Wide projector screens dropped from the ceiling, displaying a curvy woman draped over a padded bench, naked except for sexy red stilettos. Ropes secured her arms as her round ass stuck up in the air. Her toned legs spread so far apart that I could see her pussy.

What the hell? This wasn't something I wanted to see. "Are we almost done here?"

His eyes were cool when he responded, "Nope. Sit back and relax."

"But…"

"You need to see this," he said flatly.

My belly fluttered when I realized Harper was the woman, and Ryker—wearing a crisp white shirt unbuttoned at the neck and sleeves, rolled up to reveal his muscled, tanned forearms—was wielding the paddle.

I held my breath as Ryker ran a hand over her body, from shoulders to butt. He leaned in and said something to her.

I jumped when he cracked the paddle on her ass.

Harper cried out as her body twitched. He rained two more blows on each cheek, causing her to jerk against the restraints.

The stage rotated, stopping at each booth for a full view of the action.

The display mesmerized me.

The harder Harper fought, the harder he spanked her. My heart raced when she begged him to stop. I looked on with wide eyes when the stage stopped before our booth. I could tell she was in pain.

My fingernails bit into my palms, fighting the urge to leap onto the stage to save her. Knox flattened his palm on my abdomen, holding me in place.

His lips brushed my ear. "This is what she wants, pain."

"She likes pain?" I glanced at him incredulously.

He held out another forkful of rice for me to eat before responding. "See her face? She trusts him to take her to the point her body desires." He licked the shell of my ear, sending a delicious shiver down my spine. "Would you like that too,

Stormy? Your lovely ass bared for me to admire? To stroke before spanking it?"

I chewed the rice, trying to rationalize my reaction, when his fingers squeezed my thigh, sending a tingling hot sensation up to my pussy, making me press my thighs together.

He gripped my thigh, gently pulling my legs apart. "First lesson, always sit with your legs open. I want access to you at all times."

My mouth dropped open. "Excuse me?"

"You heard me." Steel laced his voice as he tapped my leg. "Spread them."

I glanced nervously around the restaurant before spreading them slightly.

He arched a brow, so, shakily, I spread them wider.

This was ridiculous. I was sitting in a restaurant with my legs wide open.

Picking up my glass of water, I drank thirstily. "I'm no good at this." I shifted, ready to close my legs, when he leaned in closer.

"Stormy. Keep them spread—wide."

"Knox, really."

He caressed my thigh. "Quiet," he ordered. "Continue drinking." His voice became husky and seductive. "Does it make you uncomfortable that you're wet?"

I bit my lip, remaining silent.

"What's your answer?"

I stared straight at him. "You know the answer. Yes." I shrugged my shoulders. "I don't like this feeling."

He kept his voice low. "You don't enjoy feeling vulnerable."

I nodded.

"Despite what you think, Stormy. I would never hurt you. Yes, I have a particular sexual taste. But I'm not into pain." He ran his fingers over my thigh before stroking the spot between my legs. "I'm glad you're completely bare. I want nothing to hide what belongs to me."

I groaned, stifling the need to trap his hand between my thighs.

"Let me show you how it will be between us."

When he thrust his middle finger deep into me, my ass shot clear off the seat.

"Hold still."

I couldn't help the pant that escaped before responding. "Knox, I can't do this. Not here."

"You can and will do this. Right here, right now," he said against my cheek. "Do you want me to stop?" His hand froze.

A whimper escaped my mouth.

This can't be right.

My body was begging and throbbing for him to continue.

"No. Please." I swallowed hard as my hand slid to his muscular thigh. "Continue."

He growled, "Very nice, Stormy." He arched a brow. "But did I tell you to move your fucking hand from the top of the table?"

He waited until I slid my hand back to the table then leaned in, brushing his lips across mine, completely covering them and forcing them apart. Sliding his tongue inside with a caress, his finger thrust into me.

I spread my legs wider, not caring about the surrounding people.

I needed this too much, so to hell with the ramifications.

With a groan, I tilted my face like a willing sacrifice, sliding my tongue against his, drawing him deeper.

He nipped my bottom lip, and with one last twist of his finger, a jolt of pleasure raced through my feminine mound. My lips parted to cry out, but his lips quickly covered mine, swallowing my cries. I trembled as he pulled me close, caressing my back until I settled.

He drew back with a slow, sexy smile as he licked his finger covered with my wetness. "Delicious."

That was when the reality of this situation came crashing back, and I realized what I had allowed Knox to do. I struggled to move away, but he tightened his arm around me.

"It's too late for regrets, sweetheart," he said.

I glanced away.

"Eyes on me, please."

My gaze snapped back to him.

"Stormy, never be ashamed of how your body reacts to me. I'm in tune with your body. The result is you coming by my hand on command."

That's what I'm afraid of—losing all my control to him, the last man on earth to whom I should.

I was speechless when Knox fisted my hair with one hand, roughly kissing me. My legs fell wide open as he worked the fingers of his other hand in and out of my hot cunt. I was so lost in his touch that I didn't realize the stage had turned until I heard the thump.

Embarrassed, I pushed at Knox. "Stop. I can't."

"I'll allow you to run this time. But after tonight, there's nothing to stop me but one word. Do we understand each other?" he asked in a rough voice.

I nodded because I did.

We hadn't talked about my safe word, but that was exactly what he was referring to, the only word that would stop him from going full throttle on my ass.

CHAPTER 9

I GRABBED my ringing cell but didn't recognize the number. "Yes?" I answered impatiently while pacing back and forth across the floor of my apartment.

"Hello, Stormy."

I recognized the husky voice immediately. "Hello, Harper. How are you?"

She laughed. "Frankly, very irritated by having to make this damn call," Harper explained. "But such is the life of a well-paid personal manager to a pain-in-the-ass rock star."

I stiffened.

What the hell?

Knox didn't even have the respect to call me himself?

"Okay, Harper, no offense to you, but I'm not doing this, all right? Tell him to call me himself."

I wanted to smack him in the face for the balls on him.

Stick a finger in me at dinner, and I'm not even worth a personal call the next day?

"Please, no drama," Harper pleaded. "It's too early. Believe me, he would've called, but he's doing a live interview as we speak. Hence, the call from his blond and simply gorgeous minion."

I tapped my bare foot. "Okay, so what does he want now? A pint of blood? The promise of my firstborn?"

"Not today, love. Maybe tomorrow," Harper jested. "He's sending over a dress he wants you to wear to Ryker's charity foundation gala. The rock god said, and I quote, 'Her sweet ass is mine, so she better get ready to spend the weekend on her knees.' End quote. If you ask me, it sounds like a damn hot weekend." She purred dramatically. "Can I join?"

Damn, I hate him.

"How about you take my place? I don't relish being on my knees for hours. Not that I object to doling out a good blow job, but I don't think I have the knee or jaw stamina to handle it."

Harper chuckled. "You're too funny. God, I hope he has the smarts to keep you."

"Yeah, that's me, a regular comedian."

"Knox mentioned you're a dancer, so—"

I interrupted her, "Former amateur dancer."

"Same thing. All I'm saying is you'd better do some leg and mouth stretches because it's going to be an enjoyable but long weekend."

"Yippee." I whirled my finger in the air. "I'm really feeling the excitement."

"I would gladly join you on the journey if you were remotely interested in women. Truth be told, that would be the only way I could stomach being around a bare-assed Knox." She made a loud sound as if she were shuddering at the thought.

I laughed. I liked her and hoped, after my Knox fling, she and I could remain friends. Goodness knows, having Harper as a friend would make life entertaining.

"Well, I think you're the only woman on the face of the

earth who would say that. Thanks for your willingness to sacrifice yourself for the cause, but again, as gorgeous as you are, I'm still not interested in women."

"Damn, that's a shame," Harper teased, jostling her cell. "Okay, I have to hurry before Knox finishes his interview. He can be an ass if I'm not standing around at his beck and call. One more thing before I go. You know about what goes on at Ryker's charity galas?"

I swallowed hard.

Everyone knew what went on, which was why getting an invitation was like winning the lottery. It was impossible.

It was one of the hottest invites in the human and Other social circles. He only invited his wealthy associates, who were more than willing to give generously to his charitable foundation, all for the privilege of taking part in an event notorious for its indulgence in freaky, sensual escapades. Each year, the event got bigger than the year before. He was also such an arrogant ass that he was infamous for leaving guests wondering if he would even show up to his own event. Nine times out of ten, he hadn't.

"Unfortunately, I do. I'll be there with one caveat. You must provide accommodations for my cousin and business partner, Light Credence." If I had to suffer through this, she was going to watch—well, not literally.

"Done," Harper agreed. "I've got to run. I hear Knox bellowing like some sort of cave dweller. See you tonight, Stormy."

I went downstairs, walking into the serving pantry off the reception area, and quickly prepared an espresso before making my way back into the office. I didn't move when I heard the elevator door open. There was no point. Light was coming in, and there was no stopping that tornado of chaos. I continued sipping my coffee, staring through the three large windows overlooking the neighboring gardens.

"That bad, huh?" Light asked.

I turned around to see her tapping her foot peevishly.

I sighed heavily before responding. "I just got off the phone with Harper."

Light arched a brow in question.

"Knox's manager. King Knox summoned me to play submissive for an entire weekend at Ryker's charity event."

Light clapped her hands with delight. "That sounds wonderful. I wish I were going." She sat down on the couch, pulling her knees up to her chest.

I plopped down beside her. "You are. Pack for the weekend, sweet cheeks." I pinched her cheek, earning a sharp smack on the hand.

"What's the big deal? I get to enjoy a weekend filled with my three favorite things—alcohol, sex, and men." She rubbed her hands together excitedly. "Now tell me what happened last night."

"Last night, I witnessed an act so hot, I was practically climbing Knox like a tree."

"Sounds about right. Redemption is the hottest sexcapade in town." She scooted down, resting her head against the fluffy throw pillow. "Go on," she prompted. "And don't leave out a thing."

"Picture it," I teased. "I'm not going into details."

"And why the hell not? When I was Light, the sexy witch on the prowl, I gave you blow-by-blow details of my sex adventures."

I made gagging sounds. "Uh, yeah, but I begged you not to. I still can't get the image of you spread-eagled on my desk, having sex, out of my mind. I sanitized my desk over and over again for weeks."

Light stared into space with a dreamy smile on her face. "Those were good times. Lots of sex everywhere. Oh, how I miss sex, glorious sex."

"You can still have sex, Light. You didn't take a vow of chastity."

She pursed her lips. "Believe me, I would if I could. But just like Demi predicted, the mood swings have only gotten worse. Sadly, I'm on a no-sex lockdown."

Light's empath symptoms were getting worse. One minute, she would be bawling her eyes out; the next, she would be dripping with rage. There was no middle ground anymore, and there wasn't shit I could do about it. What had once worked at controlling her intense migraines and wild mood swings—her large consumption of alcohol—seemed to be failing.

Sensing her mounting anxiety, I lifted her legs onto my lap. "You know Demi's premonition that your empath gift will balance with a Bringer of Death is total bullshit, right?"

Even though I loved Demi, one of our best friends and the daughter of Mom's best friend, our coven leader, I wasn't a one-hundred-percent believer in all Demi's visions, which were sketchy.

Light sighed. "That's what I said before my empath issues started getting worse. Demi specifically said I would beat this empath crap if I just kept my legs closed while waiting for the Bringer of Death. And what did I do? I thumbed my nose at the ridiculousness of her prediction. And guess what happened?" Her fingers trembled. "The more men I slept with, the worse my empath issues got. Look at me. I'm a damn emotional mess. And the alcohol? You can forget that shit. It's not buffering the onslaught of human emotions like it used to. There's nothing worse than being drunk and assaulted by whiny humans and their emotional angst." She sniffed. "As much as it pains me to do it, my legs will remain shut until I figure this crap out."

"Uh-huh." I gave her a skeptical look. "So, in the meantime, my sex life is your porno fix?"

"Hell yeah. Do you know how depressing it is to live my sex life vicariously through you?"

"Excuse me?" I shoved her legs off my lap. "I had plenty of hot sex before Knox."

"Jesus, how many times do I have to say toys don't count?" She waved at me dismissively. "Can you please move on with the details from last night?"

"Ryker was onstage, wielding a paddle," I revealed.

Light perked up. "Holy shit! With his submissive?"

"Nope. Harper. But the scene was the prelude." I looked at her from the side of my eye. "The finale was Knox getting me off so hard I swore I saw stars."

She clapped. "Good for you, girl. You needed it."

"Did you even hear what I said? At the table, finger in me, followed by his tongue down my throat with some heavy tongue action." I bit my bottom lip. "Then he abruptly called his driver to escort me out of the restaurant without even an 'it-was-great-fingering-you' wave farewell."

Light frowned. "And what would be the point of that? By the time he got you off, he knew you'd riddle yourself with buyer's remorse, and you'd be ready to fuck up a good thing by belittling the whole beautiful experience. No, he made the right choice by hustling your tight little ass out of there. He was priming you for round two." She waggled her eyebrows suggestively.

My mouth flopped open because she was right. "Why do I constantly underestimate your cunning wisdom for all things pertaining to men?"

"Don't know. I'm brilliant with three things—shopping, sex, and desirable men."

I curled my legs under me. "Talking about men, how did the Wyatt escapade go?"

"God, boring. I caught myself nodding off twice. All he talked about was his music and money. If that weren't bad enough, he started coming on real strong, like I was going to pull off my panties right there at the table and let him have at it." She exhaled. "No avoidance. Get back to the more interesting stuff. Like how long do you think it will be before you give it up to Knox?"

My shoulders slumped with defeat. "I'll be on my knees by the end of the night."

"He's that good? One night, and he's converted you?"

"Nope, I'm just realistic about my sticky predicament." My cell buzzed. Lifting a finger, I said, "Hold on a sec. Let me take this." I swiped to answer. "Stormy Credence."

"Hello, Ms. Credence. I'm Detective Burrows," a man offered.

I put him on speaker.

Burrows continued, "I'm calling because, unfortunately, we have some bad news. Your employee, Celina Rouse, was found dead last night."

Light sat up.

"What?" The room spun around me. "I mean, how?" I croaked.

"We know there was foul play, but the case is still under investigation."

My heart raced as I scrambled to pull myself together. "Have you notified her family? Because we—"

"We called them. Pardon my language, ma'am, but I don't think they give a shit," he disclosed. "And strangely, they were eerily silent when I asked about Celina's employment. Thank goodness Jeff Hunter offered her employment information."

"Jeff Hunter?"

Light motioned to me frantically.

"He's a reporter. He said he was doing some exposé on Ms. Rouse," he elaborated.

A long pause followed, so I pressed forward. "Exposé?"

"Let me be blunt. Mr. Hunter claims you're running some sort of escort business, Ms. Credence. Is there any truth to that accusation?"

"None," I lied. "I'm not sure who this Jeff Hunter is, but I can assure you Credence O. is not involved in anything of the sort. And if Mr. Hunter goes down this road, it will force me to get my lawyer involved," I pointed out. "Now, I think there are bigger issues here, like finding out what happened to Celina. Is there anything else, Detective?"

"No, Ms. Credence. That will be all. For now," he said before ending the call.

Light was eyeing me nervously. "Celina's dead?"

"Yes, and the reporter is talking to the police."

"Why didn't her family call us?" Light exploded.

My eyes filled with tears from anger. "They didn't give a shit about her when she was alive. Why the hell do you think they'd give a shit about her death?"

"Sad but true," Light agreed. "The bastards are probably dividing up her assets as we speak."

"More than likely."

That was the problem with most of our escorts. They had no family. Or if they did, they were estranged from them.

"Do you want to call our moms?" Light asked.

"What would be the point? They won't answer their cells. I'll call Reason and ask her to do some poking around. The best thing we can do right now is act normal and not raise any red flags. As far as we know, we could be under investigation—something we just don't need."

CHAPTER 10

PEERING out the car's window, I tried not to fidget in my seat as the limo driver navigated the road.

I crossed my legs as uncertainty crept up on me.

Am I really going to do this?

There was a mental box inside my brain with Knox's name on it, and tonight, I was going to open it, enjoying the contents.

But when I'm done, will I have the emotional and mental strength to replace the lid on the box and place it back on the shelf?

That was a question I'd never asked with any other man because no man was ever close to getting into the dark recesses of my heart.

But with Knox, I had nowhere to hide.

Not that I was ready to admit it aloud... But I craved Knox. And if I could keep our fling firmly in the temporary category, then I would have no fear of the Credence Curse rearing its ugly head.

Light pressed the button, closing the privacy divider. "As much as I hate to say this, I really think we should try to get in touch with our mothers. There's just something about this whole reporter situation that's not sitting well with me."

Turning to peer at her, I explained my position. "Believe me, it's not pride that keeps me from calling them. It's self-preservation. If they find out how bad we messed this up, they'll kill us. Let's give ourselves some time to work this shit out before we go into full panic mode."

Light rubbed the invitation printed on expensive ivory card stock with a pensive expression. "Agreed, but after this weekend, if things don't improve, I'm flying over to Hawaii and dragging their asses back here." She started fanning herself with the paper. "God, I'm burning up because my stress level is at an all-time high."

"Relax." I rubbed her arm. "Take a deep breath."

"I can't relax without copious amounts of sex or alcohol or both."

"There are much healthier ways to relax," I offered.

She batted her eyelashes almost comically. "So says the woman who's going to get fucked tonight."

"Fine, you got me there," I agreed. "But I still maintain that this situation with Knox is stressing me out."

"Why?"

"Because there's so much about him that's still a mystery," I pointed out.

"Like?" Light demanded.

"Like, why is Knox so important to a powerful alpha like Ryker?"

"Ain't nothing mysterious about a shifter and a human being friends," Light exclaimed.

"Unless there's something more..." I proposed. "Like, maybe he's hybrid or has alpha blood, which explains why I can't see his aura and you can't sense his emotions."

"If that's the case, then why didn't Ryker or Knox just say

so?" Light questioned. "What's the big secret? Especially since everyone in the New York Other community knows our family are hybrid Other."

"True, but something feels off." I nibbled my bottom lip. "As if I'm not connecting the dots."

"Stormy, why are you making this out to be some big Scooby-Doo mystery? If he's hybrid or alpha, so what? If he's not, so what? You're not trying to have a committed, long-term relationship with him or fall in love. It's just straight-up sex, so relax and enjoy the adventure."

"You're right." It didn't matter what Knox was or was not. Our current status was just a sexual hookup, nothing more.

The driver drove through an open private-gated entry that led to a circular drive, then he pulled up to the front of a pala-tial mansion with a fountain in a private courtyard. Turning off the vehicle, the driver stepped out, hurrying over to the back passenger's door to open it for Light and me.

Wasting no time, we both followed the crowd. Some women wore expensive-looking black capes that covered them from their necks to their ankles. Other women were scantily dressed, leaving nothing to the imagination.

The dress I wore was daring, seductive, feminine, and something I never would have picked out for myself, some-thing Knox knew even after all these years. See-through panels of my black gown hugged my curves like a glove. The sleeveless bodice pushed my full breasts up, and the hem swirled around my ankles as my stilettos clicked against the pavement.

Bones stalked over, giving me a wink before his eyes wandered up and down Light's curvy body encased in an ornate cream lace gown, a perfect foil for her smooth, glowing skin.

Light pursed her full lips with displeasure. "Hey, cowboy."

She snapped her fingers in his face. "You're staring at my damn breasts."

"I'm appreciating the view." His eyes sparkled.

Light glared at me. "Stormy? Really? I have to put up with him all weekend?" She pushed past him. "You owe me big-time," she mumbled under her breath.

I winked at him. "Okay, that's not a good first impression, Bones. And for the record, it's impolite to leer at a woman's breasts before you acknowledge she has a face." I pushed past him, suppressing my laughter as I walked up the stairs.

Bones took long strides, easily catching up with me. "Is she seeing someone? Because she sure doesn't smell mated," he asked in a low voice.

Two men pushed open the doors with a flourish, and we stepped into the grand foyer. The high ceilings and stone flooring with cherry accents thoroughly impressed me.

"Let me give you some advice, Bones. If you want a shot with Light, don't crowd her space. She'll run the other way. Trust me on this. Credence women have a thing about aggressive men. We're allergic to the testosterone. It makes us crazy."

"So, you must have a hell of a time with Knox."

We weaved through the glittering women and cigar-smoking men who were sizing one another up.

"Yep. But he's like a tiger who's been chasing me around the Serengeti, and this zebra is tired and resigned to the fact that she's going to be eaten, literally." I winked at him saucily.

Bones chuckled. "Why do Ryker and Knox get all the hot, feisty ones?"

I liked Bones, so I looped my arm through his leanly muscled arm. "Have no fear, shifter. There's a Credence running around here, unfettered and wild. Let's see if I can help you catch her."

The party was in full swing as we blended smoothly into

the crowd of humans and Others. The high-octane mixture of new and old money was intoxicating.

"So, where is the man of the hour?" I asked, snagging a glass of champagne with a canapé from the passing server.

"Knox and Ryker had some business to attend to. They should be here shortly."

"Interesting, but I don't get this relationship between Ryker and Knox," I stated casually, trying to get some gossip out of Bones because I really didn't understand how they knew each other.

Bones nodded at a guest before responding, "How so?"

I stepped closer. "Come on, Bones. They come from completely different worlds." Knox and Ryker moved in totally distinct social circles. Then there was the fact that Knox was human and Ryker a wolf-shifter. Their worlds didn't mix on a personal level.

His eyes narrowed. "Wow, isn't that hypocritical? Especially given all the prejudice crap your family has endured for being fae witches?"

"There's no bigotry involved. It's a logical question that's been bugging me. I just don't get why Ryker was so adamant about getting Knox an Other escort. You and I both know it's just too dangerous."

Bones raised an eyebrow. "What's so strange about it? Humans and Others hook up all the time. We just don't talk about it." He nudged me forward to escape a throng of exuberant partiers. "All I can say is that Knox is vital to Ryker."

I didn't ask how before I saw Knox moving through the crowd, wearing a tux obviously made to accommodate his muscular frame. His green eyes narrowed on Bones.

"Whoa! Relax, Knox." Bones stepped away from me with his hands out. "I was just keeping her company while we waited for you to get here. Now, I'm gone." He hurried away, disappearing into the crowd.

Knox's eyes caressed me greedily. "You look beautiful." His husky tone skated across my nerves, arousing my senses.

"Thank you," I responded, deliberately keeping my tone cool.

My breath caught in my throat when he pressed a hand against my lower back, ushering me through the crowd and into a secluded corner. Once there, he turned me to face him. "So, are you good with the paperwork I sent over?"

I squirmed, remembering the documents that confirmed he was disease-free and healthy, a process we required for all clients and escorts as a matter of procedure, not necessity. Others, by nature, did not carry diseases, and females couldn't get pregnant unless they had sex with their fated mate.

"Yes. And you got mine, I gather."

"Yes. So, we're both healthy and disease-free. I'm glad we got that bullshit out of the way." His eyes held mine. "Because I want nothing to interfere with my pleasure when I take you tonight."

His words sent a zing of lust to my core.

"Let's begin with a little foreplay."

My heart raced as he pinned me to his side, navigating us through the excited crowd, then weaving us down a hallway that led to stairs blocked by two men. They nodded at him, making way for us to go up the winding staircase.

My mind was whirling, thinking about all the things I knew he would want from me tonight.

He briskly pushed open the huge, ornate wooden door, leading me inside. "This is my suite. And that's the outfit I want you to wear." He gestured over to the scraps of material lying on the bed. "Once you're done, Harper will be up to escort you down the back stairs to the show."

My eyes widened. "Outfit for what?"

"Your sexy dance performance."

I pushed at his chest. "You are out of your damn mind. I'm not dancing, Knox."

He crossed his arms, looking down at me like I was some misbehaving child. "Of course you are. I volunteered you to perform onstage like all the other females brought here by their Doms. It's for charity."

I marched over to the bed, glaring at the black leather and lace corseted bodysuit ensemble. "You think I'm going to do some strip show just so perverted old men can get their rocks off?"

"Don't forget the women, too." He smirked.

I tapped my foot. "You're a fucking mean bastard. You know that, right?"

Just when I'd thought we were making progress on the forgiveness front, we'd taken three steps back.

"Knox, what kind of game are you playing now?" The thought of being put on display rankled my nerves.

He strode over to me and studied me for a long moment.

"When will you realize this is not some game, Stormy?"

He pulled me closer, entwining his hand in my loose hair. "Call it liberation." His touch felt right... It felt like home. A faint breath escaped me. "I'm unchaining you from your vanilla life." I curled my hands around his forearms. "You want this. You want to be onstage, for me to see you touching your body in all the naughty ways you can imagine." His tongue flicked against my bottom lip. "Call it foreplay, baby." Hot lust curled in my belly. "Getting me all ready to bend you over that bed and take you to heights you've never been." He pressed his mouth against mine. I parted my lips, granting him access to explore my mouth. Sweet memories of how it used to be with him washed over me, and I couldn't stop the low groan of want that escaped me as my tongue boldly met his. My passion for him was escalating sharply, and then I realized that his touch, his kiss, his taste was nothing like it had been years ago... It was better, more potent, more seductive, and my control swiftly began unraveling.

Someone knocked on the door before shouting through it, "Knox, it's time!"

He pulled away, then licked his lips as if savoring my taste. I had to bite back a groan of pleasure.

"To be continued," he promised. "Now get your sexy ass in gear." He strode toward the door, opened it and slammed it behind him.

I slumped onto the bed, staring at the walls and not knowing what to do. Being with Knox again tested my restraint in ways that unnerved me. My first instinct was to walk out of here and never turn back, but I knew that would only make him angry—so angry he might do something I would regret, like destroy Credence O.

And then there was his high-handed order for me to dance tonight, which was wrong on so many levels. Adding to this clusterfuck, I hadn't danced in years, and taking my biweekly cardio dance class didn't count.

Kicking off my heels, I stripped out of my dress, pulling on the tighter-than-hell bodysuit cut so high in the back my ass hung out.

I'm going to kill that jackass. Gritting my teeth, I slipped on the shoes provided.

This was freaking maddening. Not only was I Knox's private sex toy, but I was also his public one. To make matters worse, nothing was more frightening than a roomful of rich alpha men and women waiting impatiently for a balls-to-the-wall strip show, like I was some agenda item at their quarterly board meeting.

A knock on the door sounded loudly before it opened, and Light walked in, slamming the door behind her.

Her eyes widened. "Damn, that's hot."

"Oh, shut up! I'm freaking out here. They have volunteered me to 'shake my moneymaker'—" I made air quotes "—for charity."

Light smiled, blinking her eyelashes dramatically. "But it's for the children. Just think of all the families you'll provide with affordable homes just by shaking that ass. Besides, it will be an enriching experience for all involved."

"Then why the hell don't you do it?"

Light fingered the bodysuit I wore like it was a piece of art. "Are you out of your mind? You know I'm rhythmically challenged. But you know if I could, I damn well would. I'm an exhibitionist, baby. Not a shy bone in my damn body."

That much was true.

It annoyed me that I was panicking like some coward.

I wasn't even a panic kind of girl.

"I can't do this. I haven't danced since college."

She smirked, walking around me. "Oh, give me a damn break. You shake that toned ass twice a week in dance class. Shit, you could probably teach the class. That's how good you are."

I adjusted the back of the bodysuit in vain. My ass was determined to make a guest appearance. "This outfit is horrible."

"Lies. It's H-O-T." She dragged me over to the full-length mirror tucked in the corner.

I stared at my reflection in shock. The tight leather corset I wore made my waist look tiny and pushed up my breasts appealingly. The high-cut sides made my legs appear long and sleek. Light twirled me around grandly. The lace-up back revealed a naughty glimpse of skin. My apple butt was tight, with my cheeks peeping out suggestively.

Light gestured to my black crystal cutout booties. "And I want those damn shoes when you're done."

"Light, this isn't funny. I'm going to make an ass of myself."

"You know he's testing you."

I wanted to laugh hysterically. "Testing me to see if I'll break? Or testing me to see if I'll walk over and slap him for treating me like some dime-store stripper?"

"Neither. He's pushing your limits. Doms and Dommes are very competitive. It's the whose-submissive-can-leave-you-wanting-more showdown. And he's going to put you on full display in front of a room packed with experienced Doms and Dommes, who'll be drooling when they see you on that stage. He wants them to know you're his little sub." She danced around me. "I think I'm in love with Knox," she sang off-key. "He has a sadistic streak that is so enticing."

I stepped forward and wrapped my hands around her neck in a playful choke, and she gagged lightheartedly.

"Will you stop fucking around? I'm really stressed here."

Totally ignoring me, she looked at the clock. "We've got to go. I promised Harper I'd get you down in time." She hustled me out of the room and down the stairs into some backstage area packed with scantily dressed women.

Sensual music whirled around me in a prelude to the major event as I glanced at the stick-thin women with obviously fake breasts. And here I was, curvy with a not-so-flat belly, dressed in a leather corset so tight my ample ass cheeks were hanging out, saying, "Hello! Nice to meet you."

Light narrowed her eyes on the fit blonde brigade and then came back to me. "Nope, you are not doing that self-conscious shit. You see them?" She pointed at them with a disdainful glare. "They need more bread in their lives. Their bodies look like young boys with fake boobs. Look at how they're looking at you. They're fucking jealous. You know why? You are fucking hot. So hot, if I weren't your cousin, I'd switch to the other side." She waggled her eyebrows cheekily.

I slapped her arm softly. I didn't know what I would do without her. She wasn't just my cousin and best friend; she was my biggest supporter.

"I can do this," I declared.

"There's no doubt about that," Light retorted.

My eyes locked on two bodyguards leaning against the wall, glaring at me. They were reporting everything to Knox via earpieces. And from the smirks on their faces, they were enjoying watching me squirm. I glared right back. If Knox was trying to teach me a lesson, then I'd teach him one too. I'd show him I wasn't the stuck-up socialite he pegged me as.

Women skirted around me, looking at me with barely concealed disdain. Some smiled in admiration of my outfit. Some barely missed maliciously pushing me as they bustled over to check their makeup. It was a regular cat-fest.

My eyes narrowed with warning on a woman who deliberately bumped me.

"I do not know what song to dance to. Maybe a circus theme?" I asked cheekily.

"Don't worry." Light winked at me. "Harper and I worked that out."

Biting my bottom lip, I got really nervous.

What if I trip?

What if I get stage fright?

I got a queasy feeling in my stomach, like I was on a roller coaster.

Light grabbed my hand. "Don't overthink this, Stormy. You both want each other. So, go out on that stage and show Knox exactly what he's getting."

I sighed heavily. "I'm the one who has to prance around that stage, all exposed. So, he's clearly in the position of power this time."

"True, but that's just part of the power dynamics—to make you feel helpless. And that's the misconception about D/s relationships. The truth of the matter is, sexual submissives have all the control in the relationship."

"I'm not a submissive, Light!" I wanted to stamp my feet in frustration. "Please, will you stop saying that?"

"What do you think all this is about, Stormy? Deny it all you want, but right now, you're his submissive."

I pursed my lips with disapproval. "And when did I agree to that?"

"The minute you agreed to become his escort. Come on. Let's be honest. You want this. Shit. You might as well put a big red bow around your ass and sit on his lap, declaring yourself his gift."

She is right.

I wanted to grab the freedom of not having to think every second. He was giving me that choice.

And after spending a lifetime overthinking everything in my life, it was liberating but scary to put my trust in his hands.

I wasn't there on the trust issue, but I knew, despite his sadistic streak, he wouldn't hurt me.

Light cupped my face. "You can stop this play anytime you want. I don't give a shit about saving our business if you're unhappy. He won't hurt you, Stormy. I can read him, and everything about him says he wants you. But it's up to you to take this leap of faith, knowing if you do, you'll end up on your knees before him as his sub."

I calmed my breathing. "How is it I can walk into a roomful of business executives and give an off-the-cuff presentation without blinking an eye, but the thought of getting on that stage scares the shit out of me?"

"Because getting on that stage means you have to let go of that leash you have on your emotions."

Arching a brow, I looked at her, annoyed. "There's a reason I don't get emotionally involved."

"Don't go there, Stormy. He's giving you an out for however long this lasts. Take it. Just live in the moment for once in your damn life."

I wanted Knox. There was no need to deny that fact anymore.

But if he thought this trip down memory lane was all about him, then he was dead wrong.

The gloves were off, and I would make sure I ruined him for any woman after me.

My taste would always linger on his tongue and body.

That was a promise.

"All right, let's just do it," I announced.

"Yes." Light clapped her hands, bouncing up and down with excitement. "The old kick-ass Stormy is back. Knox is in trouble now." She reached over and snatched a jet-black fedora and a black men's tie off the dressing table. "Here are your props. Use them and abuse them as you strut your stuff."

Slapping the hat on my head, I made quick work of loosely tying the tie around my neck. "Okay, so how does this strip-a-thon work?"

"There's no stripping involved," Light emphasized. "It's really a bump-and-grind show that's almost burlesque." She pointed over at a gorgeous curvy redhead strutting across the stage. Light called attention to the black button in the hands of each man and woman. "When they like what they see, the Dom or Domme presses the button to bid on the woman. The winning bid gets to have drinks with the woman after the show." She directed me to the wide-screen anchored discreetly near the ceiling. "You track the winning bid up there."

We looked back at the woman who was bumping and grinding, her body off-beat to the music.

Frankly, I'd seen nothing so bawdy and unimaginative. And I guessed the audience agreed because the men and women looked absolutely bored as they ignored the dancer, loudly talking business.

They blew cigar smoke in the air and slammed alcohol-filled glasses on the stage. The woman's eyes widened as she tried to maneuver around glasses without sloshing them. It was a mess.

The redhead glanced up at the wide-screen, her mouth tightening at the flashing $1,000. She gave the women and men the middle finger before stomping off the stage.

"What happened?" I looked at Light, perplexed. "A thousand is good, right?"

"No. The woman before her got ten thousand." Her cell buzzed. "That's Harper. She said you're next."

My stomach fluttered nervously. "Okay, what song will I be making a fool of myself to?"

"Don't worry about it." Light urged me forward. "We got you."

The music lowered as Harper sauntered across the stage. "Doms and Dommes, the next beautiful submissive to take the stage is brought to you by Mr. Gunner. He calls her Breaking the Storm."

I tapped my foot grumpily. "For the last fucking time, I'm not a submissive."

"Oh, shut up and dance," Light said before shoving me through the curtains.

"You little..." I sputtered.

Then I froze. All eyes were on me.

My eyes panned the dimly lit room, and I counted at least thirty men and women of every ethnic background and age sitting in expensive leather chairs surrounding the large stage designed to look like an actual boardroom table.

I instantly recognized the heavy, carnal beat of the music as it thumped and echoed throughout the room.

Damn those two.

They'd picked Knox's hit single for me to dance to.

I blew out a breath anxiously, feeling like I was about to throw up.

Damn, maybe I should just concede victory to Knox and go home with my tail between my legs.

That was when I saw Knox with his broad, brawny back deliberately turned to me in what I knew was an intentional you-are-not-even-worth-paying-attention-to slap in the face.

Okay, Mr. Gunner, it's on.

"Let's get ready to rumble, New York-style," I mumbled under my breath.

Releasing all the tension, I relaxed my body, fully taking in the magnitude of the sheer power and waves of sexual energy emanating from my captive audience.

Unleashed dominance pulsed around me, but I knew I could do this.

It was Seduction 101, and judging from the lustful, hooded stares of the dominant men and women who were now sitting up at attention, they were very interested in seeing exactly what I'd brought to the freaky boardroom.

I flipped my hair, sashaying forward along a strip of lights running from upstage to downstage with a deliberate swing to my hips.

Unlike the previous dancer, my dance would be soft, feminine, and sensual. A celebration of women's bodies and arousal.

Chest out. Head up.

My gaze swept to every person as a hush filled the room.

Knox turned around, giving me a blank stare.

Lights flashed while the music wove a hard rhythm around me. Knox's voice intertwined salaciously with the thump of the drums and guitar, lending the music a satisfying lewdness.

Loosening the tie, I ran it through my hands then over my shoulders rhythmically to reflect the music.

A man with chin-length waves of chestnut hair tucked behind his ears and a blue aura—Other—beckoned me with a nod. Placing one foot directly in front of the other, I swayed over, proud, confident, and sexy.

Twirling the tie in my hand a couple times before leaning forward with my stomach in and ass out, I swung the tie around his neck to draw him close, gracefully moving my hips from left to right as his eyes followed them in perfect synchrony.

"Absolutely beautiful," he said with a sexy drawl.

Releasing my grip on the tie, I did a mild backbend as the music changed to a fast and animated drum ensemble. Gliding up from the position, I lifted my leg, digging my heel into his shoulder. His lips curled up into a smile.

Shimmying my hips in a continuous motion, I glanced at the wide-screen.

The bid was at $80,000.

Mr. Other pressed the button, moving the highest bid to $110,000.

"You, I definitely want," he growled.

"You might be asking for way more trouble than you can handle," I responded with a wink before deliberately digging my heel farther into his broad shoulder. I knew the pinch of my heel would give him what he wanted—pain.

A growl rumbled deep in his chest as his hand clenched around his glass. Just like I'd thought, Mr. Other was into pain. He pressed the bid button again.

"Thank you for the donation," I cooed before spinning around, leaning over from the waist and giving him a full view of my ass. With one smooth move, I snaked my body up and winked at him before walking toward the chair sitting in the middle of the stage. Circling around it to build anticipation, I hooked my calf around it, then twirled it with long, fluid movements.

The music and atmosphere were liberating. I felt triumphant, bold, and very confident.

I was the ringmaster, and these men and women were my circus to control any way I wanted.

Knox lifted his glass to his lips, scrutinizing me pensively.

I twirled gracefully before allowing my butt to spin on the chair. With a sultry swing of my hips, I worked that chair like a professional dancer. Our eyes locked as I fluffed my hair with an air of satisfaction before sliding off the chair to dance before a woman who winked at me while sliding her business card across the stage.

I felt dizzy from the power as I worked the men and women hard.

I had them in the palm of my hand when the bid hit $240,000.

Now it was time for the man I really wanted.

Knox's eyes lit with amusement when he held out his hand to me. I didn't take it immediately. Tossing my hair, I dropped low in front of him with a provocative smile.

"Temptress," he muttered around his cigar.

"The best," I said with an air of confidence, swaying my way up.

Leaning forward, I snatched the cigar from his mouth, letting my hair softly brush against his face. Stubbing it out on the stage, I put it into my mouth like a boss in charge as I popped my hips, spun, and bent over, looking between my legs and giving him a full-on display of my ass.

I flicked my tongue around the cigar. His eyes widened with desire. My breath hitched when I saw a pea-sized glow—the color of amber—twinkling in his eyes, then it vanished.

Did I imagine that?

Or was it just the reflection from the stage lights?

I stored that quandary for later dissection. Right now, I had to get my head back into my dance.

I extended my hand to Knox, which he grabbed firmly. Using his hard thigh as a step stool, I stepped down onto the floor. His face was like granite. No emotion showed as his hands clenched and unclenched, like he was fighting the need to touch me.

Stepping between his splayed legs, I twirled around, giving him my back, as I started a slow sway of my hips from side to side, winding them in a figure eight. My butt moved in circles as it hovered over his crotch.

Leaning back, I whispered over my shoulder, "Are you enjoying the show, rock star?"

He was silent, but the pulse along his jaw beating in a rapid rhythm said it all.

I lowered myself onto his lap, grinding against his body, glancing at him over my shoulder.

"I'm sorry. I can't hear over the loud gnashing of teeth. So, is that a yes or a no, baby?"

His hand brushed down my back, sending delicious chills up and down my spine. "Now, little submissive, it's not smart to mouth off to the man on the edge of making you get on your knees in front of guests—" he nipped my ear hard "—and showing me exactly what that talented, dirty mouth can do."

I swallowed hard as my pussy pulsated with desire at the thought of myself on my knees, at his mercy, with my lips around his cock. "Just so you know, I'm an avid believer in giving as long as I'm also receiving."

"Not an issue, darling. In fact—" his tongue flicked my neck "—I look forward to it." Wrapping his arms around me, he effortlessly lifted me onto the stage with a hard tap on the ass in parting.

I spun around to look at him one more time before the music ended. With my head held high, I strutted across the stage and nearly tripped at the sight of men and women giving Knox blatantly challenging glares as they extended their business cards toward me.

Knox's face was thunderous as I paraded across the stage, touching and caressing each Dominant's hand as I took their card.

Glancing up at the wide-screen, I saw the winning bid hit $390,000.

Not bad for a rookie.

I bowed grandly before prancing off the stage, knowing that Knox was going to make me pay for my little victory lap, and I didn't give a shit.

I accepted his dare.

And won fair and square.

Game over, Knox Gunner.

CHAPTER 11

I WAS PRACTICALLY GIDDY STROLLING down the hallway wearing my dress again, with Harper and Light talking excitedly about my performance. With their arms looped through mine, we almost skipped down the stairs.

"You don't understand how pissed off Knox is for losing the bid to Abe Calum," Harper said with way too much excitement.

"Who's Abe Calum?" I questioned.

"The sexy guy with the gorgeous chestnut hair. You know, the one who was salivating on your stilettos."

I nodded. *Mr. Other.*

Harper continued, "Sheesh, I was choking on the testosterone as they battled it out for you."

I grabbed a glass of champagne from a passing server. "Well, that's what happens when you underestimate the power of a sexy ass," I explained.

"Oh, he didn't underestimate it," Light interjected. "He miscalculated how much he would have to shell out for it, which just means more money for their charity foundation."

"Doms and Dommes have been pulling me aside, asking many questions about you." Harper waggled her eyebrows. "They're very interested in getting to know you better. And Knox is stomping around and glaring at them, trying to scare them away from you."

"Good. He's way too cocky," I pointed out coolly, even as my pulse raced with excitement.

"I'm surprised he didn't whip out his cock and mark her as his," Light said.

"I'm not his," I said with way too much bravado.

"Yeah. Okay." A smile curved Harper's lips. "Light and I have bets on how long it'll take before you're up in his bedroom suite, assuming the position." She laughed, leaning forward with her ass poking out. Her laughter suddenly died in her throat. "Oh shit! Knox is heading over here, and he looks like he's about to snap, crackle, pop. Light, let's get out of here before he snarls at us."

Light kissed me on the cheek before whispering, "Have fun, cousin."

They weaved their way through the crowd, giggling like two teenagers.

"Stormy Credence?" a nasal voice inquired from behind me.

I glanced over my shoulder and saw a short, frail-looking man studying me.

I turned to face him. "Yes?"

"I'm Jeff Hunter." He adjusted his black wire-rimmed glasses. "I'm a reporter working on a story about the death of Celina Rouse. I believe she was your employee."

Shit! I don't need this right now.

"I have nothing to add to your story, Mr. Hunter. This matter is for the police to solve. Now, if you'll excuse me." I turned to walk away when his words stopped me.

"I know all about your company and its clientele, Ms. Credence." His beady black eyes narrowed. "Wealthy clients looking for escorts to hire." He leered at my clothes. "Seems like it's a pretty lucrative business."

"If you print anything of the sort, I'll have my lawyer crawling up your ass like a proctologist."

Knox walked up with two burly bodyguards. "Trouble?" Steel laced his tone.

"None," I said simply. "I believe Mr. Hunter is leaving."

The bodyguards towered over Hunter. "Yes, I was." The reporter stepped back with eyes darting toward the exit. "You really should take it, Ms. Credence." He held out his business card to me.

I snatched it from his fingers before he scampered away.

"He must have snuck in." Knox nodded toward the bodyguards. "Make sure he gets off the property."

"Got it," they said in unison before hustling away.

"Sleazy reporter," Knox grumbled.

With an aggrieved sigh, I asked, "You know him?"

"Yes. He's a freelance celebrity gossip reporter." His eyes narrowed. "Was he asking questions about me?"

"No." I took a shaky breath. "One of my escorts was killed. And he's on the trail of the story. But with time, he'll lose interest," I said with more confidence than I felt. I'd seen the determination in Hunter's eyes. He had something up his sleeve, and it wasn't good.

"If you need me to help, just let me know. I have some contacts who can make him disappear." Knox's voice was forbidding.

I touched his elbow. "Thank you, but I don't want your name attached to this mess." Suddenly mentally and physically exhausted, I looked around at the thinning crowd. "I'm going to go up. I'm a little tired. See you upstairs."

"I need to talk to Ryker for a minute." Knox nodded toward Ryker as he towered over Light, who was pointing in his face with jerky motions before stomping away. "Then I'll be up." He kissed me hard on the lips before striding away.

When I arrived in the suite, I'd worked up another bought of anxiety about Hunter. Pacing the floor, I called Light's cell. "Light?"

"Stormy? What's wrong? I thought you'd be knee-deep in cock by now."

"There's trouble. The reporter was here, snooping."

"I know." She sighed heavily. "I saw the guards throw him out on his ass. The little asshole snuck in here."

I sat on the edge of the bed, tugging off my shoes then wiggling my toes. "I don't have a good feeling about him."

"I don't either," Light admitted.

Knox walked in, shutting the door with a resounding click.

"Um, Light? Knox is here. Let's talk in the morning, okay?"

"Sounds like a plan." Our call ended.

The suite was eerily quiet while Knox and I assessed each other.

Breaking the silence, I asked, "So how does it feel to be the biggest loser, rock star?"

"I didn't lose."

He smiled, and my heart skipped a beat. The man was beyond handsome when he smiled.

"I beg to differ," I objected. "You lost the bid to Calum."

"He and I came to an agreement after your dance."

I frowned. "Care to share the details?" I didn't like the idea of two men negotiating for me like I was property.

"No," he declared before prowling toward me.

When he reached me, I tilted my head back, staring up at him.

"No?" I made a face.

He rolled his shoulders. "Stop stalling, Stormy. I've been waiting too long for this moment. Strip."

My breath became ragged because I wanted this. I wanted him.

Standing, I reached for my zipper with trembling fingers.

"Stop." He twined his hand in my hair. "I've seen how good you are at swaying that ass for strangers. Now, it's just you and me, baby, and this better be the greatest show on earth. Dress off...slowly." He released me, stepping back.

His eyes raked over me before he twirled his finger, a silent demand for me to turn.

I wasn't a shrinking violet, and sex and seduction were nothing new to me. If he wanted a show, then he was going to get it.

I spun around until my back was to him. Glancing over my shoulder, I unzipped my gown unhurriedly. Keeping it clutched against my breasts, I turned back toward him with a wicked expression on my face.

In one smooth motion, I removed my hands from my breasts, wiggling my body until my gown slithered to the floor, pooling at my feet. Lifting my heavy breasts in both hands, I kneaded my hardened nipples.

Knox watched me with those devastating green eyes, his expression giving nothing away.

"Was that good enough?" I asked with a husky voice.

"The best show on earth." He reached out and touched the side of my face, leaning down fast and pressing his lips to mine before pulling away. "Now, let's talk hard limits."

I knew enough about the BDSM world to know these were negotiations—a verbal contract between us, binding our play with my limits, his desires, and our needs.

"No anal," I responded.

"Have you ever tried it, sweetness?" he countered. "Believe me, I will make it worth your time."

Years ago, I'd never had the chance to see him fully naked, but I remembered enough about the size of his cock from our many groping sessions after his shows. He was big, and there was no way in hell I was going to let his enormous cock back there—at least not yet.

"No, I haven't. And I'm not going there."

"But that ass of yours is so sexy." Knox smiled, and my heart skipped a beat.

"Not on the table tonight. My other hard limit is no other women."

"Harper will be so disappointed." Amusement filled his eyes. "Go on," he ordered, never taking his eyes off me while removing his cuff links and tie.

"And no public scenes between us," I insisted.

"Well, that puts a kink in my wicked plans."

My eyes widened when he removed his crisp white shirt, tossing it over the chair. I traced the hard muscles of his chest with my gaze. He flexed his tattooed forearms, showing off the intricate details of wolves chasing one another.

He strode over to me. "Now, let's talk safe words."

I knew safe words were the best way of ensuring that, in the heat of the moment, I could communicate to him how I was feeling.

"I respond to red, yellow, and green," he said, never taking his eyes off me for a second. "Red means stop. Saying it will mean you want me to stop everything I'm doing immediately. Use it when you're not comfortable, things are getting too much, or you no longer consent."

"Got it." I raised my chin, placing my hands on my hips.

"Yellow means you want me to slow down." He brushed a

hand against my breast, and my nipples stiffened immediately. "It also means you're reaching your limit or are edging on physical discomfort."

"So, it's when I like what you're doing, but then it becomes a little too much?" I asked.

"Exactly." He reached up to run his fingers over my hair. "And green means go for it. Use it when you like what I'm doing, you feel totally comfortable, and you want me to continue."

"Understood."

"Good. Let's proceed." He brushed his lips over mine, nipping hard. I inched my hands up to his shoulders.

"Hands by your sides, Stormy," he clipped out, forcing my hands by my sides. "Turn and face the wall."

His command made my breath ragged, nipples tighten, and warmth pool between my thighs, but my mind rebelled against his demand. Then Light's words echoed in my head, *"What I do in the bedroom does not reflect who I am in everyday life. I am a feminist, and Dom/sub play does not impact that. I don't feel diminished or lesser because I'm a sub. In fact, it's quite empowering. It makes me feel very sexy and turned on."*

Now I understood what she meant.

I was a successful woman, but there was no shame in wanting a man to satisfy me in bed.

Frankly, I don't want to decide in the bedroom; I want to surrender, knowing that if I do as I'm told, Knox will look after me and give me what I want.

Whirling around, I shivered as he ran a finger over the tattoo of a naked woman riding a broom on my lower back.

"Interesting," he muttered. "Tattoos? Still a fucking rebel under that wall of steel." He trailed his finger up and across the black rune tattoo between my shoulder blades.

I responded, "It means—"

"Fire," he interjected. "The end of darkness in your life."

I inhaled sharply. No one had ever understood the meaning of the symbol before.

"Is that what you're looking for, Stormy? A man to end the darkness?" He pressed a lingering kiss against it.

The intimacy of his low tone was like a tug on my nipples. "Yes."

"Very good." He bit the slope of my shoulder hard. I whimpered.

"Safe word?" he asked sharply.

"Green."

He grabbed the back of my head, gently turning me to face him.

His eyes lingered on my breasts, making them feel swollen and heavy.

He traced a finger between them before saying, "Good girl."

Reaching out to cup my breast, he covered my mouth with his. I swallowed a moan as his fingers plucked at my beaded nipple. Pinching lightly, he rolled it firmly between his thumb and forefinger. Jolts of piercing, fervent desire burned in my core. His touch smoldered with possession and feral hunger.

He cupped my jaw, his other hand flicking a finger over my pulsing nipple. I locked my knees, preventing them from buckling, as I waited for the next stroke that never came.

He covered my lips with his, nibbling them hard. Forgetting the rules of engagement, I leaned in, kissing him back with equal fever.

He retreated and waited.

I stilled.

He captured my lips again, and I remained motionless, submitting to him.

I almost smiled when I was rewarded with a rough kiss. A

stinging nip of his teeth made me open my mouth, and he plunged in, his tongue stroking mine. His kiss was slow and deep—the stamp of his possession. Not even when we were younger did he kiss me like that.

Jesus, I'm so fucked.

A rush of heat flooded my entire body. Lust curled deep inside me. Knox was slowly crumbling my resolve to remain emotionally detached.

The taste of submission was intoxicating. I needed this, craved it. I wanted to follow, contradicting everything I knew about myself.

He broke off our kiss, growling in my ear, "Safe word?"

"Green."

"On your knees," he ordered.

Sexual desire coiled in my stomach, but I was afraid to breathe, to move. I knew once I did as he demanded, I would be his forever.

"Stormy, get on your knees." His voice was deep and caressing, sliding across my skin like silk. "I want to fuck your mouth."

My stomach rolled with anxiousness as I leaped into the pits of scorching hell and slid to my knees. With trembling fingers, I unbuckled his belt and unzipped his pants.

Sweet Jesus, no underwear.

He stared at me with his penetrating gaze. "Release my cock."

I shivered as I touched his hardness. He was long and beautifully thick. When he was all out, I stroked him gently. His engorged, thick cock stretched taut, almost past his navel. The broad, round crown glistened with a small drop of moisture. His balls were tight with arousal.

My cunt tingled, and my peaks puckered as I craved the

salty taste of him. I grabbed his manhood with both hands, feeling the hardness swell. Massaging the smooth, hot column of flesh between my fingers, I leaned forward, taking the swollen head into my greedy mouth. Knox threaded his hands through my hair, as though savoring the feel. The low groans coming from him spurred me on.

He tightened his hand, jerking on my hair. He grew bigger in my mouth as I bobbed my head up and down over his wide shaft. The more I tasted, the more I hungered. With every flick of my tongue, the hard grip of his fingers against my head seemed to turn me on even more. I fed him into my throat, taking it all. His hard shaft was thick, like him. My lips stretched around his cock.

He spread his legs wider.

I hummed as he started a slow slide in and out between my lips.

A fog of desire clouded my vision.

All I could think of was bringing him pleasure.

His groan deepened, becoming more of a growl, charging the erotic tension even more. "More tongue. Suck harder," he hissed.

His dark words sent me spiraling to the edge of a lust-induced frenzy. My body quivered with a fire I'd never felt before. I didn't give a shit about how wild and out of control he was making me.

I didn't think.

I just felt liberated and bizarrely in control of Knox.

I closed my eyes briefly, letting out a strangled sound. My tongue stroked every bump and ridge of his flesh. Moving up and down on him, I sucked him harder. It thrilled me when his hands moved to my head again, positioning me over his member.

"Wider." He tightened his fists even further in my hair. "Open your mouth wider."

I did, and he pushed his staff until it hit against the back of my throat. He was huge, the size of my wrist, but I didn't back away or struggle. Holding still, I relaxed my throat to keep from gagging. My tongue slid along his length as I breathed through my nose and swallowed around him.

"Fuck. Do that again." His voice was hoarse and thick with arousal.

Heady with power, I swallowed around him. The sound of his harsh breath filled the room. It drove me on as he thrust into me with a slow rhythm that was rough and primal. His tangled fingers in my hair held my head still for his deep thrusts.

Class was in session, and he was teaching me what he demanded. And like a good little student, I was eager to learn.

My lips danced over him. My hips swayed in tandem.

"Beautiful," he whispered before a guttural groan erupted from his mouth. "Swallow it all," he commanded a second before he shot into the sweet depths of my mouth.

I continued to suck, swallow, and lick him with gentle strokes until he gradually softened in my mouth.

After inching from between my lips in one smooth motion with a heartfelt sigh, he helped me stand. My legs were trembling under me, and he cradled me against his chest with an unexpected tenderness that left me speechless. My body jerked involuntarily, and a mental switch flipped from lust-induced haze to lucid reality. This was the way he used to hold me.

My body stiffened. I felt raw, exposed, and confused.

What the fuck am I doing?

He stroked my hair. "Don't overthink this. Just feel," he coaxed.

I squeezed my eyes shut for a moment, trying to do the opposite of what he'd demanded.

Feeling was exactly what almost made me fall in love with him.

Credence women didn't feel. We fucked and ran.

We understood the price of love and that there was no winner in the game of love. Only losers.

No, it would be better to keep whatever we had strictly sexual. Sex, I understood. Relationships and emotions were not in my vocabulary.

"I don't want to fucking feel." My voice broke.

I cleared my throat. "I want to fuck you and be done with all of this." I wanted him to get angry. I needed his rejection to fuel my will to hightail it away from him and away from this intimacy.

The muscles jumped near his jawline. "We will never be over," he clipped out.

The truth of his words resonated within me, not because he wanted it to be so, but because deep inside, I wanted it too. But the risk was too great.

"There is so much you don't know about me, Knox."

I swallowed hard and bit my bottom lip to hide the emotions—longing to have something real with him that couldn't be, regret that I'd hurt and lied to him years ago, and resentment at the Curse that held me prisoner.

Clamping my fingers together, I tried to remember how to breathe.

This was why so many of the Credence women—past and present—walled off their heart, because it was too painful to love a man we could never have.

"You don't trust me enough to share." His voice was low and soft.

"This has nothing to do with trust, Knox."

He could never understand that the reason for my inability

to share the truth with him had nothing to do with him and everything to do with the Credence Curse.

"It has everything to do with it, Stormy." For a brief second, I saw hurt and anger in his eyes before it vanished. "Trust means everything to me. Without it, we have nothing."

The weight of his words cracked open the wall around my heart. This connection with Knox was frightening.

"How the hell did we move from just sex to this?" I protested huskily.

"You're still not ready to accept everything I long to give you." He lifted my chin with a flick of his finger and kissed me hard and deep before breaking it off abruptly. "So, we'll play it your way—for now. You want just sex, then I'll give you what you want, not what you need."

"Knox, I..." Confusion, frustration, and scorching-hot sexual need coursed through my veins.

"Get on the bed." He looked every bit a dominant male with his hands on his hips.

I wanted him, so I moved, lying on my back.

"Panties off," he directed, and I obeyed.

He was now standing between my legs. "Assume the position."

I arched a brow. "What?"

"On your knees."

Getting on my knees, I spread them wide. I was panting, feeling more vulnerable than I'd ever felt in my life, so I closed them.

"Open those legs. Close them again, and I'll keep you aroused all night."

Shit, I'll never survive the night turned on like this. I opened my legs.

He ran a hand across the curve of my ass before parting my cheeks.

"Are you protected?" he questioned.

I nodded—in more ways than one.

He was human.

There was no way in hell I could conceive with anyone but an Other who was my true mate.

"Good."

"Knox..."

He curled his fingers in my hair, snapping my head back. "Don't worry. I know it's just sex for you," he whispered into my ear.

Just sex for me?

Isn't it just sex for us?

Releasing my hair, he pressed me facedown onto the bed, burying his cock so deep inside me that my entire body quaked from the sheer force.

"Oh fuck!" I cried out as he stretched me ruthlessly.

His engorged flesh sank deeper between my sensitive folds, and his balls slapped against my womanhood, sending tiny shocks through my body. My hips bucked, and my pussy burned from the width of his big, thick cock.

With fingers buried into the flesh at my hips, he held me still, giving me time to adjust to his girth.

My body tensed from the burning fullness in my cunt.

"Relax," he ordered.

I took a deep breath, forcing my rebellious muscles to loosen.

He pushed forward, slowly at first, and then he increased his speed from a sensuous slide to hard, forceful pumping.

"Fuck!" he cursed.

I couldn't move as he rocked into me.

The feeling of helplessness ran through me, heightening every sensation in my body.

He was driving me crazy with lust, and each stroke brought me closer and closer to the edge.

"Knox," I groaned as he continued to fuck me like a man possessed.

He squeezed my hips with his fingers.

Again and again, he pulled out and plunged back inside me with an intensity that drove me over the edge, and then I came brutally hard, shattering into sweet oblivion.

CHAPTER 12

MY EYES SNAPPED open when Knox pressed me into the mattress with his nude, muscular frame. "You are too beautiful for words, Stormy." He tenderly brushed his lips across mine.

Tears sprang to my eyes as he took my mouth so gently and thoroughly that he rendered me speechless.

Lifting his head, he just stared before sweeping my hair from my forehead. "Damn, I love that well-fucked look on you."

My heart pounded. *This is not good.*

He was cracking open a part of me I didn't want to reveal.

A part of me that wished I could spend a lifetime in his arms—protected, happy, and loved.

But this sappy shit had to stop.

This weekend was a perfect solution to indulge in my arousal, get it out of my system, and then leave.

"Knox, I'm an escort who just violated a fair number of Credence O. rules." I licked my lips, tasting him all over them. "Last night was good."

"Just good?" His lips twitched into a mockery of a smile.

"Okay." I scowled. "It was fucking great. You rocked my

fucking world. But this is a no-strings, no-promises weekend of pleasure."

There, I said it.

Now he'll get angry. Put on his clothes. And walk away.

Problem solved.

But his reaction was quite the opposite.

He rolled me, pulling me over to straddle him. My pulse raced as I stared down into his sea-green eyes. My damn betraying body craved to have him inside me again.

"Let's get one thing straight," he stated flatly. "You belong to me."

My mouth opened with shock. "Fuck you, Knox. I don't belong to anyone. This. Is. A. Fling."

"Being with me scares the shit out of you." His eyes narrowed as if this were the first time he was really seeing me. "Why?"

"You don't know me, Knox, so don't pretend you do." With my chin tilted at a stubborn angle, I held my ground. "Besides, where do you think this thing between us will go?"

I swallowed around the emotions bubbling to the surface.

I was doing this for him, not because being with him scared me.

"I live in New York. You live..." I gestured wildly. "I don't know. Everywhere but here. You're on the road all the time, and I need stability, someone who will be here for me. You're not that man." I held my breath, waiting for him to roll me over, leaving me cold and safe from drowning deeper in this emotional abyss.

"That's bullshit, and you know it. You belong to me. That is a fact."

He was just too thickheaded to get what I was doing—saving him from me and the Curse.

I pounded on his chest. "Fuck you, Knox. I'm not property. I don't belong to you or anyone."

"I see right through you, Stormy." He slapped my ass hard before running his hands over the globes, softly soothing the sting. "This time, trying to push me out of your life will not work," he stated calmly before rolling me over onto my side and moving off the bed. "I'm going to run us a bath. Stay here." His voice was crisp, eyes warning me not to move.

What the fuck just happened?

I lay there, paralyzed, focused on his muscular butt and wide shoulders. My eyes trailed to the large, silvery-gray wolf tattoo on his back with eerie green eyes that looked like it was daring me to move.

Nothing is going the way I'd planned.

This was a no-expectations deal, but Knox was acting as if he wanted to keep me like I was some puppy. There was no way I'd allow that to happen.

I'm out of here.

When he disappeared into the bathroom, I scrambled off the bed, making a beeline for my gown, frantically snatching it up.

Knox might not believe in self-preservation, but I did. He was just too fucking stupid to realize I was doing this for him.

My inner voice mocked me. *No, Stormy. You're doing this for you. You're a damn coward.*

Ignoring the voice, I grabbed my shoes and cell. I didn't know how in the hell I was going to get back home, but I was going to walk.

Knox appeared in the doorway, still naked and looking like some well-chiseled, tattooed Greek god. "Going somewhere?"

Shit! Looking at him with more bravado than I actually felt, I announced, "I'm going home." I licked my dry lips. "I have work to do." My voice cracked.

"Not yet. I'm not done with you. I have plans, wicked plans."

I jumped nervously, trying to figure out if I could make it past him without being caught. He crossed the room, snatching the things from my hands, and threw them onto the floor.

"Knox, stop being such an ass."

My breath caught when he grabbed the back of my head, tangling his fingers in my hair and angling my mouth, leaning down to kiss me. My mouth dropped open, and his tongue thrust in.

"Stay with me, Stormy," he whispered against my lips.

My pulse sped up at the softness of his words.

God help me, but right now, I'm willing to give him anything.

To hell with this...

I'm in control here.

I'm not some fickle college girl who can't separate sex from love.

I'm a grown woman who enjoys sex, and frankly, sex with Knox is as good as it ever gets.

"Knox, I'll stay as long as we can experiment. I think I've got the hang of this Dom/sub thing." I ran my hand across his tight ass. "How about letting me top you?" I grinned, imagining all the hot, naughty things I'd make him do.

He snorted. "No."

I ran my tongue across his lips. He nipped my bottom lip so hard that I pulled back.

"Shit! Ouch!" *On to sensual persuasion tactic number two.* "Why?" I cupped his tight sac. "I know how it works. Spanking, exposure, degradation, licking my pussy. Come on, baby, let me give you a well-deserved submissive experience."

"Not going to happen. I don't bottom."

"Are you sure about that?" I stroked his cock.

His cock grew hard. "You give good head, but not even that can persuade me."

I released him. "Mmm, well then." I sat on the bed, crossing my legs., "If you don't want to compromise, I'll just take a nap."

In a flash, I was swung through the air and slung across his shoulder, cave-dweller-style.

"What are you doing?" I wasn't one of those thin women, but he carried me as if I were as light as a feather. "Put me down."

"Quiet, woman." He slapped my ass hard, shutting me up. "The water is getting cold." He strode across the room and into the gorgeous Italian marble bathroom with a double vanity, a deep soaking tub, and a separate shower without breaking a sweat.

"How did I not remember how pushy you were?" I remarked with a smile on my face.

He laughed in that husky way that sent chills of delight down my spine. "Because you were too busy trying to run away from the inevitable." He eased me into the lavender-scented water and settled behind me.

I sighed with pleasure. The combination of the lavender's fresh, floral scent and the way my body molded against him filled me with way too much bliss. Closing my eyes, I just relaxed, ignoring the plethora of reasons being with Knox wasn't a good idea.

He cupped my full breasts, gently squeezing them. His enormous shaft hardened and pressed deliciously against my back.

Grabbing a handful of my hair, he twisted my head to meet his lips before thrusting his tongue into my mouth, taking what he wanted. Our tongues tangled. Dueled. Retreated. I moaned, not caring that now I would refuse him nothing.

Breaking off our kiss, he reached forward, hooking my legs over his knees, stretching them wide. "Ready to fuck?"

"Yes," I admitted.

There was no sense in lying. I wanted him, and there was no damn shame in that.

He lifted me up slightly, impaling me on his hard cock. I settled into his embrace as he wrapped his arms around me, burying his face into my neck, softly nipping it as I rode his cock like a surfboard.

Shaking with desire with each stroke, I knew that, despite my best intentions, one night with him would never be enough.

Double damn.

CHAPTER 13

WHAT IS THAT ANNOYING RINGING?

Forcing a droopy eye open, I raised my head from the pillow and then put it back down. I was deliciously tired. My body was recovering from a thoroughly sensual ravishment in the bath and then several more times when we got out. Knox was insatiable, with extraordinary stamina for a human. And I'd loved every bit.

I rolled over onto the other side of the bed. It was still warm from Knox's body. Flipping over onto my stomach and pressing my nose into the pillow, I inhaled his lingering scent of sandal-wood mixed with lavender.

The last thing I remembered was Knox kissing me before saying he had to go to his concert dress rehearsal and would be back to take me out to dinner before we went to Ryker's charity fantasy ball.

I closed my eyes, ready to go back to sleep, when someone pounded on the door.

"Go away," I mumbled before I heard the bang of the door

slamming into the wall. My eyes snapped open to find Light standing in the doorway, looking frazzled.

"Damn, I'm so jealous," Light said before swaying forward on wobbly legs. "You look well fucked."

Damn. She had been drinking.

"You're drunk already?" I challenged.

"I'm entitled to get a little drunk. I have Bones sniffing around me like a lost puppy and Ryker acting like a pissed-off bull ready to choke me to death." She made a face. "It's confusing."

I scooted up into a seated position. "And?"

Light plopped down onto a chair. "And you'd better put on your clothes because shit just hit the fan."

Utterly mystified, I stared at her. "What happened?"

"Well, if you'd answer your damn cell, you'd know." Her mouth compressed into a thin line. "That call you didn't answer was the security company saying someone had tripped the house alarm in our office."

"Holy shit!" I scrambled off the bed, frantically looking around the room. "I can't find my dress. Why didn't you bring my overnight bag in here?"

"That was the last thing on my mind, Stormy. Anyway, Knox left clothes for you over there." Light pointed to the dressing table.

Running over to the table, I snatched up the dark jeans, quickly putting them on. Then I pulled on the black tank top that was body-hugging tight. If I weren't so worried, I'd kill him. He dressed me like some rocker chick. Annoyed, I picked up my stilettos, putting them on.

"Do we have a ride back?" I asked.

"Yes, pain-in-the-ass Ryker has a car downstairs, ready to take us home."

"Pain in the ass?" I asked, hustling out of the suite.

"Argh, just don't ask. Dislike doesn't express what I feel for that arrogant man."

Minutes later, we left the mansion, getting into the waiting vehicle. Speeding through the traffic, all I could think of was how shit had just gone from bad to worse. And a sense of dark foreboding weighed heavily on me.

Things got even worse when we arrived home and spotted the crowd gathered on the sidewalk outside. I didn't even let the vehicle fully stop before jumping out in sheer panic. Pushing through the throng, I headed to the door when a uniformed police officer blocked my entrance. "Back up, lady," he ordered. "This is a crime scene."

"This is my damn home," I protested, pulling out my identification.

After scanning my ID, he grumbled, "Okay," then stepped aside.

I rushed through the open front door to find a short, heavy man wearing plainclothes and a badge scrutinizing several framed portraits of my ancestors that hung along the foyer wall.

"What's going on?" I asked.

He turned to stare at me. "Ms. Credence?"

"Yes?" I looked at the sloppily dressed man impatiently. "What happened?" I asked sharply. "Was anything stolen?"

The man looked at me curiously. "I have some questions to ask. First—"

"Oh, to hell with this…" I had neither time nor patience to stand around chatting. I ran into our office and skidded to a stop when I saw all the uniformed and plainclothes police officers.

The annoying man from the foyer hurried up beside me, wheezing like he was about to pass out.

Light walked up to my side. "Holy hell," she whispered under her breath.

My knees nearly gave out at the sight of the wide-open double doors to our custom-designed luxury estate safe.

I took a visual inventory of the gold, cash, jewelry, and coins left by the thief. I sucked in a breath when I realized the real valuables were all gone—every single document we had on our clients and escorts.

Light gawked at me in shock before letting her face blank out.

My mind raced while surveying the rest of the office.

All our expensive laptops were still where we'd left them. We encrypted the information on the equipment, but it wouldn't take a sophisticated thief long to decrypt it. And without a doubt, this burglar was sophisticated. To have the skills needed to break in to the complicated house security system along with bypassing the biometric lock on the safe door spoke volumes of the robber's ingenuity.

"Strangely, the thief left all the valuables." The bizarre man glared at me with icy brown eyes. "So, it begs the question, why would someone break in to a safe and leave valuables?" He eyed me suspiciously.

I tapped my foot impatiently. "Who are you?"

"Detective Burrows." His eyes narrowed and his nostrils flared. "I called you yesterday about your murdered employee."

"She had a name—Celina," Light protested crossly.

"Yeah, right. Celina," Detective Burrows muttered before eyeing me. "So, tell me, Ms. Credence, what exactly did they take?"

There was no sense in not telling the truth; it would only raise more suspicions. "Company documents," I clipped out.

He raised a brow. "Documents? What type of documents?"

His tone ignited my temper. "Look, Detective Burrows, our documents contain sensitive data about our financial holdings and investments. My family has investments in all the major industries." This was true. Our family had amassed a fortune from being savvy investors.

"Uh-huh. So, there's no truth to that reporter's allegations?" he demanded, disbelief clear in his expression and tone.

"Reporter?" I commented with more calmness than I felt.

"Jeff Hunter," he elaborated. "He alleges there's some dark secret society made up of rich, powerful men who your employees—escorts—" he leered at me suggestively "—provide sexual services to."

I'd had enough, and I wanted Burrows out of my face.

Pulling out my cell, I called the one woman who could make this horrid man go away. "Hi, Reason. There's a Detective Burrows harassing me. Would you like to explain to him in lawyer talk why that's not such a good idea?" I extended my cell to him.

He backed away from my cell like it was a snake. "Come on, guys. Let's clear out," he ordered, then turned to glare at me. "I know you're hiding something, Ms. Credence. And I won't stop digging until I find out what it is." He strolled out of the room with way too much confidence.

I held my breath until I heard the front door slam shut.

"Let me make sure they're out," Light said before rushing out of the office and then coming back. "It's clear."

I put my cell on speaker. "Okay, Reason, they're gone."

"What the hell happened?" Reason demanded.

"Someone broke in to the office and stole every single document we had on our clients and escorts," I divulged.

Light's hands were trembling as she gathered her hair, pulling it into a high ponytail. "This is bad. They were thorough. They stole our contracts, along with records documenting what client booked what escort, places, times, agreed-upon service fees. It's all gone."

I felt faint when I thought about all the information our safe had held, documentation going back centuries.

Paper documentation was not my preferred method of doing business. I was more of a technology girl, with documents encrypted on my laptop. But the contracts our family had with our clients were agreements dating back centuries, when paper had ruled and a physically signed document was the only thing honored. And that practice was a recipe for disaster in the wrong hands.

"I don't understand. I thought you had a safe," Reason remarked.

"We do," I pointed out. "With a burglar alarm, including a silent alarm function. The safe also has glass plate relockers and redundant time locks that keep the safe inoperable for a time. And it has a biometric fingerprint-reading entry keypad."

"The thief bypassed it all," Light confirmed tiredly.

"Holy shit!" Reason exclaimed. "This requires major damage control, Stormy."

"Major? Why?" I protested. "We don't even know what the thief plans to do with the documents." We didn't, but this was no common thief. He or she targeted the heart of our business, the real treasure trove, our documents that contained secret information on many of the rich and powerful Others. And shit would hit the fan when the Other Council found out someone had stolen such important information.

"Stormy, it doesn't take a genius to figure out what the thief intends to do." Light threw her arms up in the air in her exasperation. "The robber is going to blackmail us."

"Don't say that." I pointed at her. "Don't even think it." I knew what she surmised was probably the truth, but thinking about the consequences of that probability was freaking me out.

"Stormy, you can't stick your head in the sand and pretend

that shit won't happen," Reason insisted. "We have to prepare for an impending shitstorm."

"I know..." I agreed. "I'm scared, Reason. When news gets out, and there's no doubt in my mind that it will, it will ruin our business."

"Let's be optimistic," Reason countered. "We won't know what the thief intends on doing with the documents. But as your best friend and lawyer, my advice is to tell the Council about this break-in before they hear about it from someone else. By putting off this disclosure, you're damning yourself to further scrutiny."

"Understood," I responded. "Just give us time to discuss next steps, and we'll get back to you."

"Okay, but don't wait too long. The clock is ticking. In the meantime, let me know if you hear anything about this robbery. I'll keep my ears open in case I hear something. Talk to you later." Reason ended our call.

The doorbell rang, making both of us look at each other. No one should ring our bell without calling.

"I can't stomach the thought of that detective asking any more questions," I grumbled.

"Take it easy." Light gave me a quick side hug. "Let me see who it is."

When she left, I paced back and forth, recounting everything that had gone terribly wrong since our mothers left for the convention. Frankly, I wasn't so sure we were ready to take over the family's business. Everything I'd thought it took to run Credence O. had been wrong.

Mom and Aunt Lia handled all the work that I'd thought was so simple—dealing with the escorts, schmoozing with the clients, making compromises that kept our business successful. And none of those duties was easy. Now, I was terrified that

Light and I would go down in Credence history as the incompetent witches who destroyed our family business.

"So, this is where the infamous Credence O. empire lives," Knox drawled.

I stopped in my tracks. "What are you doing here?"

"Ryker told me what happened." He strode over, kissing me hard on the lips. "I'm concerned." He wrapped an arm around my waist.

"Thank you." I leaned into him, inhaling his clean scent. His being here meant a lot to me.

There was a loud commotion outside of the office, then Bones walked inside with a very annoyed Light arguing with him.

Light looked over at Knox. "What's with your friend here?"

"She's freaking out. What did you do, man?" A smile curved Knox's lips.

"Nothing. I was a perfect gentleman." Bones tried to look innocent but failed. "She tripped, and I saved her from falling flat on her face."

Light slapped Bones on the arm. "By grabbing a handful of my ass, which he continued to hold longer than necessary."

"You enjoyed it, sweetheart." He winked at her.

Light crossed her arms over her chest. "I'm not your type, pretty boy." She looked him up and down. "Isn't there some hot New York model you should stalk?"

"I'm tired of pretty women with nothing to say. I'm looking for a pretty woman to give me hell." Bones's lips twisted into a smirk.

"Well, keep on looking." Light shoved him then glared at me. "Okay, I'm out of here." She turned on her heel with a little too much sway in her hips.

I knew she liked Bones, much to her annoyance.

Bones hollered after her, "See you tonight, Light!"

Light didn't pause as she gave him a one-finger salute over her shoulder.

Bones smiled at me. "She's warming up to the possibilities." He clapped Knox on the back. "Meet you in the car." He sauntered out of the office, whistling loudly.

I shook my head with disbelief. "They're both insane."

"That's nothing but foreplay," Knox said before cupping my face. "Are you okay?"

"I'm so totally screwed, Knox," I blurted out. "The thief stole documents that contained client and escort personal information. This is a massive data breach, and if they do what I think they'll do—blackmail us—this will be the end of our business."

"I can help. I have well-connected friends who could do some digging and find out who was behind this. Just say the word."

I didn't need Knox, or any human, getting involved in Others business.

"Thank you, but no." I shook my head. "My lawyer is making some calls. But I'm not sure where this break-in will lead, and your name was included in the stolen documents. This might be a public relations nightmare for you."

"I don't give a shit what people think or say about me." He grazed the side of my cheek with the back of his hand. "But you, I'm worried about. That's a lot of heat to take if the truth about Credence O. leaks to the public."

"It is," I agreed. "But my family will fight to the bitter end to protect our legacy and business. Knox, I know tonight is important to you, but I'm really not in the mood to be social."

"Come tonight," he said in a low tone. "Because if you don't, the only thing you'll do is sit here mentally berating yourself for something that was out of your control." He kissed me softly before retreating. He bit my lower lip and said, "Besides,

I have something special planned for you tonight. It involves lots of decadent desserts."

A smile twitched across my lips. "That sounds absolutely naughty, Mr. Gunner."

"It is very naughty." He squeezed my ass. "I left something in the foyer for you. Wear it. Be ready by nine. I'm sending a car for you." He brushed my hair away from my forehead before stepping away. "I'll lock the door behind me."

He walked out of the office, leaving me wondering how the hell my life had gotten so freaking complicated.

CHAPTER 14

KNOX USHERED me through the crowded party with a hand pressed against the small of my back. "You look beautiful, baby."

I adjusted the black leather gloves that went up to my elbows. "Thank you." I had to admit, I felt beautiful, wearing a stunning statement necklace paired with a scarlet-hued wrapped-bodice gown.

Several guests looked curiously at the way Knox kept me pinned to his side. Women eyed me with outright jealousy, but I didn't care. This was my time with him.

"I didn't know you were so involved in charity," I mused. In fact, there was so much I didn't know about him.

"Charity is important to me, and this is a cause that means a lot to Ryker and me. All the proceeds from tonight will go to building homes for single mothers and their children. It will be the first time these children have a safe place to live without the threat of gang violence and crime."

When I heard the passion in his voice, I stopped short and

studied him. "It is a very worthy cause," I agreed while touching his cheek. "And my part in this lovely event?"

He ran his hand across my back. "To work the dessert table, of course."

"You want me to hand out desserts?"

"Nope. Just be beautiful, darling. And remember, it's all for charity."

Harper came strolling over, looping her arm through mine. "Time's up, sweetheart. We need you in the dining room. It's time for dessert."

He winked at me. "I'll be right in."

I sauntered away with Harper, then she hustled me into an enormous room with ten beautiful women milling around excitedly. Frankly, their unusual giddiness was making me nervous.

"What's going on, Harper?" I scrutinized several long tables draped with crisp white linens.

She pulled me over to a table. "Strip," she demanded.

I backed away. "Are you out of your damn mind?"

I contemplated the distance from the table to the entrance, wondering if Harper could catch me before I made it out, when I noticed the other women were undressing and handing their garments to the waiting attendants. Some women were already naked and lay across the tables like it was the most normal thing in the world to do.

I blinked in horror as servers delicately laid canapés on the women's bodies. I'd never seen anything like this in my life.

"We're going to be human buffet tables?" I remarked.

"Yes."

"I'm out of here." I made for the door.

"Come on, Stormy." Harper wrapped her arm around mine, halting me. "You're wasting time. We're behind schedule."

A tall, thin young man dressed impeccably in a well-fitted tuxedo bustled over to us.

"This is Michael," Harper informed me. "He's here to provide anything you need to make this more comfortable for you."

"Nice to meet you, Ms. Credence," Michael greeted.

"Hello," I answered, still in shock at the naked women draped across crisp linen-cloaked tables. I wasn't shy, but I wasn't an exhibitionist either. And me lying out there for everyone to see, like some human platter, was a concept beyond my depth.

"Harper, this is Knox's sick joke. A joke I'm going to kick his ass for. But this isn't me. I'm sorry, but I can't do this."

"Stormy, it's for a noble cause. And at fifty grand per guest, this will give a lot of deserving children a real home for the first time. Some of them have been in foster care for so long, they don't know what a normal life feels like. Believe me, I know how that feels." Her voice ended on a sad note.

Damn, she had to remind me about the children. That was the decider for me.

I unzipped my gown, stepped out of it, then stripped off my lingerie and gloves and handed over all my items to Michael's outstretched hands. Two men marched over to assist me onto the table.

"Thank you, Stormy. This means so much to me." Harper smiled widely before waving impishly. "Have fun, honey. I saved the best for last. You're going to be the dessert table."

Squirming on the table, I waited like a sacrificial lamb until Michael gently touched my shoulder.

He smiled politely. "Is this your first time?"

I laughed before responding. "Yes. And I'm so glad I shaved, or this would have been a really awkward situation."

"Just relax. I'm your assistant for the night."

"So, what will you be assisting me with, Michael?"

"I'll guide you. Make sure the server keeps the desserts well stocked on your body. Answer questions the guests might have when they stop by your table." He moved my hair, spreading it around my shoulders. "There. You have gorgeous hair. We want to make sure it looks as sexy as possible." He moved my legs without lingering. "Legs uncrossed and together. Arms at your side. No moving at all when the guests take desserts from your body."

I didn't get this at all. "Are they allowed to touch me?" I wouldn't like that one bit. I wasn't up to being groped all night long.

"No, that's not permitted. They will pick up the desserts and admire you, but no inappropriate touching. Most of these guests have been to this event before. And at fifty grand per person just for the invite inside this room, they understand the rules of engagement."

"I see," I responded.

"Now, how the fundraising part works is that the table with the most guest visits accrues additional money for charity. They pay for the privilege of eating from each table."

This was simply genius. Freaky but genius. It also added to the pressure. No visits meant no additional money raised for charity.

I pursed my lips. "So, I'm the dessert buffet table. I lie here, looking beautiful, enticing them to linger and come back. The more they linger, the more money I raise for this event." I wasn't going through this angst and turmoil for nothing.

He smiled. "Exactly. They are free to talk to you and you to them. The server will be here shortly to place the delectable items on your body. So, relax."

The cold air kissed my body as the server carefully and strategically laid an assortment of sweet delights on my body.

With the ultimate embarrassment, a cup of fondue-like sauce was placed precariously on my mound. It was dead quiet until I heard the door open and music pumping. I just lay there, relaxing and staring at the ceiling, concentrating on making sure not to move.

"Well, it's the beautiful Stormy," a woman purred.

I carefully turned my head and smiled. "Hello, Vivica. Fancy meeting you here."

Two gigantic men hovered protectively by her side, both handsome as hell—one with impeccably cut chestnut-brown hair and the other with black.

"Knox is such a lucky man," the chestnut-brown-haired man remarked with a smile.

"Oh, hush, Victor." She rubbed his arm seductively. "Stormy, these are my mates—Victor and Alexandro."

"Hello, Stormy," Alexandro said in a Texas drawl.

The tips of Vivica's fingers were light on my thigh when she picked up a chocolate truffle.

"Thank you for stopping by, Vivica."

Her gaze roamed up and down my body. "Oh, darling, it's my pleasure." She walked away with her mates in tow.

As the night wore on, guests visited my table frequently; I actually had fun talking with the partiers. I wasn't normally a social butterfly, but there was something strangely liberating about just lying there, being admired by both men and women who seemed to enjoy flirting with me outrageously.

But the man I wanted to see—Knox—was nowhere around. His no-show perturbed me. Then I saw him walking toward me with Ryker. I blinked because, for the first time, I saw them standing side by side, and they looked remarkably similar.

"Are you tired?" Knox demanded.

"A little. But I'm all right." I shivered as his fingers grazed across my breasts.

"You did a lot tonight. I'm proud of you. But anytime you want to call it a night, it's fine," Knox reassured.

Ryker winked at me. "Did Knox tell you your table raised the most money tonight?"

I arched a brow. "No, he didn't."

"I didn't want to give her an enormous head," Knox declared.

"Sure." I rolled my eyes.

He trailed his fingers along my abdomen before picking up a gold-covered chocolate truffle. He bit into it before popping the rest into my mouth. The slightly bitter flavor of the dark chocolate was what my taste buds craved. He leaned down, thrusting his tongue inside my mouth, kissing me hard.

"Delicious," he whispered against my mouth. "I'll be back in a few for you." He stepped back, giving Ryker a perturbed glare for the way his eyes lingered on me with appreciation.

They walked away, surrounded by several men from Ryker's pack. This strange friendship between Ryker and Knox was something I didn't quite understand.

I sighed, relaxing my body and closing my eyes, letting the cool, fragrant air soothe my nerves.

"It's time, Ms. Credence." Michael's voice was smooth.

My eyes popped open to see him standing with a black silk robe open and extended toward me. Two men eased me off the table, stepping back as I put on the robe.

"Ms. Credence." Michael gestured toward a door at the other end of the large room.

I smirked. "It's Stormy. I think after you've seen me naked, first-name basis is more than appropriate."

"As you wish, Stormy." He smiled. "Shall we?"

I followed him past the other women putting on robes, and we exited the banquet room.

"Harper has placed your dress and lingerie in a private

room. It's the last door at the end of the hallway. Here's the key." He handed it over. "Mr. Gunner has requested your presence downstairs when you're done."

"Thank you, Michael," I responded before walking down the hallway.

"So he's finally made you his whore," a voice taunted from the shadows.

I recognized the voice. Turning around, I staggered back with my eyes wide. He was the last man I'd expected or ever wanted to see again.

"Luke? What the hell are you doing here?" I nervously peered around, relieved to see a smattering of guests.

"Watching him treating you like his personal sex toy," Luke snapped.

I didn't know what to make of his presence. He looked the same as he had in college—blond, handsome, and crazy as hell.

Women in college had loved him. In fact, they'd hung on his every word. But I'd quickly realized something was very wrong with him. It had taken me months and an order of protection to shake him from my life after college. Now here he was, standing before me after all these years, looking cool and focused on me—again.

I popped my hands on my hips. "What I do with my life is none of your business, Luke. Were you invited, or are you stalking someone else?"

"You forget, my family runs in these circles, Stormy." He strolled around me, checking me out. "Still beautiful. No woman could ever compare to you. I've tried to forget you but failed miserably."

"Uh-huh." I edged away from him. "Look, I'm seeing Knox again."

His lips curled up into a cruel smile. "And exactly how long do you think it will last this time? Face it, you're nothing but his fuck toy."

"Oh, shut the hell up." His words ignited my temper. "What I do and who I do it with is none of your concern."

"No man will ever love you the way I love you." Surprising me with his quickness, he slid his hands around my neck in a weird gesture of ownership.

Oh, hell no.

Enraged, my palm connected with his face.

"Ouch!" he growled.

"Don't touch me, Luke," I protested. "I'm not the woman for you." I took several calming breaths, trying to soothe my anger.

His creepy smile widened. "Let me take you out to dinner and prove how wrong you are. We're meant to be together. I was born to love you."

He's certifiably insane.

"No! I'm not going out with you. Don't come near me again." I strode away from him.

"Stormy. Stay away from Knox Gunner!" he shouted after me. "You know what happens to human men around the Credence women."

I stopped dead in my tracks, turning around to face him. "What did you say?" I demanded.

"You're getting too close to Knox. Stay away from him. I won't be responsible for what happens to him if you don't."

I clenched and unclenched my hands. "You're sick and delusional. That's exactly what you are."

He shrugged. "Call me what you want, but history is a funny thing. It has a habit of repeating itself."

"Not with me, it won't."

"You belong to me, Stormy. And you'd better not forget it."

He was a very sick man.

It took me a few seconds to speak. "You and I will never happen."

He shook his head. "It's really sad you think you'll win this battle when the truth is written in stone. You're mine. The only one who doesn't know it yet is you." He blew a kiss before strolling away.

CHAPTER 15

I RAN my hands through my hair, hoping I didn't look as stressed as I felt.

I hadn't seen Light all night, which was strange.

Luke had materialized from the past like some demented psycho ghost.

And I was milling around, searching for Knox—my current fling—like a strung-out junkie hunting for her next fix.

Feeling a tap on my shoulder, I turned around to see Luke standing behind me with a champagne glass in his extended hand. "For you, love."

Yeah, like I'm going to drink anything he gives me.

"No, thanks." I tried to sidestep him.

He blocked my exit. "Don't be rude. I'm trying to be polite here."

"And I'm trying to do the same," I maintained. "Please don't spoil this charity event by causing me to make a scene."

"You don't have to. I'll do it for you," Knox snapped, flanked by three of Ryker's men.

Knox started removing his jacket, and the crowd parted curiously.

"Déjà vu." Luke smirked. "Haven't we done this before? Last time, it ended with you losing the girl." He glanced at me slyly. "I believe this will end in the same way."

I stepped between them. "I think not, Luke. This has to stop." I nodded toward the men. "Can you please escort him out before Knox does something I know he won't regret?"

"Stormy, step out of the way," Knox cautioned.

"No. Not this time." I wrapped my arms around his waist. "I don't want to see you all over the evening news. Let Ryker's men throw him out."

They shoved Luke.

"Don't touch me!" Luke exclaimed. "Do you know who I am?"

One man said, "We know who you are. You're an ass who's making a scene. Now, either move on your own or get tossed out. You decide."

Luke brushed off his jacket. "I'll see you soon, Stormy." He walked away, his head held high.

Knox nodded toward the men. "Ensure he gets out."

"On it," they said in unison, striding after Luke.

Knox turned to me with a hardened expression. "What was that all about?"

Utterly mystified, I stared at him. "I didn't invite him, Knox. So, stop with the cave-dweller tactics."

"It didn't look like you were trying to stop him from practically pawing at you either." Steel laced his tone.

"Okay, I'm not doing this." I threw my arms up in the air in my exasperation. "First, I'm not your girlfriend. Second, despite the obviously low opinion you have of me, I only sleep with one man at a time. Third, if you don't trust me, there's no point in taking whatever this thing we have going on any further."

"You don't leave me feeling warm and fuzzy when your fucking ex-boyfriend shows up to my damn party, touching my property."

I stared at him with my lips pursed in disbelief.

"Well, I'm not your *property*," I stated flatly. "And I'm tired of having to explain myself." I sighed heavily. "Damn, just when I thought we were making progress, you take us fucking five steps backward. Knox, it's hypocritical to ask me to trust you when you're unwilling to trust me. Please let me know when you're willing to do that and raise whatever this thing we have going on to an acceptable level of civility."

I shook my head with disappointment before walking away with a heavy heart.

CHAPTER 16

I AWOKE with a start when my bed tilted.

My eyes popped open, and I glared at Light, who was extending a large mug of coffee that smelled absolutely scrumptious. Scooting to sit up, I crossed my legs yoga-like, before snatching it greedily.

"Where did you go last night?" I demanded over a mouthful of coffee.

I'd spent a sleepless night working late just to take my mind off my argument with Knox. The time spent working hadn't been productive. In fact, it had been depressing. I'd gone through the documents on my laptop, trying to figure out what records the thief had stolen, and I concluded the person had gotten everything.

"I had no support as I portrayed a human buffet table. And no support when Luke the Stalker made an appearance."

"Luke?" she exclaimed.

"Yup."

"Holy shit." Light shook her head. "Sorry, Stormy, I got a call from Reason. She had a lead, or so we'd thought, on the thief. And she swung by to pick me up so we could chase it, but it turned out to be a dead end." She kissed my cheek. "You know I'd never leave you hanging like that."

"I know you wouldn't," I muttered over another sip of coffee. "Don't mind me, I'm in bitch mode because I had an argument with Knox. After that shitshow, and his driver took me home, I ended up going through our records to see exactly what they had stolen, which was pretty much everything of importance. Not to mention, we have a ton of voice messages from irate clients, complaining about that reporter asking them uncomfortable and embarrassing questions about Celina." I took another sip of coffee.

Light waved the folded newspaper in her hand. "Well, I don't think you're going to like this, then." She handed over the newspaper. "Turn to page five."

Doing as instructed, I widened my eyes as I read it aloud.

"The rich and famous got rocked by a Credence O. Corporation scandal. After the recent unsolved murder of Celina Rouse, an employee of Credence O., a confidential informant has reported that the headquarters of Credence O.—alleged image consultant to the rich—were robbed. Stolen items include a black book containing the client names—powerful figures in politics and entertainment, including ultra-wealthy families. A verified source has come forward, providing a copy of their client list. Among the names on the list: none other than mega rock star Knox Gunner. Is this robbery linked to Celina's murder? And is there any truth to the rumors that Credence O. is running something more than an image consultant company? None of the calls made to Credence O. and their alleged clients have been returned."

I literally wanted to throw up.

"Holy hell!" I yelled. "No wonder none of the escorts

returned my calls." My cell buzzed, and I recognized the number.

"Hello, Ryker," I greeted tiredly.

"I gather you read the newspaper this morning." His tone was harsh. "So, I'll get straight to the point. We have issues to discuss. The Other Council is not pleased with the recent developments. I expect you and Light at my penthouse in an hour." He ended the call.

I scooted off the bed. "Ryker summons us to provide answers we don't fucking have."

"This is not happening," Light complained testily.

"I'm afraid it is. I'm going to take a shower," I declared before walking into the bathroom.

And for the first time in years, I broke down in a fit of hysterical tears.

CHAPTER 17

THE ELEVATOR OPENED DIRECTLY into a grand foyer leading to a magnificent living room and dining room with floor-to-ceiling windows that hosted panoramic views of Central Park and the city.

"Follow me," Bones ordered. His face was the most solemn I'd seen since meeting him.

Light and I walked into the luxurious penthouse side by side, not uttering a word. We followed him past an impressive collection of artwork, into a large living room with a small gathering of men standing around. Instantly, all eyes focused on us.

Ryker turned around to examine Light. His eyes lingered on her curiously and then landed on me.

"Men, leave us," Ryker commanded without taking his eyes off us. "I need to have a private conversation with the Credence women."

The men left the space without a word.

"Ryker," I rushed out. "I know what you're going to say."

"No, you don't, Stormy." He tilted his head as he considered me. "You have no clue about the shitstorm that's brewing as we speak."

"We do, alpha!" Light bellowed.

He pinned Light under a hard stare. "I would advise less tone and more humbleness for your current predicament."

Light rebutted. "We're not your pack minions, Ryker. So, my advice is that you tone down that bass in your voice." She plopped down into a chair, crossing her arms defensively.

His mouth twitched into a smile. "No fear, I see. That's what happens when you're sober. And judging from the last time I saw you, that's not too often."

Light glared at me with outraged eyes. "Stormy, I don't care if he's an alpha. I'm not dealing with this jackass. Handle him."

I held out a placating hand before saying, "Ryker, what would you have us do? Someone stole our documents, and we did everything in our power to prevent such a situation."

"I don't doubt that." He regarded me coolly. "But I'm disappointed you didn't come to me first with the fact that someone had stolen Others' information."

I sat beside Light, crossing my legs. "Come on, Ryker. This is bullshit."

"No, what's bullshit is I have my pack business to deal with, and now I have to deal with the influx of fucking complaints from Other families demanding immediate Council action."

"And what action is that?" Light requested.

"Closure of Credence O.," he stated firmly.

"What?" I shouted. "They have no right, Ryker. They've been chomping at the bit to close us down for years."

"And your carelessness has given them the ammunition to do it," he retorted. "This is all your doing. They have stolen information. The exposure of what we are could be next. Don't you think the Others have a valid concern?"

He was right, but I would not say that aloud.

"But lucky for you, I'm a fair man. I've convinced the Council to investigate before rushing to judgment."

"Investigation?" I yelled.

"Yes," he affirmed. "With the full understanding that after such an investigation, if Credence O. is found guilty of negligence, it will mean closure of Credence O., including a hefty fine and expulsion from Other society."

"Why don't you just order us to be executed while you're at it?" Light argued.

He glowered at her. "As the bearer of the Sword of Souls, that possibility is not off the table."

Shit! This situation is getting ugly.

"Just so we're clear. Our family will fight any move to close us down or expel us," I explained. "So, you better have this investigation conducted by a neutral party. We have many enemies among the Others, and I'd hate to have this process contaminated, and us railroaded, by centuries of unfounded hate."

His eyes went frosty. "If you're implying I'm among your enemies—" he assessed Light and then me "—then that couldn't be further from the truth. But I have a responsibility as leader of the Other Council to ensure we keep order. This investigation must happen. I also have a duty to my pack, and we're going through troubling and dangerous times with an impending Others war. I cannot risk further damage by exposure of our kind. Fix this," he ordered before turning his back on us, staring through the window without another word.

Being thoroughly dismissed, Light and I got up and marched away, but his voice stopped us at the elevator. "And, fae witches, I'd advise you go visit that reporter. Convince him, using any method you deem fit, to cease his dangerous investigation. His meddling is adding tension to a contentious situation."

CHAPTER 18

AFTER I MADE a call to Reason, she'd reached out to her contacts and got the reporter's address. Wasting no time, Light and I drove over to Hunter's place.

Pulling up to his brownstone, I parked, then we hopped out of my car.

"Okay, so what's the plan?" Light asked as we walked up the stairs.

"We find out what he wants and take it from there. I have a feeling there's not much we can do to stop him from digging further. But if we warn him of the folly of printing anything else without substantial evidence, we might have some leverage."

When we arrived at the door, I held Light back when I noticed it was open. My senses were ringing off the hook. Something wasn't right.

I nudged it open with the tip of my shoe. "Come on," I whispered, urging her to follow me inside.

The brownstone was eerily quiet. That was when we noticed the total disarray of the apartment. Papers scattered across the floor, furniture ripped and broken, and glass shattered. And last but not least, Jeff Hunter was lying facedown in a pool of blood in the middle of the living room.

I rubbed my eyes. "Damn. Someone got to him first." I leaned over his body when I saw the paper clutched in his fist. Carefully pulling it out, I examined it. "It's a copy of our contract."

"We have to leave," Light demanded, huffing and puffing like she was on the verge of hyperventilating. "Jesus. My heart is beating so fast. I might have a heart attack."

Taking her face in my hands, I stroked her hair, bringing her back from the brink of crazy. "It's going to be okay. Take a deep breath. Calm down."

Light swallowed hard, nodding. "Okay."

"Good," I soothed before stepping away. "Get all the documents you see, and then we'll leave."

We revved into action, picking up the strewn documents with jerky, disconnected motions. I kept my eyes on Light, worried that her ability to maintain sanity was getting weaker. And there was nothing I could do to stop it.

I ran around, picking up all the papers in my path. "Hurry, get everything," I ordered.

We fanned out, snatching everything we saw.

After collecting the documents, I strode over to his landline. I didn't want to get involved in the investigation of his death, but the decent thing to do was call the police. Flipping over the phone receiver with the pen I dug out of my bag, I punched 9-1-1 with the tip. When someone answered, I disguised my voice and whispered, "Hurry! I heard gunshots at..." After giving out the reporter's address, we hurried out of his home like the hounds of hell were at our heels.

CHAPTER 19

WHEN WE ARRIVED HOME, we leafed through the stack of documents we'd found at Jeff Hunter's place, but they led to nothing but more questions.

"These are all copies," I declared while feeding the documents into the shredder. "We are so fucked right now. The thief still has the originals."

Light's fingers fumbled around a glass of water, splashing it everywhere. "As far as we know, they could have created handouts for the news media," she babbled.

"Agreed." Running my trembling fingers through my hair, I racked my brain for a rational explanation, which was an exercise in futility. "This just feels all wrong, like somehow, we're not connecting the dots."

Light gulped her water thirstily. I knew she wished it were numbness-inducing alcohol, but she was trying to keep a clear head, an effort I respected.

"We should start by making a list of our enemies." Light pursed her lips. "With Lacie at the top."

I bit my bottom lip. "I'm pretty sure it's not her. We have

more dirt on her and her family than they do on us, and they know it. Besides, exposing us to humans would be bad for all our businesses, something neither of us wants. No, this plot seems too calculated."

"But that's what the Others do—hide in the shadows and plot. A prime example is the war brewing between the shifters. There's been a peace treaty between them for years, and then out of nowhere, it's raining shifter bodies."

"Since when have you been interested in Other business?"

Light shrugged. "Since bodies started piling up at such alarming rates that humans have noticed. It's just dumb."

Pushing away from the desk, I walked over to the window and stared. "Dumb?"

She snorted. "Yes, dumb. It's like they've forgotten what happened centuries ago when Others were hunted and killed by Hunters—the few humans who knew of our existence. And you know what happened to the Hunters. Others banded together, exterminating most of those whacked-in-the-head humans."

I turned to smile at her. "Look at you. My very own Other historian. Nice!"

She rolled her eyes. "All I know is if bodies continue to drop, humans are going to figure out that Others exist. And *poof*, there goes the veil of Other secrecy. Exposure central."

"Exactly." A thought formed as I paced back and forth. "It makes little sense. Others don't like attention. Could you imagine the chaos if humans found out we existed?" Humans believed Others were folklore and fairy tales.

"Total anarchy. Never mind the fact that history would repeat itself with humans hunting Others and Others hunting humans. It could mean the extinction of all races."

History. Something about the word kept echoing in my head.

"Last night, Luke said something that bothered me." I sat on the edge of my desk. "He was rambling on about history repeating itself."

Light shrugged. "Maybe he was talking about you and him."

"Highly unlikely. No, he had this real snarky look on his face, like he was dying to let me in on some secret."

Light scoffed. "Luke was born with that snarky, elitist look on his face."

"No, I'm pretty sure it's something else."

His showing up out of the blue was bothering me. His crazy history remark compounded that. Maybe "history" was the key to unraveling all this shit. If that were true, then I knew where to start, a place I avoided like the plague—the Credence library.

"Let's go," I urged.

With trepidation, I walked out of the office with Light by my side. We headed toward the library, directly off the gallery at the front of the house. I examined the dreaded heavy mahogany door, the portal to the scary Credence archive.

Taking a calming breath, I punched in the door code, then I pressed my thumb over the custom-made lock. The lock whirred, delivering a quick prick to the fleshy skin of my thumb, sampling my blood for entry. We took a step back when the lock clicked.

"What are you looking for?" Light demanded.

"Answers." Pushing open the door, I shivered as the cold air in the temperature-controlled room brushed against my skin.

The dark, expansive room was quiet, except for the whisper of air circulating. Floor-to-ceiling bookshelves lined every surface of the walls.

"It must be really serious if you decided to woman up and

come back after the alleged—" Light made air quotes "—'incident.'"

I shot her an annoyed stare. "There's no *alleged* about it. Elizabeth was standing in here eyeballing me."

Just the thought of that day still made me want to piss on myself.

I was only thirteen when, as clear as day, I'd seen the back of a strange woman wearing a long frilly skirt and a puffy lacy blouse walking into the library. Naïve and, yes, just plain stupid, I'd followed her, only to find her standing over the *Book of Mirrors.*

I'd instantly recognized her from the painting in the foyer, and then she turned and stared at me. A ghost, Great-great-great-great-grandma Elizabeth Credence.

Pointing to the book, Elizabeth said, *"Solista. The truth shall set me free."*

That day, I'd nearly fainted from fright because Elizabeth had died eons before I was born. But I'd run out of the library, screaming bloody murder. No one in my family believed me, then or now.

But I knew who I'd seen—Elizabeth.

And there was something in that book she'd wanted me to see. Only now was I brave enough to find out what.

Even now, standing before the ornate pedestal was intimidating. But touching the large, antique, brown leather journal lying on top of it sent a shiver down my spine. This was a treasure passed down throughout the centuries—the Credence *Book of Mirrors.*

I ran my fingers over the gold filigree decorating each corner of the book. Then I traced my finger over the gold Celtic dragon carved from genuine gold, framed in the center. The book was beautiful, and it filled me with awe. Centuries of Credence women had scribed their important spells, thoughts, feelings, and experiences into this book—each woman adding on, preserving the rich history of our bloodline.

Tears welled in my eyes as I opened it carefully. The first name signed at the top of the page was Elizabeth.

"I know what I heard, Light," I recalled. "She wanted me to read something Solista wrote in this book."

"Stormy, you're wasting your time." Light yawned. "They declared Solista insane."

I didn't care. All I knew was Great-grandma Solista was a shrewd businesswoman. She'd set the Credence women on the path of wealth and success. But she'd become so consumed with some insane theory about the Credence Curse being a lie.

"She wasn't crazy, Light. She was eccentric. How the hell can a woman as smart as her be a lunatic?"

"Do you know how many geniuses are stark raving nuts?" Light countered.

Ignoring her comment, I flipped through the book, stopping at the start of Solista's entries. I began reading where she'd written about her carefree youth and her love for her family. Her love for her childhood friend named Tiber Alfero, the only son of the alpha from the strongest wolf-shifter pack in North America. Then there was a gap in dates, but the entries resumed months later with her listing every Credence born and their subsequent mates, with X marks next to each name the Credence Curse had touched, besides noting the date they'd died.

I read her next entry aloud.

"Mother is the most foolish Credence alive. After only months of warlock Morpheus Brasson courting her, she's suddenly agreed to marry that most vile man. The family's pleas to call off the wedding have fallen on deaf ears."

Her next entry noted,

"I hate that man. Morpheus is evil and conniving. He's tried

everything in the book to break the Credence family. No topic makes me angrier than the fact that he married Mother to elevate his standing within the coven, and then he killed her with a death spell when he got what he wanted—Credence money and power."

I skimmed through, stopping at a curious page and read it out loud.

"I have my suspicions about the Brasson family. Morpheus's nephew, Tomas, has taken a liking to me, but I have refused his disgusting attempts to court me. Even though Tiber has broken my heart, I'm happy for once in my life. Edison, the village doctor, has shown quite an interest in me. He's human and far removed from the prejudices and inner workings of the Others."

Then something clicked in my head. "Brasson, that's Luke's last name," I revealed.

Light snorted. "Are you serious? Luke is *not* a warlock. An idiot, yes, but most definitely not a warlock."

"How can you be sure?" I countered. "For centuries, Others have been blending into human society for survival. They're like chameleons. Even with our magical abilities, an Other could hide their true nature from us if they wanted to."

Light rolled her eyes. "I'll give you two reasons he's not a warlock. One, everyone in the New York Others community knows our name, so he would have outed himself day one of meeting you in college. And two, warlocks are notoriously powerful. And as desperate as he was to keep you back then, he would've thought nothing of trying to use magic to bind you to him forever."

With an aggrieved sigh, I agreed, "Okay, that's true. I guess there goes that theory." I went back to the book, reading the next passage.

"So it begins again. Tomas is dead, and I'm accused by the

Council of having a hand in his demise. They have brought me before the Council for judgment, but I know the truth..."

I flipped to the next entry.

"Only the truth shall set me free. That statement struck fear in Tomas's heart, just like I'd expected. It was more of a warning to him and his secret cohorts—drop the false charges against me or face the wrath of a vengeful Credence. I will not stop until I expose his plan to bring down the Others."

Farther down the page, it read,

"Morpheus and Tomas have mysteriously disappeared, leaving the Council gnashing their teeth in frustration. No Morpheus and Tomas means no trial against me. Mercy wept openly with relief, foolishly believing this is the end of their witch-hunt, but the Brassons are not done with the Others or the Credence family. That much is written in stone. The pieces of the game of the Shadows have been reset. I am one step closer to discovering the root of the Curse and eradicating it forever. This is the truth that will set the Credence family free."

The date of the next entry skipped a couple months, and I read aloud.

"I am inconsolable. They have finally destroyed my world. My Mercy is dead, and the Other Council refuses to find the culprit. Sadly, my pleas to Tiber have fallen on deaf ears. No one will listen. No one cares. They have labeled me a raving lunatic. But I will make them all listen. Soon, they will understand how it feels to lose everything."

The next page listed all the names of the Brasson family, like some sort of family tree. At the bottom of the list was one line.

"The truth will set the Credence family free. Vengeance will be mine."

"I told you she was insane," Light maintained.

I pointed to the writing at the bottom edge of the page with a strange symbol drawn over it. "It's Latin, but it doesn't make a bit of sense."

"Like I said, she was nutty as a fruitcake."

"Wait." Flipping the *Book of Mirrors* upside down, I translated the words. "Beware, the Shadows are watching."

"Okay, I'm done with this Scooby-Doo mystery. Let me know when you find something remotely credible." Light sauntered out, mumbling to herself about needing two shots of tequila.

I knew everything that I read made no sense on the surface, but I refused to give up on finding a solution.

"Come on, Solista," I mumbled. "Give me something here. Prove you're not some crazy woman." I paged through the book, perplexed at not finding any other entries from Solista. My mind instantly went into puzzle-solving mode as I tried to piece together everything she'd written.

What does she mean by "the Shadows"?

I read the line again, then focused on the word "Shadows."

The S was capitalized, which could mean that Shadows was a proper noun or a name used for a specific person, place, company, or other thing. My heart raced with excitement because I felt in my gut that I was onto something.

Are the Shadows people?

And if they are, who are they watching? And why?

My cell buzzed, interrupting my brainstorming session.

"Yes?" I answered.

"Come to my concert tonight," Knox demanded.

"No." My tone was cool, but my body immediately reacted to his voice. I craved him, but I refused to cave to him so easily.

Knox had to work if he wanted me.

Plus, I wanted—no, needed—his apology for his hurtful behavior last night.

He cleared his throat loudly. "That thing I said last night was rude and uncalled-for. Can we just get past it?"

"You're a prick. You know that, right?" I was learning to pick my battles with him, and this was the most I was going to get from him as an apology.

"They have called me worse." His voice held amusement.

"I bet they have," I countered. "And since I've recognized you're mentally incapable of apologies, give me one reason to overlook your fucked-up behavior."

"I miss you. I want you. And I need you by my side."

"Okay, that's three." I placed the book back before walking out of the library, slamming the door shut. "What time should I be there?"

"Eight o'clock. I have a backstage interview with some reporter named Gigi Bordeaux, but I want to see you before I go onstage. I miss your sexy ass."

Just like that, my core clenched from the allure of his voice.

"I wouldn't mind seeing you either, Mr. Gunner."

I stepped into the elevator, taking a quick ride to my apartment. "They mentioned your name in that trash article this morning. I'm sorry."

"No one believes it, Stormy. The likelihood of me needing an escort service is slim to none. The media laughed that shit off. Besides, Jeff Hunter is known in media circles as weird and disreputable at best."

"Well, the irony of this mess is, this time, everything he reported is actually true."

Walking into my spacious closet, I riffled through all my clothes, but I found nothing remotely appropriate to wear to a rock concert.

Plopping down on the cushioned chair, I stared at my rows of shoes.

"I'm worried, Knox. When we went over to Hunter's place

to talk with him today, we found him dead, with copies of our contracts all over the place."

"Why did you risk going over there?" he exploded. "They could have hurt you."

"We needed to talk to him. Maybe persuade him to stop his one-man campaign against my family. But I guess he's made another enemy because now he's dead."

"Did anyone see you going inside or leaving?"

"I hope not, but I alerted the police to check out his place." It was a relief to confide in someone besides Light.

"I'm worried about you," Knox confessed. "Let me provide some security for you and Light until this whole thing blows over."

My back stiffened. "I don't want some strange men following Light and me around. Really, I appreciate the gesture, but this whole thing will die down soon. I'm sure of it." I didn't know if it was dreaming or my slow slide into a delusional state, but I knew the words were hollow.

"Stormy, it's not a good sign when you lie to yourself."

"Yes, I know." This crap wasn't going away; it was just the beginning of the chaos and madness. He knew it, and so did I.

"After the concert, you're coming to my place."

"Yes," I agreed because I needed to be with him tonight, and I needed a momentary reprieve from the churning turbulence of my life.

"Finally, submission," he quipped.

I shrugged. "It was inevitable. But my submission extends only to the bedroom. I don't have time to play coy games. That's not who I am."

"And that's why you're the woman for me. I've got to go. Harper will wait to escort you backstage. See you later."

Our call ended, and as I sat there contemplating a shopping spree, a gust of frigid air rushed into the closet.

The temperature dropped so low that the cold air caused my breath to appear like a small, misty cloud.

What. The. Fuck?

"The Shadows are watching..." a woman's voice that I didn't recognize whispered in my ear.

I jumped to my feet with my heart thumping wildly.

I swung my gaze around, expecting to see a woman standing inside my closet, but no one was there.

"Who's there?" I croaked.

No one answered, but I hadn't imagined the voice.

Someone didn't want me to forget that the Shadows were watching, but the *why* eluded me.

CHAPTER 20

LIGHT GRINNED AT ME, checking out my outfit—a biker jacket with a T-shirt, pair of super-tight leather pants that I finished with lace-up black ankle boots.

"Now this is the girl I used to know. You look smoking hot." She hip checked me. "That Knox must be royally putting it down in bed for you to shed your boring clothes for something finally fitting the real you."

I shrugged, not letting the curious stares of the backstage crowd distract me. "I'm all for any opportunity to shop," I remarked with a deliberately neutral tone. "Nothing more."

"Holy shit." Light stopped with her hands on her hips. "Wait a minute." She narrowed her eyes as if she were finally noticing something. Her mouth dropped open, then closed, and then opened again. "You're falling in love with him again?"

I gave her a silly grin.

"Really?" Light whispered, touching her throat.

"Yes." And this time, there would be no running away and no denial, because Knox wouldn't allow it. And neither would I.

I closed my eyes, calming my racing anxiety, and then snapped them back open, looking like a deer in headlights.

Damn, this is too new, and I'm scared shitless.

She pulled me into a tight hug, and I wrapped my arms around her, needing her emotional support.

"You do what's necessary to snare your man," she whispered in my ear before breaking away. "And I'll stand by your side, regardless of what our mothers have to say about it."

"Did I tell you I love you?" I replied.

"What's not to love?" She winked at me before looping her arm through mine as we continued to walk through the backstage chaos.

Both of us skidded to a stop at the sight of petite Harper squaring off with another blast from the past—Portia.

Harper pointed in Portia's face. "Your artist is the opening act, not the headliner. There will be no 'perks,' other than what's stated in the band's rider. Last, Knox is not interested in seeing you, something you should've gotten a clue about by now, given your countless unanswered attempts to contact him."

"You little bitch." Portia's face twisted. "Without me, there wouldn't be a Knox Gunner."

Nothing had changed about Portia. She was still revolting and obnoxious.

"Uh-huh." Harper looked her up and down. "Look, ice queen, you've milked that cow for all it's worth. That's why Knox granted your artist this opportunity. Well, that, and they have a number one that's hot right now. All good for making Knox and *me*—" she smiled spitefully "—more money. Now get yourself back to your band's dressing room, and I won't have to tell security to throw your skanky ass out."

"You little..." Portia sputtered.

Harper rolled her eyes. "Yeah, yeah, whatever." She turned

her head, spotting us. "Hey, my girls are here. Sorry I couldn't greet you, but…" She looked over at Portia with disgust. "I had some trash to deal with."

I placed my hands on my hips. "I understand. Believe me."

Portia looked me up and down with a cruel smile. "What are you doing here?"

"Unlike you, we invited her," Harper explained.

Light snickered. "Damn, I love you, Harper."

"You're back together?" Disapproval turned down the corners of Portia's mouth.

"Uh-huh." I pasted a smile on my face and delivered my next words in a saccharine-sweet tone. "He can't seem to get enough of the Storm. I just can't get enough of him either. That little stunt you pulled years ago can't stop the inevitable—us."

"It won't last." Portia tightened her fists. "I'll make sure of that."

For the first time, I really looked at her, and she had crazy written all over her. "Oh my goodness, how desperate are you? You'll never have him, a fact proven by you standing here, foaming at the mouth. I'm looking at you and loving it," I stated calmly.

"So, Portia, what's it going to be?" Harper nodded toward security. "Play nice and go to your corner of shame? Or get thrown out on your bony ass? Either option is all good with me."

The guards edged closer, waiting to carry out Harper's orders.

Portia gave both Harper and me a malevolent stare. "This is not over," she spat before walking away.

Harper shuddered. "That woman is simply vile."

I looked at her curiously. "What is she doing here?"

"Wyatt. He practically begged Knox to give the band she manages the opening act slot tonight. She's desperate and probably doled out a blow job to Wyatt for the favor. And the band is young, talented, and clueless to the toxic waste they've hitched their wagon to," Harper said before looking down at her watch. "Shit. The interview with the piranha reporter is over. Light, security will escort you to the VIP section. Stormy, Knox wants to see you before he goes on."

"Yes." Light did a fist pump. "VIP city." She practically bounced away, talking animatedly to the guards.

Harper dragged me along as she barked out orders and asked questions of the employees about moving things in the sea of insanity. She knocked on the door and pushed it open, revealing Knox strumming his guitar and looking like sex on a platter.

His gaze came straight to me. "Come here." He moved the guitar aside and stood in one lithe move.

I strode over, stopping before him. Without a word, he cupped my jaw in his hands, pulling me to him before slamming his mouth onto mine. I gasped, making low mewing sounds at the back of my throat, burying my hands in the soft strands of his jet-black hair.

"Damn, you two are so fucking hot together," Harper mumbled under her breath before the door clicked closed.

He plundered my mouth, his tongue darting in and out, taking what was undeniably his. Our tongues dueled as he grabbed the back of my neck, controlling me and then easing me off the kiss, a warning that he was in control of the kiss and of me. I pressed into him, loving not having to think, just feel.

He tore his mouth from mine and stared into my eyes. "Now, are we clear you belong to me, Stormy?" He nipped my bottom lip. "Do you understand now what I need from you?"

I closed my eyes, fighting the tears of emotion before nodding.

"Open those beautiful eyes, baby. I need to see them

concede to me," he whispered. "This is not a fling. You and I, we will make it work. You will not run when it gets hard or when I demand more than you've ever given any man. Or when I make you angry or when you get scared." He kissed my lips hard. "You will trust me to do the right thing by you, as I will trust you to do the same."

"There are things you don't know about me, Knox." I chewed the inside of my cheek. "Things you won't understand."

"Then explain it to me." He stroked my cheek. "Make me understand."

My bottom lip trembled. "I'm so different from you."

"And that's what makes us work."

I shook my head. "It's not just that..." I swallowed hard. "There are things I can't reveal about me and my family."

"Why not?" He prodded gently.

"I just can't."

He cupped my cheek. "Because you don't trust me to accept you." It was a statement, not a question.

His words hit home because, for the first time, I realized it wasn't just the Curse that scared me but that he'd reject me because I was Other.

"Yes," I admitted. "And the last thing I ever want is for you to regret being with me."

"That will never happen." He kissed me quickly before pulling back.

My sigh was deep and heavy. It wasn't fair to let him walk into our relationship blindfolded.

"Stormy, there are things you should also know about me if we're going to make this work. But let's take it slow, and when the time is right and you trust me, then we both will reveal our secrets."

I didn't want to walk away from him.

I didn't want to spend the rest of my life with lingering romantic regrets about not taking the leap and grabbing the chance of something more with him.

Is it better to have loved and lost than never to have loved at all?

Before our reunion, my answer would have been no. But now, my answer was an absolute yes.

"Fuck it. Okay. Yes. To everything. I can't keep going on living half a life." I grabbed his T-shirt desperately. "But you'd better understand everything I've done in the past was because of my feelings for you. Because I feared the repercussions of what and who I am."

He tilted his head to the side. "I'm not afraid of who or what you are, Stormy. I'll take you as you are. Trust me on that."

I took a deep breath and let go of the baggage, and I trusted in him and in me.

Light was busy dancing and singing embarrassingly out of tune to the loud music of the opening band. She leaned in, singing in my face, pointing the invisible microphone at my mouth as she bobbed her head to the beat.

"I'm happy you're enjoying yourself!" I shouted.

Light whistled and clapped when their set ended. "Did you see those guys? Smoking hot. Pretty please, can I have one of those?" She sipped her drink, eyeing me with a wide grin. "I love seeing you so happy, babe."

"I was happy before, Light, but having Knox back in my life is the icing on the cake."

The overhead lights dimmed, and the crowd roared.

The music ripped, and the stage lights flickered.

Suddenly, the spotlight was on Knox in the middle of the stage. Women screamed as they jumped up and down.

A deafening cacophony of, "Knox! Over here. I love you!" erupted.

Light winked at me. "Your man is hot."

My lips curled up into a smile. I was really proud of him.

"Thank you, New York," Knox said with a gravelly growl. "It's been a long time,"

The crowd roared again.

"This next song is really special to me. It's a song I wrote for the one woman who believed in me when I first started out years ago. And I promised myself I'd never sing that song again until I had her back in my life. So, Stormy, baby, welcome back into my arms—forever."

My mouth dropped open as the melody rolled.

Then he sang in his toe-curling way.

"There was no me before you.

You brought me something I didn't think I ever wanted.

The roar of the Storm.

The thunder.

The lightning.

And when the clouds rolled in, all I could think about was the break in the Storm.

My Storm.

Breaking the Storm..."

Light wrapped her arm around my waist as we swayed back and forth.

It was then that it hit me.

No matter how much I'd tried to stop my emotions, I couldn't stop the love I now felt for Knox.

I needed him in my life.

And if he accepted what I was, there was no one or nothing that could keep me out of his life for as long as he wanted me.

Just like the song said, there was the break in the Storm, and I wouldn't have it any other way.

CHAPTER 21

I HADN'T REALIZED there was so much mayhem and coordination involved in shuffling a celebrity out of a location until I saw five bodyguards strategizing our way through a maze of tunnels under the concert arena.

Knox was eerily silent as the bodyguards talked logistics via earpieces. I could tell he was tired from performing, but I couldn't help but wonder if something else was keeping him mentally removed—like maybe he was having second thoughts about us.

Nope, I'm not going down this road.

No doubts and no sabotaging myself.

Three bodyguards abruptly went one way, and the other two led us down another tunnel, ending in an empty garage with one parked motorcycle.

The bodyguards smiled at Knox.

The biggest one said, "Knox, it's clear. Be safe." He winked at me before both of them stepped aside.

Knox pulled off two helmets locked to the bike and handed one to me.

I pursed my lips. "I'm assuming you're fantastic at riding this thing?"

"Of course. I'm good at a lot of things, but you know that all too well." He slapped my butt before putting on his helmet. He threw his leg over the motorcycle and gripped the handlebars. The engine roared to life as I put on my helmet.

"Come on, baby. Let's go home," he said.

My stomach clenched at the word *home* and the thought of us eventually having a life together.

A home was very enticing.

He extended his hand, and I threw my left leg over, sitting with him between my thighs.

He pushed back, and I quickly put my feet onto the footrests. Wrapping my hands around his waist, I leaned into him, pressing my breasts against his back as he smoothly pulled away. He barreled out of the garage and into the cool night air.

Minutes later, my eyes narrowed when we pulled up to the block Ryker lived on—well, not lived on, *owned*.

Ryker owned all the brownstones on this block and the building that held his penthouse, among other apartments where his enforcers lived. This was pack territory, and this pack was the most dangerous and ruthless in New York City.

I was trying to figure out what the hell was going on when the underground parking garage opened, allowing Knox to drive in. Then it closed behind us, cutting off our escape.

I was seconds away from going into interrogation mode when three terrifying looking men I knew for a fact were wolf-shifters walked toward Knox's motorcycle. I'd seen those shifters several times with Noah, and I knew they were Ryker's friends—Rip, Jackal, and Soar. They didn't look too happy to see us.

Soar looked at Knox coolly. "Ryker's not here," he said, while Rip and Jackal gave me the stare-down.

My fingers clenched anxiously against Knox's shoulder.

He pulled off his helmet, arching a questioning brow at me over his shoulder.

My fingers fumbled as I pulled off my helmet.

"What's wrong?" Knox asked me.

What the hell is wrong with him? I just stared at him, dumbfounded.

These guys were huge, mountain-sized men. And from what I knew, they were US Special Forces veterans.

Soar's grim face broke out into a wide smile as he clapped Knox on the back. "It's the rocker man, adored by thousands of oversexed screaming women and *men*."

Knox shoved away his hand. "Yeah, okay. Fuck off, Soar," he said with a smile. Then he looked over at me. "Come on, baby. Get off. I'm hungry."

Rip winked at me. "I bet you are, but not for food."

Their camaraderie with Knox was puzzling. Wolf-shifters despised humans and only embraced their own.

Could Knox be a wolf-shifter?

I quickly scoffed at the idea because if he was, wouldn't he have told me by now?

But my mind wouldn't let go of my nagging feeling that there was more to Ryker and Knox's relationship that I was missing.

I just sat there, looking at them suspiciously, when Knox reached back, caressing my thigh. "Don't let these Neanderthals scare you. This happens when friends come to visit for a week and decide to linger indefinitely. They become unruly guests who have overstayed their welcome."

Jackal nodded toward me and then looked at Knox. "May I?" he asked.

Knox and Jackal maintained eye contact, with some kind of

unspoken message passing between them before Knox nodded his head with consent.

What the fuck?

I sat there, stunned, swinging my head to look at all of them, only to receive blank stares. Something was going on here, and I was determined to figure it out.

I gave Soar my helmet and Jackal my hand. Jackal pulled me off the bike before quickly releasing my hand and stepping back with deference.

Contemplating Soar, Jackal, and Rip, I asked, "So, will you guys be staying in New York long?"

Rip grumbled, "Apparently."

I asked Soar. "Where's Noah?"

Rip, Jackal, and Soar stared at Knox with raised brows before loudly clearing their throats.

"We thought you knew Noah took a position in England," Soar responded.

"No, I didn't know." I narrowed my eyes. "I've been trying to get in contact with him for days. Is everything okay with him?"

Now I was really concerned. It wasn't like Noah not to return my calls or leave the country for good with no goodbye. Something about this did not sit well with me.

Rip's mouth twisted sardonically. "Nope."

Soar elbowed him hard in the ribs.

"What? She asked me a question," Rip responded indignantly.

Knox swung his long leg off, locking his helmet and mine to the motorcycle. I was so engrossed in trying to figure out what in the hell was going on when he gently grabbed me at the back of the neck, a gesture used by wolf-shifters as a sign of possession. My mind revolted, but my body had a mind of its own. My neck tilted to the side, giving him access to the crook of my shoulder, where he nipped harder than I'd thought he was even capable of.

"A little rough there," I whispered in his ear.

Then I looked over at the wolf-shifters, feeling stupid. With their keen shifter hearing, they could hear a pin drop. But they just looked on like this was the most natural thing in the world for them to see, because it was.

"Knox, we'd ask you to join us for drinks, but we can see you're busy, very busy," Jackal said sarcastically.

"Uh-huh, very busy," Knox responded without even looking at them.

He kissed my neck, sending a jolt of lust straight to my sex, making me rub my thighs together. *Jesus, I'm about to come right here in the garage.*

Jackal's, Soar's, and Rip's eyes narrowed. Their noses twitched, no doubt smelling my need. I wanted to sink into the floor with embarrassment. Knox's head slowly came up, and I swore his eyes did the weird amber glow, flashy thing before turning back to sea-green.

"Let's go," he said gruffly while pushing me toward the elevator, away from the more-than-interested stares of Jackal, Soar, and Rip.

Leaning against his side on the ride up, I probed for information. "So, you seem to know Ryker's friends well. Do you also know Noah?" I asked with a forced infusion of nonchalance.

The elevator opened directly into a foyer with a brightly hued hallway and a view of a private gallery. He nudged me in front of him. "Noah's not an option, Stormy." He followed close behind me. "A fact that he is more than aware of now."

I almost tripped over my feet. "You have no right to tell me with whom I can be friends. He's a good friend and workout buddy."

He snorted, walking around me. "Like I just said, Noah's not an option."

I stood there, watching him walk away, my mouth hanging open. It took a minute for me to snap out of it, chasing behind him to finish this dispute, only to skid to a stop. My mouth dropped open again as I stared at the open floor plan with an expansive living room and gourmet kitchen equipped with marble countertops and stainless-steel appliances.

My eyes narrowed on the stunning, raven-haired woman holding out a spoonful of sauce for Knox to taste.

Knox licked his lips in the most indecent way. "Delicious, Rosa."

Rosa patted his cheek affectionately while I took off my jacket, watching the I-adore-Knox-fest. Rosa glanced over at me with a ridiculously gorgeous white smile that made her look even more stunning.

"So, this is the one," Rosa stated as some sort of fact. "And you're right. She is exquisite, inside and out." She handed over the spoon to Knox before walking over to me determinedly.

In one smooth move, she tugged me into a big bear hug. For a few seconds, I just stood there awkwardly. But the woman patiently waited for me to hug her back, and only then did she let me go.

Stepping back, she held my hands, peering warmly at me.

I stared right back at her.

Rosa couldn't be over thirty, with tanned skin and green eyes that seemed to reach into my soul, reading everything.

"She needs more meat on her bones to have healthy bambinos," Rosa stated simply.

I sputtered. "Who the hell said I'm having any kids?"

Knox picked up a slice of garlic bread, tearing into it. "And I want at least three children, so you'd better eat up, Stormy. I need to fatten you up."

I gave him an evil glare.

Rosa pinched my cheek. "She will give you pretty bambinos." She patted my cheek like some doting mother before swaying over to grab her designer bag from the white granite countertop. "The lasagna is in the oven, and the spaghetti is on the stove." She slapped Knox on the hand. "And stop eating all the bread. She needs all the carbs she can get." Rosa winked at me saucily. "To have enough energy to make it through all the depraved things you will, no doubt, do to her tonight."

"Bread down." Knox slammed the bread that had been making its way into his mouth back onto the plate. "I need her energetic and ready for the baby-making marathon to begin."

Rosa winked at me. "My Knox is so bad." She laughed before walking over to the elevator and pressing the button. She stepped into the car when it slid open, but she stopped to look over at me with a weird, assessing stare that lasted longer than I was comfortable with. Her eyes twinkled as she stated, "This one's a keeper, Knox. Please don't fuck it up."

"I don't intend to, Rosa. Now, if I can only keep her from running away again."

Rosa stared at me for a few seconds before her lips curled up into a wide smile. "This time, she will stay and fight for you." She stepped into the elevator, waving at me until the doors shut.

A shudder went down my spine. It was like some eerie prediction of things to come.

"What in the hell is going on, Knox? And who is that woman?" I walked into the kitchen, prepared to ask a ton of questions, when he handed me two glasses and a bottle of red wine.

His eyebrows furrowed. "Rosa."

Now he was just being fucking annoying. "Yes, I know her

name. But who is she? The housekeeper? Personal chef? Lover? What?"

He came up behind me, wrapping his arms around my waist. He kissed my neck as I poured wine into glasses, and then he mumbled against my skin, "Rosa is Ryker's aunt. And when she's really bored, she cooks for us. Her husband recently died, so she's at a loss for things to fill that void. What can I say? It's a nurturing thing."

She was a wolf-shifter. That explained the fact that she looked like she was in her thirties, with the wise eyes of a woman three times that age.

"Okay, so back to the Noah conversation."

He picked up a glass, making me take a drink before he tilted his glass for a long sip. "Can we eat before we get into this complicated conversation? It's been a long night."

I started feeling guilty because he had just finished a grueling concert, so I backed off a little. "Okay, let's keep it simple and eat here."

I quickly set up the plates and silverware in front of the stools surrounding the granite countertop. Then I walked to the stove to help him put everything on the serving platters. I didn't even dwell much on the fact that he and I worked together in perfect domestic bliss or that there was a comfortable, relaxing silence while we ate.

"Knox, I'm serious when I say Noah and I are friends. It's been that way for years. And I don't like the idea of you saying whom I can be friends with."

He quietly assessed me before feeding me another bite of lasagna and then taking a bite himself. He chewed silently. Then he picked up a glass of water, drinking slowly. But I was patient, waiting for his response. This conversation had to happen. This was what rational couples did—talked.

He leaned back with his eyes locked on me. "I know how

far back your relationship with Noah goes. And I'm not controlling you—at least, not in that way." His jaw tightened. "Unless there's a logical reason, and believe me, there is."

I wiped my lips with a napkin. "And that is?" I took a sip of water.

"Noah and I had a conversation where he confessed he had hoped for more than friendship with you."

I choked on my water. "What? Uh, no. Wait. No, we're just friends."

"He was giving you time to warm up to the idea of more," Knox disclosed.

I started rewinding back to all the times Noah and I had been together. And he'd never once hinted that he wanted more than friendship.

Damn, how could I be so naïve?

I'd just automatically assumed he would mate-claim a full-blooded wolf-shifter and not a hybrid like me. Noah being interested in a romantic relationship with me was bizarre. In the past, I had given him advice on how to handle his many sticky romantic relationship issues. He could have told me how he felt about me many times before.

"This is fucking crazy." I rubbed my head. "All these years? And why the hell would he tell you and not me?"

Knox got up and started clearing the dishes. "Maybe because he thought you wouldn't accept him."

There wasn't anything about Noah a woman wouldn't want. He was caring, intelligent, funny, rich, and handsome. He was the whole damn package. But I considered him to be like a brother.

"There's nothing about him I wouldn't accept."

Knox stopped cold with narrowed eyes.

I shrugged. "He's hot. It's a fact."

After calmly placing the dirty dishes on the counter, he

turned, reclining against it with his arms crossed. "And?" he asked calmly.

I leaned back in my chair with a smirk. "What do you mean by *and*? I never slept with him, which I don't doubt he already told you." I paused dramatically. "But I'm kind of kicking myself right now for missing out on the *Noah* experience." I tapped my chin. "Hmm, maybe he's not called Big Noah for nothing." I waggled my eyebrows suggestively.

I was laughing at my joke, waiting for Knox's angry reaction.

Nothing.

In fact, he looked at me with such nonchalance, I would've sworn I'd been talking about the weather.

"Uh-huh." He widened his stance. "Anything else you'd like to add before you assume the position?"

Uh oh. My brows rose. "What position?"

"Come here, baby." His voice was husky, like he'd just woken up.

Dammit! "And if I do? Are you going to make it worth my time?" I ran my tongue across my lips.

"Yes."

I playfully pursed my lips. "Well, okay. If you say so."

I stood up slowly, walked over to him, and cupped his cheek. He nuzzled my hand. *Damn, it's hard to believe this man is all mine.*

I bit my lower lip, holding back my smile. "Why aren't you upset?" I asked.

He pulled me closer by the waistband of my leather pants. "Because he can't give you what you need."

Wrapping my arms around his thick neck, I relished his comforting body heat. "And what do I need?"

"This." He swooped down, kissing me with gentle strokes.

His tongue ran over my teeth and dueled with mine,

rendering me speechless. He was sensual. Stoking the flames. Building the anticipation fluttering in my stomach. Daring me to let go. Showing me he'd give me everything I needed, if I gave him all of me. I knew he'd accept nothing less.

I reveled in the many sides of this man—hard, gentle, demanding, funny, and dominant. I wanted it all.

He was right. No man could give me what he could.

I sighed, letting go.

It was the only way I could have him with no reservations, just trusting he would give me everything I needed.

I knew then I couldn't live without him.

I couldn't go back to a life of loneliness, living half a life.

Not living much at all.

Fearing love.

Knox pulled off my T-shirt and unhooked my bra with unhurried fingers. He was savoring the moment. As soon as he grabbed my breasts with his rough, enormous hands, my stomach clenched with need.

My head dropped forward as he fell to his knees in front of me, unzipping my pants and yanking them down, along with my sheer panties. He bent down, resting his head against my stomach, gently kissing it. My knees almost buckled when he ran his tongue around my belly button.

In one swift movement, he lifted me, setting me on the large granite countertop. He grazed his lips against my neck. I glided my teeth against his throat, kissing him.

I nipped and licked him. "I want you, Knox."

He whispered against my neck, "And you shall have me, baby, once you understand one thing. I'm a selfish man. I don't share."

I swallowed hard. "And I'm a selfish woman. I don't share either."

He cupped my face between his hands. "Now that we have

that out of the way, let me show you how much I need you." His eyes were dark and sensual.

I desperately clutched his shoulders, wrapping my legs around his waist, clasping him to me. I dug my nails into him, and Knox growled, pulling away from my hold to settle his face between my legs. He slid his tongue into my cunt. I gasped with pleasure, grabbing his head with my hands, my fingers digging into his scalp. The tip of his tongue circled my nub, licking and teasing it.

"Yes," I panted, arching my back.

He flicked my clit with such a delicious force that my ass lifted off the granite. My hips surged against his face. He pushed his tongue deep into me, making a low, growling sound. Its hard vibration made me tremble, and I moved my hips faster.

Oh. My. God. "Yes, Knox."

"Yes, Knox, what?" He pulled back, a thick finger replacing his tongue.

"Give it to me now."

He inserted a second finger into me. My thighs quivered. My head fell back as I panted like I'd just run a marathon.

"Now, is that nice?" He continued to move his fingers in and out with such precision that, for the first time in my life, I was speechless.

My mind went blank as I thrust my hips forward, riding his fingers hard. The need to climax was building, but he deliberately kept me in limbo.

"I don't give a fuck about nice. I need you now, Knox."

When he looked up at me, his sea-green eyes were hard. "Beg for it, Stormy. I want to hear you say it." He grasped my sex between his forefinger and thumb. "Out loud. I want your utter submission."

Spreading my legs wider, I pushed against his fingers.

My body was begging to come.

I knew he would keep me hovering for as long as it took me to submit. I pushed down all the fear, the doubt, and I accepted that my life would change forever with my submission. Now I was finally ready to make it happen. Something in me snapped as I recognized and accepted his dominance.

"Please, Knox, make me come." The words rushed out of my mouth. The relief of my submission made me dizzy. My fingers tightened in his hair.

He growled before returning his tongue to my throbbing nub while pumping his fingers inside me.

My pants and moans became louder. My body shook, needing more. He knew exactly what I desired. With a twist of his finger, he sent me over the cliff. I shouted and groaned.

I looked down with wide eyes as he unzipped his jeans, stepping out of them. He was commando, so his thick, long length was standing at attention. *Damn*, I still couldn't get over how huge he was. Without pause, he pushed into me with no mercy, stretching me.

"Take all of it, Stormy," he growled in my ear.

I wrapped my arms around his neck, letting one leg curl around his waist, the other around his thick calf. "Give me everything you have."

"Always, baby."

His rough fingers tightened around my body, digging into my back. He thrust faster, mercilessly, giving me all of him, pushing me hard toward the edge of pleasure. My arms gripped him with each rough pant and growl.

"You are mine. And I am yours," he whispered.

He spoke the words with such reverence, such heartfelt emotion, that they anchored me.

Something deep inside me broke open. I loved this man.

And for the first time in my life, I actually felt what the

Others who had been fortunate enough to find their mates talked about—the glorious but elusive feeling that overtook the body as the mystical silken tendrils wrapped around it, snapping the mate bond into place.

I'd never understood the glazed look that came over the Others' eyes when they spoke about mating—saying no words could describe it—until now. I felt the natural, seamless slide of my mind and body bonding with him.

Now, not only could I feel him deep inside my body, but also in my soul and my mind. We were one.

He nipped my neck before raising his head. His eyes held mine. His body tensed and then quivered, as if he felt the hard snap of our new mate bond. And whether he knew it, our souls were bound forever.

I slid my hands down his muscled arms. I was almost giddy. So, this was the feeling my ancestors had felt when they bonded with their human mate, knowing it was love and it was time to reveal who they were.

A surge of warmth flooded my body, pushing me over the edge with my mate for life. He pushed one more time, seating himself so deep inside me I swore he was touching my womb.

"Mine," he growled before lightly kissing my neck.

My body froze when I felt the graze of his teeth on the sensitive skin between my neck and shoulder.

My breath hitched when he bit down slightly, not breaking the skin. My body braced, as if expecting the impossible—the sting of canines sinking into me, completing the claiming. He lightly sucked the area as he pumped every bit of his essence into my womb.

He gently kissed my neck before whispering against it, "Are you okay?"

I smiled, running my hands across his muscled back. "Never better." I reached over, caressing his jaw. "Now, don't go getting a big ego over this, but you were absolutely amazing."

He kissed me on the forehead. "You inspire me to give my best." He kissed me hard on the lips. "Are you thirsty?"

"You just defiled me, rock star, depleting me of energy to even think. Of course I'm thirsty." My legs felt like rubber. I wasn't sure how I was going to walk after this.

"That was just round one, baby." He winked at me. "It's going to be a really long but enjoyable night for us. Wrap your arms and legs around me. Let's get you hydrated and ready for round two." He wound his arm around me, easily picking me up and walking over to the huge stainless-steel sub-zero refrigerator. He pulled open the door and grabbed two bottles of water before shutting it.

I laughed against his neck. "You think that's going to be enough?"

"I'll be back for more. I'm keeping you locked up in my bedroom until one of us passes out—and it will not be me."

"That confident, huh?" I smirked.

"It's not confidence—it's fact." He strode out of the kitchen, past the massive hallway that cut across the elevator.

The elevator doors swooshed open.

Knox whirled around. "Slide down, Stormy," he ordered. "And stay behind me."

Sliding down, I got behind his massive back. His legs widened, allowing his body to shield me from the prying eyes of the unexpected visitor.

I peeked around Knox to see Jackal and Rip briskly stepping off the elevator.

"What the hell? Where are your pants?" Rip asked.

"I'm busy," Knox snarled.

Jackal and Rip sniffed the air, then stepped back. I cringed, knowing that their sensitive noses picked up the fact that we'd just had sex.

Jackal cleared his throat loudly. "We're sorry to disturb this very delicate time between you and Stormy, but Ryker needs you, pronto. There's been a serious attack at headquarters."

Knox sighed heavily. "Give me a minute alone with Stormy, and I'll meet you downstairs."

I opened a bottle of water, drinking thirstily, watching as Jackal and Rip hustled into the elevator. Knox's body relaxed from its protective posture when the elevator door closed.

I bit my bottom lip worriedly. The attack had to have something to do with a wolf-shifter war. I hated that shifters were always fighting. If it wasn't power, it was the territory. The strife between them never ended.

"I don't understand," I started. "Why do you have to go?"

This was wolf-shifter business.

Knox had no place in it.

And the thought of him getting involved or hurt set my teeth on edge.

He didn't respond but reached around, hefting me over his shoulder before striding down a long hallway.

"Put me down, Knox." I pounded on his back. "You didn't answer my question." All I could think of was some wolf-shifter tearing him apart, killing him.

"And I'm not going to," he responded gruffly.

We entered his luxurious master suite with the largest bed I'd ever seen in my life. He put me down on it, grabbing the bottle of water from my hand, gulping it down.

Now I was livid. "What do you mean, you're not going to?"

My heart was racing out of control. The mate bond was too new to separate us.

If he were a wolf-shifter, he'd be consumed with sealing our bond by sinking his canines into me, finalizing the mate-claim while pumping me full of his seed.

I jumped up, agitated. "So, you're telling me what we just had together meant nothing?" I blurted out.

Catching my chin, he bored his eyes into mine. "It meant everything, and you know it." He lowered his head and took my mouth in a demanding kiss. He gave me one last swipe of his tongue before he retreated. "When Ryker needs me, I'm there, no matter what. So, you better get used to it. Now, I've got to go." He strode away and into a large custom-fitted walk-in closet. He came back out with jeans and a black T-shirt. His jaw was tense as he tugged on his clothes.

He just didn't understand. Ryker's world was dangerous. It incensed me. *How could he be so reckless?* This was inexcusable.

I raised my chin, placing my hands on my hips. "And what if I don't want to get used to it?" I was bluffing, but I was desperate to stop Knox from leaving and getting involved in shifter business.

He stalked over to me with a calm demeanor. "What did I tell you about my loyalty? I will not change who I am, Stormy. And I don't expect you to either."

He was right. Loyalty was important, and it was one of the many things that I admired about him. I was embarrassed and annoyed that I let my fear turn me into this needy, cloying woman.

He cupped my face. "I know you're scared for me. I see it in your eyes. But believe me, I can handle myself. Trust me on this."

I trusted him, but it terrified me that he might walk into a shifter war that could get him killed.

Am I already paying the price for loving him?

Is this the prelude to the Credence Curse claiming him?

I placed my hand over his heart, comforted by the vigorous thump. Those three words, "I love you," were on the tip of my tongue, but I declared, "We need to have a serious talk when you get back. There are things you need to know about me, about us, and about Ryker."

It's time.

I'm in love with him.

I'm duty bound to tell him everything now—about my family, Others, the Credence Curse, his impending death, and me.

"I've been ready for that conversation with you forever, Stormy." He kissed me hard, dragging my body against his, comforting me. "Promise me you'll stay here until I get back."

I nodded. "Yes, I'll be here. So, don't get your ass killed, rock star."

He slapped my butt before grabbing his leather jacket and swiftly walking away. It surprised me when he came back into the room with my clothes, shoes, and cell, tucking everything on a chair except for my cell, which he handed to me then kissed me again before disappearing.

I crawled onto the bed, wrapping myself in his sheets. Pressing my nose into the pillow, I inhaled his lingering, familiar scent.

My eyelids felt heavy, and my breathing evened out as I slipped into an uneasy sleep.

CHAPTER 22

FOUR SNARLING wolves chased me through the dense woods. No matter how fast I ran, they were there, nipping at my heels, howling, growling, scaring the shit out of me.

The air was crisp as white puffs of smoke formed while I panted, pushing branches out of the way. Exhausted and desperate, I ran over to a large gnarled oak tree, nimbly climbing it, but brutally scratching the tender flesh of my palms.

My thighs burned and trembled as I crawled along a big limb, hanging on for dear life. Clueless how to get out of this hairy predicament, I peered down at the wolves circling the massive base of the tree. There was no way out, and for the first time in my life, I contemplated giving up.

The largest of the pack, a midnight-black wolf with red highlights running through its fur, shook violently before transforming into the largest man I'd ever seen. His skin was slick with sweat. His wild, tangled black-and-red hair cascaded down his back as he stood with arms akimbo, looking up at me.

"Fae witch, we mean you no harm," he rumbled.

Squeezing my thighs tighter around the branch, I almost groaned from the effort it took to stay put. "If that's the case, why were you chasing me through the forest with your pack of merry wolf-shifters?"

"You ran." His sea-green eyes narrowed. "Never run from shifters. It's an invitation for shifters to chase."

Noah had taught me that years ago, but amid my fear, his lesson had flown out of my head.

"Duly noted," I responded sarcastically. "Now go away."

"I have little time, Stormy. Please come down."

My palms slipped, causing my chest to bang against the branch. "Ouch! That really hurt."

Nothing about this nightmare felt right.

How was I feeling pain in a dream?

I glared down at the other four wolves, who had shifted into men and were staring up at me.

"Stormcloud Credence!" the black-and-red-haired man shouted. "Descendant of Solista Credence. I am Tiber Alfero, alpha of the Alfero pack and bearer of the Sword of Souls."

Holy shit, this is real.

He'd lived eons before I was born. This was like history leaping off the pages.

"How?" My stomach was a queasy, churning mess. "Why am I here?"

"That is irrelevant." He nodded to one man. "Get her down before she breaks her damn neck."

My eyes widened as the man gripped the tree, proceeding to scale it. I didn't bother to panic. They could have killed me long ago if that was what they wanted.

The man reached the branch. "Hand, fae witch," he demanded gruffly.

I couldn't get down on my own. Hell, I didn't even know how I'd gotten up here. I wasn't that athletic. I quickly grabbed his hand, our palms touching. My soft palms glided against his callused ones before he slung me effortlessly over his broad shoulder and scaled down the tree without breaking a sweat. Hopping onto the mossy ground, he righted me with surprising gentleness, respectfully bowing his head before stepping back.

Tiber and I stared at each other silently.

So, this is the infamous Tiber who had gone down in history as the most ruthless wolf-shifter who ever lived?

He was Ryker's great-grandfather and a notorious womanizer.

He'd also strung Solista along for years.

"Remarkable. You look just like her," Tiber acknowledged.

"So I've been told," I agreed, nervously licking my lips. "Tiber. Alpha. Look, this dream is really freaking me out."

"This is not a dream," he informed me. "It's real."

He confirmed what I'd suspected.

"And what is this place?" I asked.

"The realm between the human realm and the Other realm. They granted me a gift, and I brought you here."

"And who are *they*?"

"Your ancestors, the fae."

"No disrespect, Tiber, but the only thing the fae gave my family is a really terrible reputation. A status that even you wanted nothing to do with." I scowled. "I know my history. You turned your back on Solista when she needed you."

He flinched, widening his stance. "A mistake that I paid for threefold."

I crossed my arms, not giving an inch. "All your issues and all your mistakes. So, if you want forgiveness, you won't get it from me." I looked over at his pack and then back at him. "Besides, shouldn't you be contacting your own bloodline?"

"I need help!" he shouted.

"If you have issues involving your bloodline, then you should get Ryker to resolve them. Not me."

"Ryker does not have fae power." He stepped closer. "You and Light are the bond that ties us together."

"Us?" I arched a brow. "There's no bond, Tiber. Trust me on this."

He looked over his shoulder sharply, then turned to glare at me. "I have sacrificed a lot for the chance to speak with you, Stormy. But this message I must bring to you is of the utmost importance."

I tried to interrupt, but he cut me off briskly. "And it involves not only the survival of my bloodline, but yours too. Listen to me closely. There are those who work to destroy all Others. They want to cleanse the world of our race."

"If you're talking about Hunters, they'll never be successful in wiping us out." Hunters were humans who knew about the Others' existence and viewed us as unnatural. Their sole purpose was to annihilate Others. "They don't have the power or resources to eliminate the Others."

He shook his head. "Not humans. Shadows devoted to the legacy of the fae and who are obsessed with creating a new race of fae using the Credence bloodline."

My mouth dropped open in shock when I remembered the entry in Solista's journal that mentioned the Shadows. Solista wasn't as insane as our family had believed.

He continued. "Our bond is the only thing that prevents this destruction from happening. Use it wisely."

"I don't understand," I answered. "What bond?"

"Tiber. They're closing the doorway," one of his men announced. "We must leave."

Tiber reached forward, touching my shoulder. "Our bloodlines are fated mates. I obliterated that legacy when I foolishly rejected Solista. I was ignorant, arrogant, and, frankly, scared to love her as she loved me. My bloodline has paid for my short-sightedness. I want to correct my mistake."

"I don't know what to do about that, Tiber," I countered.

"Your heart will reveal the answers," he replied. "He loves you very much, Stormy. Do not let ignorance or fear keep you from him. The Credence Curse has no legs if you cut them off." He turned on his heel, following his men, who headed toward the thick woods.

"Wait," I croaked, trying to follow him, but my legs felt as if they were wading through water, too slow to keep pace. "He?"

Tiber stopped, turning to look at me over his shoulder. And then I saw it. That tiny amber spark flickering in his eyes. He winked at me before rushing off and completely disappearing into the woods.

Holy hell! The amber glow was real, which meant that maybe the glow I'd seen in Knox's eyes when I was dancing onstage was not a figment of my imagination.

A heavy weight slammed into my chest, shoving me back. Then total blackness engulfed me before I jolted awake, lying tangled in the sheets, sweating profusely.

Staring at the ceiling, I tried to clear my sleep-fogged brain when I felt the tingling sensation across my hands.

Scrambling to my knees, I stared at the angry redness of my palms, a vivid reminder that it had not been a damn dream.

Easing back on my heels, I just sat there, blinking at the bright morning sunlight streaming across the bedroom.

My cell buzzed. Digging under the sheets, I reached for it, hoping it was Knox. He was going to get his ass chewed out for not returning last night like he'd promised.

I looked at the number. *Nope. It's not him.*

"Yes?" I answered.

"Didn't I warn you to stay away from him?"

I felt my back straighten instantly. "How the hell did you get my number, Luke?"

"I have my ways," he admitted.

"Lose my number, psycho." I was about to end the call when he started ranting.

"What's with you Credence women? Why do you persist in whoring yourself to humans?" He laughed hysterically. "For the life of me, I can't understand why your family insists on polluting your bloodline with inferior human genes."

"What we do is none of your business."

"Oh, I beg to differ. The Credence bloodline is my business until the day I die."

I pushed the sheets away, scrambling off the bed. I listened to him. There was something very concerning in the tone of his voice and erratic words.

"What in the hell are you talking about, Luke?"

He went on an unsettling tirade, actually talking to himself. "They continue to deny what's before them. Why do they do that? We were born to love only them. Why isn't that enough?" He switched back to conversing with me. "Stormy? Do you know how much I love you?"

"Do you know how nutty you sound right now?" I countered.

"Do you?" he screamed. "Do you even understand the things I've done for you?"

I felt myself panicking just from thinking about Knox lying in a pool of blood, dead. My stomach clenched as I tried to slow down my breathing and think rationally.

He isn't dead.

He can't be. I would have felt it through our bond. At least, I thought I would have.

But what about Celina and the reporter?

Someone had killed them, and I hoped it wasn't Luke because of me.

I reached down deep, pulling on the last of my sanity to use the firm, confident voice I reserved for hysterical escorts bitching about needing a pay raise.

"What types of things, Luke?"

He laughed in a maniacal way that grated against my nerves. "That fucking reporter was too close to the truth. Snooping, always snooping. I saw him. Outside your house, waiting. Taking photos. I did it for you, don't you see?" His voice was high-pitched and whiny.

I closed my eyes, pushing down the building rage. "So, you killed the reporter? For me?"

His voice hardened. "I did what was necessary. We always do."

My eyes narrowed. "Whose we?"

He totally ignored my question, continuing his insane outburst. "I did it to protect you. That's how much I love you, Stormy."

My stomach heaved at the adoration in his voice.

"What about Celina? Did you kill her to protect me, too?" I held my breath, waiting for his response.

There was dead silence before he responded. "I didn't kill her. But she deserves to die for betraying you."

"Betraying me? What does that mean?" I paced back and forth. "Do you know who killed her?"

"We know more than you think, Stormy."

Who is "we"?

"Did you break in to my office?" My fingers tightened around my cell. "Did you leave my business documents all over the scene of the crime, incriminating me?"

His laughter was like fingernails on a chalkboard. "Are you even listening to me? I said I love you. Why would I want to hurt you? You have no clue, do you? There are Others trying to destroy you and your family. They're very close to wrecking the world, you know. I can't let them do it. I need to protect you."

I needed to get out of here and sort out this shit. Walking into Knox's bathroom, I turned on the water, wetting a soft washcloth. "I don't need your protection. I need you to get fucking help—lots of it. So, the best thing you can do for me is turn yourself into the police. Like, now!" I needed this lunatic off the streets and in a padded cell, pronto.

My fingers gripped the cell when he barked, "No! I'm never leaving your side. I can't. Don't you realize I was born to love and serve you? I'll do what they charge Brassons to do."

"Knox is the man I want to do that. Get help."

I was about to end the call when he stopped me cold by saying, "Don't fuck with me, Stormy. I'll kill him. Carve him into pieces until there is nothing left for you to love."

My hands trembled at the passion in his words. "To hell with you, Luke."

"No, to hell with Knox, and that's exactly where I'll send him. Straight to the underworld." He cackled like a wacko. "He's the only man in the way of me having you. And failure is not an option. Not this time. This game is over. It's time to show you how serious I am." He ended our call.

The puzzle came together—Solista's entry about Morpheus Brasson. Luke Brasson *was* his descendant.

CHAPTER 23

RUNNING OUT OF THE BATHROOM, I grabbed my clothes, quickly putting them on, making sure to put my wallet and phone in my pocket. With shoes in hand, I ran out of the bedroom, careening around the corner, only to run smack into a solid wall of muscles.

"Are you going somewhere?" Bones asked.

I hopped from one foot to the other, putting on my shoes. "Look, I don't have time for this, Bones."

I stepped to the left. He followed. I stepped to the right. He smoothly blocked my path.

"Out of my way. Now!"

He crossed his beefy arms, peering down at me like I was a wayward child. "Nope. Knox left specific instructions to protect you. And that's what I intend to do. Now, if you want to go somewhere, I'm more than happy to be your chauffeur for the day."

I jammed my hands on my hips, looking him up and down. "Excuse me? Who the hell made the wolf-shifter brigade my jail warden?" I shoved at him, which was like pushing against a brick wall. I got nowhere.

"Are you done?" he demanded.

I tried to skirt past him, but he easily stepped into my path. This wasn't working, and I was wasting precious time. "Okay, look, I'm a big girl and more than capable of taking care of myself." I patted his arm. "Now, if you would just step aside, we can stop all this craziness, and you can go back to doing whatever you wolf-shifters do. Okay?"

Wolf-shifters were notoriously pack-driven, and I understood his loyalty and respected his role within the pack as an enforcer, but I had business to take care of.

"As precious as that plea was—" he smirked "—you understand what no means, right?"

I clenched my fists. "Dammit! What gives Knox the right to assign me a bodyguard?"

He leaned in, sniffing the air. "His scent is all over you and inside you."

I cringed with embarrassment. "Don't be so fucking crude. He's human, not a wolf-shifter." Or at least I thought he was. "So, what happens between us is personal. Now get a clue and step out of my way."

"No. You're the one who needs to get a fucking clue." His eyes narrowed. "He's family and, therefore, pack."

Pack?

My mind started lining up all the breadcrumbs.

Bones carried on. "So, that automatically makes you pack. Like it or not, fae witch, you are now under our protection." His eyes glowed with a fierceness not even I wanted to mess with.

The pieces to the puzzle continued to click into place.

Tiber's words, *"Our bloodlines are fated mates,"* and *"He loves you very much, Stormy."*

The "he" that Tiber mentioned, was it Knox?

Then there was that tiny amber glow in both Knox's and Tiber's eyes.

The strange feeling I had, that there was some sort of familiarity between Ryker and Knox.

Knox being summoned by Ryker to assist with what I assumed was pack business.

Ryker hiring Credence O. as a gift to Knox.

Is Knox related to Ryker?

Is he a hybrid just like me?

If Knox is Other, why is he hiding this truth from me?

It was a question I planned on asking Knox later on today.

But right now, I had a mission to complete. Protecting my mate from Luke, the psychopath. And absolutely nothing and no one were going to get in my way.

"Fine, Bones," I agreed. "We'll play it your way." I patted him on the arm. "But I need coffee. Believe me, you don't want to stop me from getting a cup. I can get darn right evil without it."

"More evil than you are right now?" he asked before stepping aside.

"Definitely," I confided.

"Go ahead." He gestured for me to go.

I strolled into the kitchen with forced nonchalance. Pressing the button on the espresso machine, I placed a cup beneath to capture the wonderful stream of black liquid gold.

My face was neutral, but my mind was racing a mile a minute, frantically plotting a way to get out of this mess, when my cell buzzed.

"Hey, Light," I answered with my cell to my ear. "What's up, girl?" I lifted the cup of coffee to my lips, taking a small sip, savoring the much-needed awakening brew.

"Uh, everything. Detective Prick called. He wants to meet with us."

I tensed. "Why?"

"Information linking Credence O. to Celina's death was found on the dead reporter's laptop."

I banged my hand on the countertop. "Dammit to hell," I snapped. "Did you call Reason?"

"No, I'm standing here with my thumb up my ass. Of course, I called her. We're meeting Detective Burrows over at her office. I need you back now because you know me. I'll crack under pressure if you're not there," Light wailed hysterically.

Shit! She was already cracking. Unfortunately, she was going to have to step up to the plate and take one for the Credence team.

"Uh-huh." I pursed my lips, shooting a discreet glance at Bones. "I can't right now. Take the meeting without me."

"What?" Light shouted. "Did you not hear what I said? He wants to talk to both of us. I'm not playing, Stormy. Get your ass over here. The last time I was around Detective Prick, I picked up some weird vibes. His emotional compass is not stable."

Damn, that was the last thing Light needed—to have her empath senses swamped by an emotionally unstable human. But this Luke problem was a life-and-death situation.

"Yep. Got it. It's still a no-go."

"What in the hell is wrong with you, Stormy? No-go?"

Tapping my fingers on the counter, I gave her a minute to get my silent message.

"Oh, wait. Someone's standing there?" Light asked.

Finally, she'd gotten it.

"Uh-huh."

"Text. Pronto." Light ended our call.

Bones looked at me suspiciously as I took another sip of coffee.

"Business problems?" he questioned.

Damn his sharp wolf-shifter hearing.

"Yep. Let me text my lawyer."

I tapped out a text message to Light.

Call Bones ASAP. I need a distraction. Will explain later.

Stuffing my cell back into my pocket, I took another sip of coffee, leaning my hip on the edge of the granite counter.

His cell buzzed a few seconds later. He glanced down at it and then at me before answering, "Hey, Light. Funny that you called." His eyebrows furrowed. "At this precise moment."

I turned my back on him. *Shit, he was onto me.* I needed another plan. I heard the elevator ding, and I swung around, expecting to see Knox. The doors slid open, revealing an impeccably dressed Rosa, looking as if she'd just stepped off a fashion runway, teetering on the hottest stilettos I'd ever seen.

I smiled widely. "Hi, Rosa." Putting my cup on the counter, I casually strolled toward her with a smile any beauty-pageant contestant would envy.

Rosa's eyes widened as she sniffed the air. "Mated. Wonderful." She reached out to hug me.

I swerved out of her way, slipping smoothly into the elevator.

After that, everything collided into one chaotic mess.

Bones threw his cell and sprinted toward the elevator. His gigantic body slammed into Rosa. Rosa stumbled forward, screeching at Bones in Italian.

The harder he tried to maneuver around Rosa, the louder she swore.

The last thing I saw before the doors slid closed was Bones's angry red face as he tried to move Rosa out of the way while she angrily jabbed him in the chest.

"Sorry, Rosa and Bones," I muttered, feeling like crap for ditching them. But Bones had left me with no choice. I couldn't just sit on my hands, waiting for fate to take what I had waited forever for—love. I hoped they both would forgive me later when I explained everything.

The elevator rode down to the lobby. When the doors slid open, I ran through the hallway. Pushing open the heavy front door, I hurried onto the sidewalk, blending in with the flustered pedestrians. There would be no way Bones could catch my scent mixed among all the Manhattan smells.

My cell buzzed. Pulling it out of my pocket, I answered, "Hello, Knox."

"What the hell are you doing, Stormy?" he growled. "I swear, if you're running away from me."

Skirting past a hot dog cart, I shouted, "I'm not running away from you! I love you. And I damn well plan on giving you those babies you and I want."

I weaved in and out of a group of tourists taking photos while standing in the middle of the sidewalk, adding to the damn pedestrian congestion.

"Then why would you leave my protection?" The tension in his voice eased a little.

"Because I have business to take care of," I revealed, annoyed with all his questions.

"What kind of business is that, Stormy?"

I scanned the area before sprinting across the street. "I can't say right now. But I promise I'll tell you everything when I'm done."

I ducked into a busy café, sitting down on one stool facing the street, waiting to see if Bones was following me. If he was, I hoped his highly trained senses would go into hyperdrive from the mixture of varied city scents. A busy Manhattan was a wolf-shifter's worst nightmare.

"Dammit, Stormy! Get your ass back to the penthouse. It's not safe for you to be alone. There's a war brewing between Ryker and his business rivals."

I pursed my lips. "That has absolutely nothing to do with me. I'm fine. Believe me."

"No, you're not fine. They know Ryker and I are close. And by now, they know you're my girlfriend. What if they kidnap you?"

"That will not happen." I waved the server over, pointing silently to the chai almond milk latte on the menu.

"I need to protect you, baby." His voice was husky with emotion.

The fierce strain in his tone pulled at my heartstrings. I was stressing him out, but I had to take care of Luke for him and me.

"What about if I need to protect you?" My voice cracked.

"What?" he asked sharply.

"Would you let me?" I didn't realize I was even crying until I tasted the salty teardrops on my upper lip. "I just need to make sure I do everything in my power to ensure I take care of an issue."

Dammit, this mating thing is turning me into a weepy wreck.

"Please, Knox. Just give me a chance to do this," I persisted.

"Shit! Stormy? Are you crying, baby?" His voice broke, alarming the hell out of me. "Come back home, okay? We'll talk this out. Then you can do whatever you think you have to." His forced casual tone set off warning bells.

If I came back right now, I wouldn't be able to scratch my ass without an entourage of Ryker's enforcers watching me do it.

"Lies," I exploded. "You won't. See you later, Knox." I ended our call.

He called back twice. I refused to answer.

I slumped against the stool, emotionally exhausted. Taking a deep breath, I smiled shakily when the server smoothly placed the chai latte within my fingertips. I sipped it while tapping on my recent calls list to find Luke's number.

"What a pleasant surprise. Change of heart, sweetheart?" Luke answered with a cheerful tone.

This was where I had to stay strong and draw the line. I refused to let him play mind games with me.

"We need to talk," I announced.

"We are talking."

"In person, Luke."

He laughed loudly. "Finally, we're getting somewhere. Come to my place."

There was no way in hell. "No. I'm in a café. Meet me here."

"My place or nothing," he countered.

I bit my bottom lip, trying to work out the scenarios of meeting with him in person, and all roads led to putting myself in danger.

"No, Luke."

"Bye, Stormy." His voice was hard.

"Okay, wait," I muttered.

This was a really dangerous move, but I was desperate.

There was no way I could live the rest of my life looking over my shoulder, waiting for Luke to come out of the shadows to kill Knox, me, or my family.

I had to stop this insane legacy of killing human men that our family fell in love with.

Solista had been unable to stop it, and where she'd failed, I would succeed. I had to. The Credence bloodline depended on it.

"Where do you live?" I asked, listening to his words,

committing his address to memory. "I'll be there in thirty minutes," I confirmed before ending the call.

I finished my latte, paying the bill before slipping out of the café and down the block to hail a taxi.

Sliding inside, I gave the driver my home address while concocting my plan.

It was simple—meet Luke and try to reason with the certified madman.

If that didn't work, I would kill him.

That was not my preferred solution, but if I had to, I wasn't afraid to protect Knox and my family.

CHAPTER 24

THE TAXI PULLED up to my house, and I wasted no time jumping out and entering my home. It was quiet inside, which was a good sign that Light had already gone to Reason's office.

Kicking off my shoes, I pulled on my sneakers before running into the office, opening the safe, taking out the small gun, and sliding it into the pocket of my leather jacket. Slipping inside the garage and into my car, I took a deep breath, contemplating my plan.

Common sense told me that what I was about to do was dangerous and reckless. No one would know where I was, which was both a positive and a negative—positive if I had to kill him, and negative if he went ballistic and killed me.

Pulling out of the garage, I zipped into the Manhattan traffic, all the while kicking myself for this rash decision. I'd seen enough news stories and documentaries where people had gone missing without a trace, yet I was making this rookie mistake. Desperation was making me do such a stupid thing.

I rolled back the convertible top, letting the cool breeze

soothe my frayed nerves. I pulled up in front of Luke's luxurious brownstone, but I wanted to keep on driving. Parking, I sat there, hesitant to leave the safety of my vehicle.

Leaning my head back, I gathered all my strength.

This is fucking stupid.

I know better than this.

Fuck it. I'm out of here.

I was about to turn on the car and leave when Luke's voice jolted me straight up in my seat.

He was standing by the driver's door, looking well groomed.

"Are you coming in?" he asked, leaning over into my car.

My hands gripped the steering wheel as I gave him a sharp stare. "You're in my space, Luke. Can you step back?"

"Sorry." He backed up with his hands up.

Pushing open the door, I hopped out, slamming the door.

"Let's talk," I ordered, leaning my butt against the hood with arms crossed.

"Outside?" His eyebrows shot up with mock surprise. "I think not." He gestured toward his house. "Shall we?"

Dammit to hell. If I refused, he'd never tell me what I needed to know. I scowled before walking up the stairs, feeling his heated stare on my ass.

"Enjoying the view back there?" I sneered.

"Of course. It's a lovely view. It always has been."

"You're an asshole," I remarked while waiting for him to open the door to his lair of doom.

He pushed open the door grandly, allowing me to step into his house. My sneakers squeaked loudly on the marble floor, with Luke following close behind me. He was so near, his cloying cologne made me want to throw up. He pressed a hand to my back, his icky fingers trailing seductively along it.

I spun around, shoving him back. "Don't touch me. Ever!"

Amusement flitted across his face. "Apologies."

"Can we get this over with?" I demanded.

He was creepy, and I wanted to get out of here as quickly as possible.

"Follow me," he directed with that weird smile that made me uneasy.

We walked into the expensively decorated living room with a roaring fireplace.

Luke gestured toward the sofa. "Have a seat."

Crossing my arms, I regarded him. "I'd rather not. I won't be here long."

"Talk," he ordered before sitting down in a large leather chair, staring at me with an indecent look that told me he was undressing me with his eyes.

"I want you to leave me alone. Leave Knox alone. And lastly, stay the fuck away from my family."

"No!" he exploded. "If I can't have you, no one can."

"I tried to reason with you, Luke." I pulled out my gun and aimed.

He actually laughed at me like I was some sort of joke.

"You won't kill me, Stormy." He got up, creeping toward me. "You love me."

"Believe me." I widened my stance. "I don't love you." My finger slowly squeezed the trigger. "And I will kill you."

He froze midstep, considering me.

"You're trying to hurt what is mine," I declared. "And that will never do."

"Do you think you can just kill me and end my family's and the Shadows' mission? I'm a warlock," he divulged. "And I'm not the only descendant of Morpheus. Nor am I the only follower committed to our agenda. We are the Shadows. We are always watching, always vigilant. The Credence women are ours to love and protect from worthless human men. Just like those humans who were not worthy of Elizabeth, Mary, Claire, or Solista—that is why we, the Shadows, killed them."

Fuck! This is what Solista meant.

The Shadows were a group of stalkers who'd been killing the human men we loved for generations.

"So, let me get this straight. You and your family are part of a group called the Shadows? A group that's been stalking my family and killing every human man we've ever loved?"

"We killed to protect your family." He reached a hand toward me. "Don't you see why our duty is so important?"

Important?

The Shadows are cold-blooded killers.

Anger surged through my veins.

There was no Credence Curse, and my family had spent centuries believing a lie.

It incensed me that the Shadows killed men just because we loved them.

"No, I don't," I objected. "What I see is the *Shadows* are a bunch of fucking nutjobs whom we need to exterminate like roaches."

"Don't you fucking get it?" he bellowed, practically foaming at the mouth. "Your family is important to our mission."

"What mission?"

"The union of my bloodline and yours. Together, we can annihilate all Others, then recreate this world."

Every hateful word that spewed from his mouth incensed me further.

"There will be no union." My jaw tightened. "Or the eradication of Others."

"Don't you realize how powerful you and Light are? The

fae blood that runs through your veins has an untapped magic that, combined with my pureblood warlock DNA, is the key to eliminating those mutt Others."

"What are you talking about?" I demanded.

He grinned. "This is the secret your fae ancestors passed down to my ancestors and the Shadows."

Holy hell. I knew the fae were evil and tyrannical, but why would they align themselves with the Shadows?

"There will be no union of bloodlines."

"You can't stop us," he threatened. "We are too powerful." He marched forward.

It was time to send him a warning message—I meant fucking business. I squeezed the trigger, and a bullet grazed his ear.

Luke squealed like a pig, jumping back hotly while grabbing his bloody ear.

"Lucky shot," he snarled.

"Luck has nothing to do with it. This just got real for you, Luke. I feel threatened by your aggressive actions. So, if I were you, I wouldn't make any sudden movements."

"Bullshit." He stepped forward again.

"Freeze," I ordered, aiming for his knee. "Do you enjoy walking? Because I'm prepared to blow them both out."

He froze in his tracks, wiping at the blood dripping from his ear. "Okay, Stormy. You kill me, and then what?"

My aim never wavered. "Dispose of your body. Then my family and I will start hunting down the rest of the Shadows, making the world safer for Others. And last but not least, my mate and I can live in fucking peace."

Taking a life wasn't in my nature, but I would do it if it meant saving Knox, my family, and countless innocent lives from Luke, his family, and the Shadows.

"What mate?" he exploded.

"Oh, did I forget to tell you? I'm now mated to Knox. Surprise!"

His face glowed red with rage. I didn't care because I was busy contemplating which knee to shoot first.

"You bitch!" Luke bellowed while charging forward, screeching hysterically like a reality-show contestant.

I got off one bullet to his shoulder before he tackled me like a football player, knocking the gun out of my hand, sending it sailing across the floor.

"Fuck!" I growled as pain ricocheted through my body, my legs splayed awkwardly as he pinned me to the ground with his body and blood dripped from his wound onto me.

I fought against him like a madwoman with the primal need to survive coursing through my veins. My blood-coated arms slipped, adding an extra complication to every move I made to escape.

A full-out fight ensued, with Luke banging the back of my head against the floor with such force that my vision swam. I fought the urge to black out.

His face was a distorted mask of sheer madness as he screamed over and over, "You bitch!"

My instincts and training guided me as I swung my knee up into his groin so hard I even felt the force jarring against my body. I followed up with an upward strike of the heel of my hand to his nose. His blood splattered everywhere.

Luke fell over onto his back, screaming in pain like a panic-stricken girl.

Rolling away, I scrambled to my hands and knees, crawling backward on all fours, trying to put as much distance between us as possible.

Out of breath, I wobbled to my feet, preparing to launch another attack, when the crazy bastard somehow got his bearings and lunged at me, yanking my foot toward him. The bite of his fingers against my ankle sent me into panic mode. I kicked him hard in the face with my other leg, jumping back.

I was a mess. His blood coated my clothes and face.

Just a little more and I win this thing, making it out of here alive.

Circling him, I got into a fighting stance.

Getting to his feet, he staggered. "I still want you, Stormy, although you sullied yourself with that human. You're strong. A fighter. Beautiful. Fae. Imagine what we could do together."

I tracked him, waiting for an opening to strike a deadly blow. "But isn't that what we Credence women do? Sully ourselves with human men?" Taking a step back, I prepared to strike him in the throat.

He charged at me wildly.

I delivered a roundhouse kick to his chest, knocking him back.

Recovering, he barreled forward. This time, he grabbed my leather jacket, tugging at it. I punched and kicked, but no matter what I did, he kept coming at me. It was like he was on some super steroids. He was taking my blows like it was nothing.

Swinging me around, he banged me face first into the wall, plastering his body against mine.

He started rubbing his groin against my butt while moaning and panting like some barn animal, all while successfully pinning my hands to my sides.

"You're a damn freak," I gritted out before butting him with the back of my head, feeling instant satisfaction at the sound of the crunch with the connection of my skull to his nose.

But he remained steadfast.

His breath came out harder against my ears as he dry-humped my ass. I took a calming breath when I felt myself on the verge of full-on panic mode.

Noah had taught me that patience was a skill in defensive fighting, so I waited for a lapse in Luke's posture and my opportunity to launch another attack.

Suddenly, loud crashing and ripping sounds filled the room. It was as if someone was tearing the door off its hinges. A terrifying growl erupted, and the ground shook.

Luke's body was flung away from mine.

Free, I turned around then froze at the sight of a huge, feral-looking midnight-black wolf dragging a flailing and kicking Luke across the room like yesterday's trash.

Luke's foot connected with the wolf's flank, which only seemed to incense the beast even more.

The wolf's hackles rose as its lips curled back, displaying nothing but canines and gums. The beast circled Luke, periodically charging forward to bite and tear into his flesh. It was almost as if the wolf was toying with Luke. Blood drops flew, and the sounds of flesh being torn echoed throughout the space.

I backed away from the fray, trying not to make any large movements that would turn the ferocious wolf on me. I was almost a safe distance away when I bumped into something hard.

"Going somewhere, Stormy?"

I yelped, swinging around, only to stare at Soar, Rip, and Jackal, standing there like a gigantic wall of muscle.

"How did you find me?" I demanded.

Rip smiled cockily. "Knox put a tracker on your cell."

That sneaky bastard. I tried to move past them.

The wolf growled menacingly with his green eyes keyed on me. I froze.

"I advise you not to move," Jackal remarked. "He seems to be a little angry with you at you at the moment."

"Rightly so," Rip added, giving me a stern look. "You need to be bent over his lap and your ass smacked, hard, for this asinine stunt."

"Oh, she's going to get more than that at the end of this little ordeal. He's fucking pissed," Soar added with a smirk.

My heart raced with fear. I couldn't deal with a pissed-off wolf-shifter right now.

"Who is that?" I licked my lips nervously, feeling like my bladder was about to fail. "Ryker?"

Soar dropped the bundle of clothes in his hand on the floor. "Nope. Guess again, sweetness."

My eyebrows rose. "Knox?"

"Yes." Jackal nodded toward the wolf tearing into Luke. "I wouldn't want to be you when Knox gets finished with that warlock."

Just as I'd begun to suspect, he was a wolf-shifter.

"All this time and no one told me?" I shouted. "Why?"

They shrugged, looking over at the wolf-shifter tearing into Luke.

I jammed my hands on my hips. "Well?"

They just stared at me before Rip said, "It ain't our business to tell."

I rolled my eyes heavenward before turning to glare at the wolf attacking Luke with such ferocity I almost felt sorry for him. The wolf looked savage, and that couldn't be good for any of us.

"Are you guys going to do something?" I asked.

"Like what? He's got this," Soar responded nonchalantly.

"He's ripping Luke to shreds." I pointed over at the blood and carnage. "The world could do with less trash, but I came here for answers, and he's killing the only person who can provide them." I needed to know more about his family, the

Shadows, about who had killed Celina, and anything else the little prick could tell me.

They just shrugged.

"Oh hell, just fuck it." I strode forward.

They blocked me.

"Are you crazy?" Rip asked crisply. "He'll hurt you by mistake."

"I'm not stupid." I shoved at them. "Move."

My abrupt movement caught the wolf's attention. He stopped and growled at them like he was going to attack.

Jackal froze. "Oh shit!"

I'd had enough of this.

If they would not stop this bloodbath, then I had to.

Pushing them aside, I moved steadily forward.

Knox snarled at Luke, who was rolling on the floor, bloody and screeching in pain.

I clapped my hands to get the wolf's attention.

The beast's eyes locked on to me with heated intensity, and a strange wave of power slammed into me. The force of the magic almost made my knees buckle, but I stayed focused on the wolf.

"Drop it, Knox," I ordered, pointing at the mangled arm he held in his mouth.

Knox dropped the limb, and Luke tried to snatch it. Big mistake. Knox lunged, biting down hard on his other arm, ripping into it.

"Baby, please shift back," I pleaded. "I want to go home. Our home."

The black wolf stood there, massive, dominant, and focused on Luke, who was backing away.

"I'm not afraid of you, wolf-shifter. She's mine," Luke croaked like a lunatic.

If I didn't put an end to this, it could go on all night.

"Hey! Shifter, look at me." I clapped again.

Knox sniffed the air, still focused on Luke.

This wasn't working.

Luke's blood saturated my clothes, masking my scent.

I had to get Knox to shift.

"Guys," I whispered. "Will you stop staring at me and give me his damn T-shirt?"

Someone put Knox's shirt into my hand. Pulling it over my head, I let it glide over my body before stepping forward again. Because there was so much animosity between shifters and witches, years ago, I'd asked Noah to train me how to avoid, de-escalate, and potentially survive a shifter attack. I knew Knox couldn't understand me in the state he was in, but he could smell the mixture of my scent combined with his.

The wolf plowed forward, sinking his canines into Luke's calf. Luke was going to die, and Soar, Jackal, and Rip were laughing hysterically like they were watching a stand-up comedy show.

Mental note to self: Payback is a bitch, and those three are on my shit list.

The wolf's nostrils flared, probably scenting my aroma mixed with his, but that didn't stop him from grabbing Luke, locking his jaws around Luke's throat.

"Stop!" I yelled with my hands thrown out. The lights in the room flickered, and an electric shock coursed through my body.

A slew of emotions—rage, disgust, fear, surprise—that were not mine flooded into my brain.

My heart raced, knowing that my fae powers had picked a real fucked-up time to surface. Magic surged, wrapping around me like a viper, then fanned out, sucking all the energy and emotions out of the room like a vacuum and depositing them into me.

My body trembled when I felt the sensation of the wolf's teeth sinking into my throat. I was feeling all of Luke's pain and emotion. Tears streamed down my cheeks as a blood-curdling scream erupted from my mouth.

The wolf's head whipped around to face me, his jaws still around Luke's throat.

"Stop," I pleaded. "I can feel everything you're doing to him."

Releasing Luke, he let loose a low growl and then a whine.

I sighed with relief when the pain stopped.

Luke rocked back and forth, chanting loudly in some sort of daze.

The wolf gave Luke a disgruntled stare before trotting over to me and circling me. I froze, not wanting to make any sudden movements that would agitate him. I grunted when he nudged the back of my legs over and over with his nose.

Taking the hint, I fell to my knees before sitting back on my heels. Knox playfully butted his head against my arm before sitting by my side, allowing me to run my fingers through his soft fur.

"You're even gorgeous as a wolf," I remarked softly.

His body convulsed, and his bones made a loud cracking sound while he shifted to his human form. Leaning back on his heels, he looked exhausted.

"Are you okay?" I asked, running my fingers across the slick, taut muscles of his back.

"Yes." His breathing was heavy when he leveled me with a hard stare.

"Who are you?" I asked in a hushed voice.

He tilted his head in a wolflike way. "Son of Ronan Alfero. Brother to Ryker. And beta of the Alfero pack." He scowled.

"And when we get home, we're going to have a serious fucking discussion about following instructions." He tugged me up with him, clutching my body against his.

Drawing back, I widened my stance, giving him a hard stare of my own. "Yes, we will. Wolf-shifter, you have some serious explaining to do, like why didn't you tell me you're a shifter in the first place." I jabbed him in the chest. "And why you put a GPS tracker on my cell. That's a sneaky asshole thing to do."

"Well, this *asshole* just saved you from getting killed by that psycho warlock."

As stupid as this disagreement was, neither of us would stand down. It was like we were getting off on fighting, like it was foreplay.

"I was doing fine, Knox."

He arched a brow.

"Okay, yes, I had some issues subduing him, but I was working on it."

"What possessed you to come over here alone?" he asked with a sharp tone I didn't like.

"I needed to know what he had to do with the Credence Curse."

"That bullshit? If you had just been straight with me, I would've told you that Curse is a bullshit urban legend."

"Bullshit urban legend?" My eyes widened. "Before I found out about Luke, his demented family, and the Shadows, every human a Credence loved ended up six feet under."

He scoffed.

"That is a fucking fact, Knox." My anxiety was rising as my chest tightened.

He crossed his arms, looking down at me with an air of disbelief. "So, you left me years ago because of some urban legend, instead of sticking around and fighting it out to the bitter end? Yep, sounds logical to me."

"You don't know what the hell you're talking about, Knox. Do you think it was easy for me, walking away from you? Because it wasn't. But that's what we do. We walk away to protect the men we love."

"Uh-huh. After you fuck them over, literally. You smile prettily, give men the 'it's-not-you-it's-me' speech, and then move on to the next unsuspecting guy. That seems like a pretty fucked-up way for the Credence family to live."

My eyes opened wider with shock. He'd figured us out. But there was way more to the Credence story, and he was oversimplifying it.

"I love how you conveniently just glossed over the fact that we were trying to protect our men from dying needlessly."

"I'm giving you the truth with no fucking chaser, Stormy. I always have and always will. It's an urban legend that no one believes but your family. Swallow it, digest it, and let's move the hell on."

"We protected humans, like I was just trying to protect you."

He seized my chin, pulling it up. Our eyes locked. "Let's get one thing straight. I'm your mate. I protect you, not the other way around." His eyes narrowed. "You Credence women weren't protecting anyone but yourselves. You all used that *Curse* as an excuse to keep every man at arm's length."

"You don't know what you're talking about. I came here to stop Luke from killing you."

"Thanks, baby, but I can take care of the both of us. I'm your mate. Next time, let me do the protecting, okay?"

It really was exhausting to always be the protector. I needed someone who wanted to protect me, a wish I would never admit to him—at least not yet.

"Whatever, Knox," I responded softly.

"Hey, guys!" Rip shouted.

"Not now!" we both shouted in unison.

"Okay, but in case you're remotely interested, the crazy warlock just disappeared into thin air."

CHAPTER 25

I WAS EMOTIONALLY and physically exhausted, angry, and hungry all at the same time. Not to mention, the tension between Knox and me in the elevator ride was so thick we could cut it with a knife.

"So, are we going to talk about the wolf-shifter thing now?" I questioned with a raised brow.

He grabbed my hand, weaving his fingers through mine. Bringing my hand up to his lips, he kissed it. "Shifting takes a lot out of me. Let me get some water, then I'll tell you everything."

The elevator doors opened, and still holding hands, we stepped out, making our way to the kitchen. Knox grabbed several bottles of water out of the refrigerator, handing me one before opening his.

I sipped my bottle slowly, watching Knox guzzle down five bottles back-to-back.

"From what I've been told," he started, "the woman I thought was my mother stole me from the Alfero pack out of spite," he said in a voice devoid of emotion.

"What do you mean, spite?"

"She was a female wolf who wanted my father, but he rebuffed her and mate-claimed my mother, making her alpha female of the pack. So, this she-wolf did everything in the book to thwart my mother's powers throughout the years. And her bitterness got worse when my mother gave birth to Ryker and then to me."

My eyes widened. "Oh my god."

"I guess the craziness ate away at her. She challenged my mother to a fight to the death for the position of alpha female. They fought. She won, killing my mother. But my father still refused to mate-claim her. That's reportedly when she went completely insane and kidnapped me."

I thought my family was crazy. His was worse.

"So, she pretended to be your mother until the day she died?" I asked.

"Yes." I sensed his anger simmering just below the surface. "And she made me pay for being the offspring of a man who had rebuffed her. Every fucking day of my life, she made me feel like shit." He bit out the words, closed-lipped. "Nothing I did was ever good enough for her. She even drilled into my head that my father had abandoned her because of me. I hated that woman. Then I started hating myself."

He took a sip of water. "For years, I was wild, reckless, and even got into some serious trouble with a gang of shifters. That's when I met Wyatt and Portia. We had something in common. We were Others—unloved and abandoned."

"Wait, they're wolf-shifters?"

"No. Hybrid Djinn."

"Hybrid? Now it makes sense why Light's and my magical abilities didn't work on them. Well, on you too, but now I know why."

He arched a brow. "Explain."

"Light can sense human emotions, and I can read auras. Others have blue auras and humans green. But our abilities don't work on hybrids or Others with alpha blood, which now explains everything. They're hybrid, and you're from alpha blood."

"Damn, that's a pretty powerful ability," he replied.

"When it works," I pointed out. "So, what made you finally fire Portia?"

"When I found out that she and Wyatt had set up that scene in the manager's office."

"If you knew Wyatt was behind that bullshit reality show between you and Portia, why is he still around?"

"Because, believe it or not, he had a more fucked-up mother than I did. Yes, he's fucked in the head, I get that, but you don't understand what it's like, not being accepted by your own kind. I now have a brother who loves me and a pack that has embraced me as their own. It's a family Wyatt will never have."

I just stared at him with my heart fucking melting. Just when I'd thought I knew everything about him, he'd unpeeled a whole additional layer.

He grabbed my face between his hands. "If there's anything you need to understand about me, it's that I don't turn my back on people I care about. We're all broken—some a little and some a fucking lot. But trust me on this. If Wyatt fucks with you again, I will not only cut him loose, I'll get rid of him permanently."

Oh shit, I didn't even have to ask what he meant. The feral look in his eyes said it all.

"And for the record." He gave me a hard stare. "I scented you outside the office before you walked in. I smelled your indecision, fear, relief, but what I hadn't expected was that petty act you put on just to break up with me." He lifted an eyebrow and waited.

I swallowed hard. "Yes, I used that opportunity to break it off with you. I had to because of the Credence—"

"Curse?" he interjected.

"Okay, don't rub it in. It's not a curse." Which was hard for me to wrap my mind around. "Let's get back to you. Did you know who I was back then?"

He shook his head. "Not at first. I mean, I knew you were a witch. But I didn't even know how important your family was until way after Ryker found me and told me everything about my own family and the woman I thought was my mother. Her name was Julia."

"When did you find out about your father being Ronan and Ryker, your brother?"

"Right around the time we started dating. My father had been searching for me for years, and Julia knew it. That's why we'd moved around a lot. When she died, something drew me to New York. I thought it was my music, but apparently, it was because my family lives here. The stars aligned, and one night at my gig, this shifter came up to me, telling me I smelled a hell of a lot like some alpha named Ryker. Of course, I called bullshit and moved on with my life, but Ryker got intel about me, and that's how it all was revealed."

"Wow." I bit my bottom lip.

"I spent my entire life not giving a shit about politics. After I found out who I really was, I got thrown neck-deep into the Others' world. Between finally getting a recording contract, my music career taking off, and getting up to speed on my bloodline, it was a crazy couple of years. That's why I took a music hiatus. I needed to get my shit right to take my place in the pack." He eyed me. "That's the only thing that kept me from coming back to claim you sooner. But you best believe, woman, I never forgot you."

I touched his cheek. "I'm sorry for hurting you. But why didn't you tell me who you were?"

"Trust."

My heart dropped. "You didn't trust me?"

"Oh, I trusted you, but you didn't trust me. I smelled the mistrust years ago, and the scent was still there when we reunited." He reached out and grazed the side of my cheek with the back of his hand. "You were hiding so much from me, and it had nothing to do with the Curse and everything to do with you being terrified to open your heart to me. I could have pushed, forced my way into your heart, but that's not what I want with you. I want love and trust given freely. So, I waited for you to come to the same conclusion I came to years ago. You and I are mates, and we are forever." He cupped my face. "Telling you I was a shifter wouldn't have changed your resistance to me. You would have just found another excuse to push me away."

He was on point with that assessment. Between my fucked-up relationship with my sperm donor, my fear that Others despised me because of my fae witch lineage, and the repercussions of the Curse, I'd built a wall around my heart to protect myself from getting hurt. It was a vicious cycle of never getting close to anyone because I expected the worst of them, and I was always looking out for something to go wrong.

"I'm not making excuses, but I have a suitcase-worth of emotional baggage that I'm working on," I admitted.

"You're not the only one, baby. I'm working on my issues every day. But it will never stop me from trusting you or make me push you away."

"You still could have told me you're a shifter."

"I could have, especially when Ryker told me about the Curse and that bullshit truce between your family and the Council about not killing humans. But again, I knew who I was wouldn't have stopped you from trying to push me away. And believe me, I had every intention of telling you today, but you ran and went to that dangerous meeting with that lunatic."

I brushed my lips against his. "I met with Luke because I'm ready to let you in, Knox."

"And I'll never take advantage of your gift of trust and love," he pledged.

I blinked back the threatening surge of tears. This man was who I'd waited a lifetime for.

His mouth closed over mine. His tongue teased and coaxed, demanding my submission. And I gave it. He was mine. My shifter, and I could deny him nothing. A fist in my hair angled my head back, granting him deeper access. His growl vibrated through me, and I clenched my thighs, aching for him to fill my pussy in the way that only he could.

He broke away from our kiss. "Let's take a shower. I need to get the stench of that dirty warlock's blood off us."

I was too tired to argue, allowing him to walk me through the living room and into the bedroom suite. Tiredly, I started taking off my pants, when he knocked my hands away, unfastening them for me. Once he undressed me, he quickly undressed himself, hustling us into the shower.

"Come here," he commanded, reaching for the shampoo.

Pouring some into his hand, he washed my hair. It was heaven to feel his fingers on my scalp, massaging it.

"I'm sorry, okay? I thought I was doing the right thing," I explained.

Knox didn't respond. I was going to make a joke, when I looked up and saw his clenched jaw and furrowed brows.

I reached up, cupping his jaw. "What do you want from me, Knox?"

In one swift movement, he wrapped his arms around me, yanking me closer to him, high against his chest and down onto his cock. As I panted with pleasure, he braced me against the wall of the shower, burying his face into the crook of my neck, inhaling deeply.

He looked up at me with emotions swirling in the depths of his sea-green eyes. "Everything," he said gruffly.

That one word broke the dam of emotions. I wrapped my arms and legs around him, clenching as I tried to adjust to his wide staff filling me completely. Leaning in, I ran my tongue along his jaw, stroking my hand over his wet hair. I blinked back the tears, knowing it was time to utter the words of my ancestors, who had dared to love.

"I, Stormcloud Credence, descendant of the Credence fae witch bloodline, give you all that I am." I swallowed hard. "My heart, love, body are yours to cherish. Now and forever."

I held my breath, waiting for him to reject me because of my bloodline, but he didn't even blink. In fact, his lips curled up into the most beautiful smile I'd ever seen.

"As is mine, Stormcloud Credence. I love you and claim you as mine—my mate—forever." His voice broke.

Shaken, I clutched on to him with my needy body tightening around him. Knox squeezed his hand on my butt, pulling me closer. His other hand collared my throat possessively, branding it as his. His eyes flashed amber, then reverted to sea-green.

"I've never seen an Others' eyes flash amber," I marveled.

"It's distinct to my bloodline."

"I'm learning something new every day." I kissed his lips hard.

He stared into my eyes. "And every day I spend with you, I find more to love."

His mouth crushed mine, his tongue thrusting forcefully into my mouth. His hard, hot length surged into me, stealing my breath away. Gasping at the power of his thrusts, I tightened around him. I moaned into his mouth with pleasure as I dug my nails into his back.

Pulling his mouth from mine, he growled, "Now that we got this trust shit out of the way, I'm ready to mate-claim my woman."

He tangled his hand in my hair and kissed me hard before nibbling his way down my throat. Resting his lips on the juncture of my shoulder and neck, he scraped his teeth over the spot before biting down hard, breaking the skin. I moaned in ecstasy when a hot flash shot through my body and up my womanhood, giving me the most intense climax I'd ever experienced in my life. He groaned, spilling his seed inside me.

I collapsed against him as he sucked hard on the spot, no doubt leaving a very distinctive mark—a mark letting all shifters know I was mate-claimed by none other than Knox Gunner.

I didn't know how to stop the tears that streamed down my face. My chest heaved. My heart was heavy, and it scared me to death that some wicked twist of fate could take everything away. With Luke's escape, I knew dark days were ahead. He was out there, waiting for a chance to kill Knox. And I couldn't lose my mate, not like that.

Knox looked up at me. His smile disappeared. "Not happening, Stormy. Don't you dare think about running away because I will hunt you down and fuck you to death."

My hands trembled on his shoulders. "I'm scared to death, Knox. It's this weird feeling in the pit of my stomach that won't go away. Something bad is going to happen." I swallowed around the lump of emotions. "I'm strong, but I'm not strong enough to live through your death."

He kissed where he'd marked me, sending a delicious shiver down my spine. "That will not happen. Please trust me on this."

I nodded, but I knew the truth. Luke, his family, and the

Shadows would never stop stalking my family and those we loved.

"I belong to you." He brought my palm to rest on his chest over his thumping heart. "And you belong to me. And no one takes what's mine." He reached up to cup my cheek.

"You're turning me into some emotional crying chick."

"There's nothing weak about showing how much you want what we have, baby." He nipped me hard on my chin as he raised my leg, pulling it over his muscular ass. "Now let me show you how much I need you."

With one hard thrust, he drove into me, sending me to a place I could live in forever—pure ecstasy.

He sank his teeth into my neck. "Damn, Knox." I panted, digging my nails into his shoulders as an orgasm gripped me.

He growled. "Mine." His nose pressed against my neck as he breathed in my scent.

I touched his cheek. "Absolutely."

He soothed the bite mark with soft kisses. As he pulled my hair away from my damp face, I took a minute to appreciate his hard body.

"As much as I love the idea of basking in my mate's presence all day..." I sighed heavily. "There's important Credence business I have to handle with Light and a detective with an ax to grind."

"So, let's go handle it," he murmured. "Together." With one fluid movement, he effortlessly hauled me over his shoulder. "After I take you again."

God, I love my shifter.

IF YOU LOVED **BREAKING THE STORM**, you're going to devour Ryker and Lightning's story. Keep reading for a sneak peek at **WHEN LIGHTNING STRIKES!**

GET A FREE SEDONA VENEZ BOOK!

https://sedonavenez.com/free-book

SNEAK PEEK AT WHEN LIGHTNING STRIKES

CHAPTER 1 / LIGHTNING

My eyes darted toward the door. *Where is Storm?*

My cousin Storm's tardiness was so out of character that my fingers trembled as I took a large gulp of tequila.

I snorted, thinking about our earlier phone conversation. There was no way in hell she'd actually been serious about me attending this meeting without her. She couldn't be, not after I'd specifically told her the last time I'd been around Detective Prick, I had picked up some weird vibes. His emotional compass was not stable. I would crack under pressure if she weren't here.

Shit! I'm already cracking.

I wasn't proud to admit it, but I was desperate. I needed her.

I frantically tapped out a text message to Storm. *Where in the hell are you? I'm not playing, Storm. Get your ass over here. Now!*

I waited. No response. *What in the hell?*

Reason Orlov, my bestie and lawyer, pursed her lips with displeasure while drumming her well-manicured nails against her desk. "So, Light, let me get this straight. She's not coming to this meeting because she had some emergency?"

Leaning back into the chair, I tried to refocus my mind by absorbing the sleekness of Reason's pristine midtown Manhattan office suite. "The last time I spoke to her, she sounded panicked, and that's not like her."

Reason bent toward me with eyes narrowed, as if she were interrogating me on the witness stand. Her drumming increased.

My lips curled up with distaste. Her loud tapping was like fingernails on a chalkboard.

"Reason, I swear, if you don't stop that, I'm going to fly over this damn desk and fucking cunt-punt you." I was already pissed off with Storm for dodging this meeting. I sure as hell didn't need lawyer extraordinaire pumping me for answers I didn't have.

Reason flashed her canines. "Watch it, Light. I'm not putting up with your mood swings today."

Irrationally, my temper flared as I leaned forward. "I don't give a flying fuck, vampire!"

Reason's hazel eyes narrowed with concern. "What's up with you lately?" She sat back, examining me like a lab rat, drumming again.

I pointedly stared at her fingers. "I'm not fucking kidding," I hissed.

I was out of control. I knew it. Reason knew it. But I couldn't rein it in. I wiped my damp forehead with shaky fingers. My empath symptoms were getting worse, and there wasn't shit I could do about it. What had once worked at controlling my intense migraines and wild mood swings—my large consumption of alcohol—was now failing. I tossed back a glass of tequila, gritting my teeth with frustration.

My symptoms were making me a nervous wreck, and even

worse, I had slowly been alienating everyone I loved with my erratic behavior. One minute, I would be bawling my eyes out; the next, I would be dripping with rage. There was no middle ground anymore.

"It's getting worse, isn't it?" Reason's tone softened. "You need help, Light. You can't continue down this path without going completely crazy."

I didn't flinch at her bluntness. I respected it. That was why she was my best friend, and I loved her like a sister. Our bond had been formed from practically growing up together. Her family, a long line of lawyers, had been handling all my family's legal affairs for centuries.

"I'm already there, Reason." I swallowed over the bitterness of being the only Credence born as a sensory empath with the unlucky ability to feel humans' energies and emotions.

"Storm thinks I can handle this meeting without her . . . but look at me." I was sweating, as if I'd just run a marathon. My fingers were shaking like a junkie's. And I was yelling like a deranged cast member from a reality show. "I won't last five minutes in the presence of that detective. He's pure evil." I knew, in a matter of seconds after being exposed to him, I'd be overwhelmed by his energy, taking his feelings and losing mine.

Reason's eyes widened with alarm. "Where is Storm? Is she with Knox?"

"She'd better not be." As much as I was relieved Storm had finally been getting some from Knox Gunner, rock star hotness, now was not the time for being knee deep in sweaty sex. We had major issues concerning a detective with a stick stuck up his ass sideways and the likelihood of me going straitjacket insane.

Storm wasn't just my cousin, best friend, and business partner. She was my sanity check from the daily strain of keeping the barrage of human emotions from sending me to Crazy Land.

I was tired of being a burden. I hated I'd been born with the worst luck of all the members in the Credence family. The constant influx of feelings was overwhelming, with no remedy to prevent them from completely making me insane. My family had tried different methods to help. The only two that worked were dulling my senses with alcohol and Storm soothing me through our bond connection. A few sips of her emotions would put my mind in a neutral, calm state.

Reason glowered. "Detective Burrows requested a meeting with both of you. It's too damn late to cancel without arousing further suspicion." She banged on her desk. "Damn it to hell. I can't believe he actually found information on the dead reporter's laptop linking Credence O. to Celina's death."

I snorted. "You and I know that's total bullshit. Someone is framing us."

Reason arched a brow. "Can you be more specific? Your family has more enemies than friends."

I couldn't dispute her point. Despite my family's wealth, we were considered outsiders among Others—wolf-shifters, vampires, and assorted supernatural beings who blended in, coexisting with humans—because of our fae ancestry.

I leveled her with an irritated stare. "Lacie Gilden. Everyone in the coven knows the Gildens are ruthless."

And it didn't help matters that they were our direct business competitors. Their business would go to great lengths to steal our clients and employees. Lacie was a spiteful, bitter she-wolf who tried everything in her power to ruin our prestigious reputation as Credence Other Corporation. Credence O. was secretly New York's most sought-after Others escort service, providing over-the-top discreetness and exclusivity to our clients. Clients included Other men with a preference for

Other women, minus all the drama of unnecessary attachments. Our clients demanded the elite of beautiful Other women as arm candy when they were in town on business.

Reason stared in shock. "This is bad. I can't believe all your contracts are missing. Records documenting which client booked which escort, places, times, agreed-upon service fees . . . all gone!"

My jaw tensed as I thought about all the information that safe had held. Paper documentation was not my preferred method of doing business. But the contracts we had with our clients were arrangements dating back centuries, when paper had ruled and a physically signed document had been the only thing honored—a practice that was a recipe for disaster in the wrong hands.

"I don't understand why Storm isn't here yet," Reason said flatly.

I rubbed my now throbbing forehead. "She'll be here." At least that was what I hoped. I'd been calling her like a stalker and had still gotten no response, which was totally out of character for her.

Reason grabbed my hand, gently rubbing it. "Don't worry. Once she gets here, she'll do that weird fae thing and fix you right up."

"I can't continue using her as my crutch," I responded.

"And you can't continue pretending you're resigned to your fate. You'll find a cure, like Demi's vision predicted."

My mouth flattened at the mention of Demi, the daughter of the Coven High Priestess. Demi was adamant the solution to my empath dilemma was a Bringer of Death. Due to her erratic personality and unreliable gift for foreseeing future events, her predictions almost never made sense.

"I love your optimism, but there's no magic fae wand that's going to save my ass."

Reason suggestively wiggled her eyebrows. "It could be a man."

I rolled my eyes. "That's the last thing I need in my life right now. Besides, I'm on a no-sex lockdown."

In the beginning, it had been hard to give up something I loved—sex—but it had become easier as the months had gone by. I didn't need the drama of a man in my life. I was too complicated, too emotional, and definitely too unstable—red flags that made the possibility of having a long-term relationship simply impossible, red flags that enabled my habit of discarding men like disposable shavers. I loved sex . . . lots of it. And I'd control the who, the when, and the how.

That was probably why one of my ex-lovers had endearingly nicknamed me the Sex Dictator for my insistence on directing every lick, move, or touch. And like I'd told him, I wouldn't have had to if he weren't such a hopeless case in bed. Needless to say, he'd stormed out in a huff, leaving me to finish myself—quite well, I might add.

"Maybe that's what you need right now—someone to take the edge off."

I scoffed. "No offense, but I'm not interested in dating advice from someone who hasn't had sex in years."

She pursed her lips. "I'm not willing to settle."

"What you really mean is you're not willing to settle for getting married to some coldhearted vampire your father picked."

Reason was the black sheep in the family. Her mother was a human, and her father was a vampire. Her birth was a shame to her blueblood family, who would do everything in their power to ostracize her. Her father, a powerful and ruthless man, loved her more than life and would do everything in his power to make her fit into the vampire world. But Reason wanted no part of it, totally ignoring his attempts, much to his embarrassment.

"Exactly. He's so obsessed with marrying off his hybrid-vampire daughter that he's willing to make a pact with the devil. Besides, I don't need a man. I'm happy being single."

I rolled my eyes before saying, "Uh-huh."

I heard Tabitha, Reason's administrative assistant, say in a whiny little bitch voice, "You all can't go in there!"

My head snapped around, and my body quivered with unease as I scooted back into my chair. My unease heightened when my body instantly went on high alert, like a cornered animal. I watched with narrowed eyes as the door slammed open. Storm and Knox burst in, followed by four men. My unease increased tenfold when my eyes were drawn to the only man on earth who could simultaneously make my sex clench with lust and my stomach roll with hatred—Ryker Alfero.

Why in the hell is he here?

His sea-green eyes darted to the empty bottle of tequila sitting in front of me. He snorted with distaste. "Oh, there she is, my beautiful drunk." He held up two fingers. "How many fingers am I holding up?" he asked mockingly.

I gave him the middle finger. "One! Now fuck off!"

Today, I refused to let him ruffle my feathers like he had at his gala the other night. This was business Light, hyper-composed Light, fashionable, elegant, in-charge Light. I'd deliberately chosen to dress the part by wearing my best designer handiwork, a dainty gray petal-collar blouse, five-inch studded black heels, and black pants.

"Baby, your dirty little mouth is making me hot," he growled.

He sauntered toward me with fire in his eyes. I refused to get up. His gaze locked on me as he trapped me against the chair with his beefy arms.

His lips grazed the shell of my ear when he grumbled, "I would love to see what else your dirty little mouth could do."

With those few words, I shivered as a surge of energy zipped into my body, unlocking something I didn't understand. My brain started functioning with a clarity I hadn't experienced in years—no warring emotions, just calmness.

Good God! This shouldn't be happening, especially not with him.

My heart and pulse raced as panic set in. The power snapped like a rubber band, and the dreaded dark emotions came flooding back with a vengeance. Sweat broke out on my forehead while perspiration trickled between my breasts.

"God, this is going to be a rough fucking ride." My voice was hoarse and ragged.

"I'll do my best to break you in slowly, submissive," he hissed, his voice dripping with raw sex.

He took my hand, gripping it tight when a jolt of electricity ran through both of us. His thumb caressed my hand.

My clit thumped against my panties as an erotic image flashed through my mind—me on all fours and those big hands all over my body while he fucked me from behind. When my tongue snaked out to wet my lips, a soft snarl left Ryker's mouth.

Shit! Shit! Shit! I was in serious trouble.

"Let go." I looked pointedly at our clasped hands.

He squeezed mine hard before releasing it.

"I guess you know each other . . ." Reason trailed off, looking between the two of us with an arched brow.

I made no move to explain. Reason turned a curious gaze to Storm, who shrugged.

Reason suddenly cleared her throat. I glanced guiltily at her. She was staring at Ryker and me with a smile on her face, doing absolutely nothing to dismiss the question in her gaze.

I was beyond exasperated as I looked at Storm. "You're late, cousin!"

"Hey, Light. I apologize for being late," Storm muttered while looking at Knox. "Something kept coming up."

She started to stroll toward me, but Knox pulled her back, pinning her to his side.

I truly wanted to choke her for being late, but damn, the girl looked well fucked . . . and happier than I'd ever seen her.

Knox nipped Storm's neck. "Damn right. I can't help it if my mate makes me rock hard."

Storm slapped his arm. "Cut the shit, Knox."

"Mate?" I raised a brow. "What the hell's going on?"

Casually, Ryker sat at the edge of Reason's desk and stared at me. "He's a wolf-shifter. Keep up, darling," he stated dryly.

I considered him from head to toe and back again to his hard lips that looked like they rarely smiled to the scar across his left eyebrow and over to the snake tattoo on the right side of his neck, which completed the don't-fuck-with-me aura. He looked more like a Viking who should be carrying a bloody sword.

Storm responded with an overly exaggerated, "Surprise!" and jazz hands.

Completely ignoring her, I shook my head with an uncharacteristic serious air. "And who are the three idiots?" I glared at the three hulking men standing by the door, staring at me in slack-jawed shock. "More members of the wild kingdom?"

They were far from beastlike; in fact, all three were handsome, freakishly so. My gaze snapped to Ryker. Those intense green eyes were staring at me in a way that shouldn't have made me want him, but I did.

Ryker growled loud enough that Knox protectively pushed Storm behind him.

"They're my enforcers—Soar, Rip, and Jackal," Ryker said

with eyes locked on me, "and, darling, if you call me or my pack animals again, I won't be responsible for the next thing I do to your pretty ass."

I moaned like a porn star. "Like what? Bending me over and giving me a spanking because I've been a bad girl?"

His mouth tightened. I bit back a smile, taking pleasure in ruffling his feathers.

I dug in like the vicious witch I was. "Not that I mind a good spanking, but I would prefer my punishment to come from one of your enforcers. It seems I'm more woman than an alpha like you can handle." I sighed playfully while winking at them.

He looked at the empty bottle of tequila sitting in front of me. "They say you can't judge a book by its cover, but in your case, what you see is exactly what you get. Isn't that right, tequila sunrise?"

My smirk fell. "You ass."

Ryker smiled, a slow lifting of perfect lips to reveal straight, white teeth. "When you play with the big dogs, you might get bitten."

I was ready with my smart comeback when one of his enforcers stepped forward, grabbing my hand.

"I'm Rip," he crowed with teeth sparkling.

His piercing blue eyes stared at me with interest—too much for my liking. There was way too much confidence in his surfer-guy swagger. He looked like something right out of a fashion magazine.

"Really?" I rolled my eyes, removing my hand from his. "My panties will not be dropping for the likes of you, golden boy."

He upped the wattage of his smile. "I like her."

A throat cleared, and the tightly muscled guy with jet-black hair cropped in a buzz cut pushed away from the door. He smiled, flashing a dimple, as he leisurely but thoroughly studied me. "I'm Jackal." He waved his hand over his shoulder and noted dismissively, "That's Soar."

Soar ran his hand over his short-cropped chestnut hair as his mouth curled downward.

Rip puffed his chest, smiling flirtatiously. "So, Lightning, are you single?"

"Rip." Ryker's voice was harsh.

I laughed at Rip's bold flirting. Through the Other rumor mill, I'd heard about Ryker's new enforcers. They didn't look as deadly as Others had made them out to be, but looks were sometimes deceiving.

I glanced at Ryker, who was glaring at Rip with murder in his eyes.

"Nice to meet you three." I leaned closer to Rip. "And I'm *very* single."

His smile widened as his blue eyes left me and moved to where Ryker was sitting on the edge of the desk.

I quickly looked at Storm. "Where's Noah?"

Noah was Storm's friend and an enforcer for the Alfero pack, the largest and toughest New York wolf-shifter pack.

Rip, Jackal, and Soar looked at Knox with raised brows before loudly clearing their throats.

"Noah decided to take a position in England," Rip responded.

I arched a brow. "That was sudden."

Storm grumbled, "Apparently."

"Rip, move," Ryker snapped.

Blinking innocently, Rip turned to him with a wide smile. "Why? If you're not interested, then—"

Ryker moved from the desk. Rip winked at me before sliding back to take his post by the door. Ryker sat back down and scowled.

"Wow. Okay, that was intense," Storm mused loudly while pointedly looking at Knox's arms.

He released her. She smiled, leaning up to kiss him hard before swaggering over to me. Her eyes narrowed. I knew she could see the frayed emotional walls around my mind—that and the fact that I hadn't slept in days.

She softly kissed me on the cheek. "You okay?"

"Not with Wolfie all up in my face."

Storm looked from me to Ryker and then back to me. Her eyes widened. "Oh, I see."

I rolled my eyes. "No, you don't see because . . . there's nothing to see."

Storm smiled cheekily. "Why don't you take your own advice and submit?"

I gritted my teeth. She was throwing back my advice to her about Knox when I'd encouraged her to give him a chance. Ryker and I were not the same. She knew that. I had issues . . . and from the smug look on Ryker's face, he did, too.

"I'll deal with you in private, Stormy Credence," I hissed.

Storm smiled widely. "I'm not scared."

Knox came up behind Storm, wrapping his arms around her waist. "Come on, baby." He winked at Ryker. "Let the alpha play with his new submissive." He pulled her toward the leather sofa while whispering something in her ear.

My eyes narrowed on Knox. "I did like you, rock star. Now? Not so much."

Reason leaned back, silently watching us as if we were some horrible experiment gone wrong. "I feel like I'm missing something here, and I can't figure out what."

I loudly snapped my fingers. "You, lawyer girl, we're paying out the ass for you to do lawyer stuff. Close your mouth and do your job." I nodded over at Ryker and his enforcers. "Get rid of the wild kingdom, and let's get on with business."

Reason rolled her eyes. "Simmer down, Lightning. My job is to get you out of trouble; it's not to prevent you from getting into it." She stood, strolling over to Storm. "I'm so happy for you, baby cakes." She tightly hugged Storm and then sternly eyed Knox. "She's one of my best friends . . . next to Grumpy over there." She nodded toward me. "You'd better treat her good, shifter."

Knox solemnly stared back at her. "I will."

Reason cracked a smile. "Good. I might be a hybrid vampire, but I can still kick your ass." She winked at him before sauntering back to her desk.

I crossed my arms. "Are you done kissing his ass?"

She raised her eyebrow before sighing. "Are you trying to test my damn patience?"

"No. I'm trying to get you to do your job," I responded snidely.

Reason stared at me with a frown before the phone on her desk rang. "Yeah? What's up, Tabitha?" she answered, hitting speaker phone.

"Detective Burrows called. He's running late."

"Good, because I'm going to need time to rein in this circus," she responded dryly while looking at me before disconnecting sharply.

"*Oh*, wait, are you actually going to do your job?" I snapped.

Ryker smiled charmingly as he grabbed ahold of my chair, pulling it in so his huge muscled legs straddled mine. "Darling, don't be rude. Adults are talking."

When he suddenly leaned in, putting his nose against my neck, I refused to flinch. His appealing aromatic smell of expensive cigars, sandalwood, and rich earth wafted around me. I almost dropped at his feet. I hated myself for this weakness.

"What is it about the Credence scent that's so alluring?" He took another sniff. "Is it the rare combination of fae and witch blood?"

I rolled my eyes. Others were fascinated by the fact that my family were the last of the fae—mystical Others with the ability to wield great power in magic.

Credence scent? God, he is such an ass.

I bit back the hysterical bubble of laughter at his cocky, sexy smile. I was positive that smile had countless women, Others and humans, melting at his feet. It was like I was some trophy he wanted to mount on his fucking wall. He thought I was some game, and fucking me would be his grand prize. I saw the eerily familiar predatory look in his eyes. It was the same predatory stare I would give to men I was determined to sample to scratch my sexual itch.

I arched a brow at him. *Oh, Wolfie is in for a rude awakening.* I wasn't interested in the bullshit he was selling, and he needed to understand that . . . now.

I brought up my knee, aiming for his nuts, smiling with glee.

Oh, alpha, this is going to hurt . . . a lot.

***

Devour Ryker and Lightning's story **WHEN LIGHTNING STRIKES!**

WANT FREE SEDONA VENEZ BOOKS?

Sign up for Sedona Venez's Newsletter and receive FREE BOOKS. In addition to the free stories, you will also get special pricing, exclusive previews and news of new releases.

GET A FREE SEDONA VENEZ BOOK!

Join Sedona's mailing list to be the first to know of new releases, free books, special prices and other author giveaways.

https://sedonavenez.com/free-book

ABOUT THE AUTHOR

USA TODAY BESTSELLING AUTHOR SEDONA VENEZ lives in New York City with her hot ex-military hubby —hooah—and their fur babies. She loves writing sizzling, sexy intricate stories about strong but broken characters who push limits, overcome their fears and risk it all for love.

Sedona loves to connect with readers!
www.sedonavenez.com